Deep in the heart of touristy small-town Spirit Canyon, South Dakota, former journalist Zo Jones runs the Happy Camper gift shop, where she sells everything from locally made souvenirs to memorabilia. She even rents out mountain bikes, and dabbles in the adventure industry—and sleuthing . . .

It's Memorial Day weekend in Spirit Canyon, and for Zo that means the return of summer shoppers. It also means the return of her good friend Beth, who's moved back to the area to reopen her family's premier hotel, Spirit Canyon Lodge. Beth and Zo spent many childhood summers there and Zo can't wait to reconnect and celebrate the Grand Opening. But the festivities go from bad to worse when a power outage knocks out the lights—and morning reveals a competitor's dead body found on the premises . . .

Soon enough, Beth is the prime suspect in the suspicious death. Fortunately, Zo isn't afraid to put her investigative skills to work and prove her friend's innocence. To start digging for information, she appeals to Max Harrington, a local Forest Ranger and unlikely ally. Though they've argued about Happy Camper's tours, in this case they agree on one thing: Beth isn't a murderer. Stranger things have happened than their collaboration. After all, this is Spirit Canyon. But as the list of suspects grows, Zo will have to keep her guard up if she doesn't want to be the next lodge guest to check out . . .

Visit us at www.kensingtonbooks.com

Books by Mary Angela

Open for Murder

Published by Kensington Publishing Corporation

Open for Murder

A Happy Camper Mystery

Mary Angela

LYRICAL UNDERGROUND
Kensington Publishing Corp.
www.kensingtonbooks.com

LYRICAL UNDERGROUND BOOKS are published by

Kensington Publishing Corp.
119 West 40th Street
New York, NY 10018

First Electronic Edition: November 2020
ISBN-13: 978-1-5161-1069-8 (ebook)
ISBN-10: 1-5161-1069-2 (ebook)

First Print Edition: November 2020
ISBN-13: 978-1-5161-1072-8
ISBN-10: 1-5161-1072-2

Printed in the United States of America

To my mom, for all the stories.

Chapter One

Zo Jones pulled open the door to her deck, convinced she'd seen her cat, George, sauntering along the back fence. *My cat—right*, thought Zo. *If he was my cat, he'd come home.* The orange-and-white fur ball had been a menace ever since she'd adopted him from the shelter six months ago. First, he shredded her one good chair, then contracted an expensive ear infection, and after he was cured, he took off at the first sign of spring. Zo was starting to think he didn't like her. Pausing in the warm sunshine, she couldn't completely blame him. The nice weather was giving her spring fever, too. Like the tourists, she wanted to be outside, enjoying the canyon.

In the heart of Black Hills National Forest, the canyon was the reason most tourists came to Spirit Canyon, the small town named for the landmark. They filled up on food, gas, and souvenirs before taking the twisty drive into one of the most beautiful byways of the hills. Zo had been here so long she could have been numb to its beauty. But she wasn't. Mornings such as these still had the ability to move her, and she stood for a while staring into the distance. Like a paintbrush dabbed in gold, the sun moved across the treetops, highlighting the jagged forest cutting along the bright blue ridge of sky.

Hearing a sound at the fence, Zo walked down the deck steps into her tiny backyard, her flip-flops slapping against her feet. As the owner of Happy Camper, an eclectic gift shop, she had no need to dress up. She wore short shorts, a long sweater, and silver earrings that hung past her shaggy inverted bob. She also wore a lovely blue scarf, one of many she splurged on at the local Cut Hut. Today's creation, tied into a headband, fell to her shoulders, brushing the Archer tattoo on her right shoulder. She was a Sagittarius.

The gate creaked as she pushed it open. If George had been there, he'd heard her and was gone. Instead, Dr. Russell Cunningham, an English professor at Black Mountain College, greeted her. Bent down near the side of his house and wearing a straw hat and leather gloves, he looked a little like a garden gnome, wrinkled but in a cute way. Unfortunately, this garden gnome talked—a lot.

"Lost your cat again, Zo?" he said. His voice was like sandpaper, rough from overuse in lectures.

"I've decided he's not really my cat. He's the neighborhood's cat." She dislodged a rock from her sandal. "Have you seen him?"

"He's been here." He pointed a leather-gloved finger toward a struggling patch of green. "Obviously."

She shrugged. She didn't see anything except Cunningham's poor attempt at a garden. He thought all English professors should garden in the summer, probably because of something he read or something a dead author said. What he *was* good at was drinking, late and often. He made the best rum cocktail—he called it The Hemingway—she'd ever tasted. "I thought you were giving up gardening after last year's fiasco."

Squinting into the sun, he readjusted his straw hat so he could see her better. "Those were bad seeds. Ms. Mork sold them to me on purpose. She's always been keen on me."

Cunningham was under the delusion that all women in Spirit Canyon over the age of fifty-five had a crush on him. He *was* handsome, in an eccentric sort of way. He had a lot of white hair and crystal blue eyes full of expression. "If that's true, why would she sell you bad seeds?"

"So I'd come back, naturally," said Cunningham, smiling.

"Naturally."

"If I see your cat," he said, "I'll let you know."

"Thanks, Cunningham." She kept walking down the hill, to the front of her story-and-a-half cedar cabin, which also functioned as her business. Happy Camper, distinguishable by its sign showing a Volkswagen van and colorful peace symbol, was below her upstairs living quarters. She sold locally made gifts, souvenirs, and memorabilia. She also rented mountain bikes and kayaks and, with advance notice and an additional charge, even gave tours, much to the chagrin of Max Harrington. Max was a local forest ranger who thought all guides should have a degree in forestry. He said a shop owner had no business dabbling in the adventure industry. But Spirit Canyon had lots of stores that were multifunctional, and Zo's was no different. Besides, no one knew the area better than she did. As far as she was concerned, she had all the expertise she needed to introduce newbies to the area.

She unlocked one of the bikes from the key on her coil bracelet. After this weekend, renters would have first dibs on the equipment. It was the Friday before Memorial Day, which meant the official start of tourist season. Though she looked forward to the increase in business, what she was really excited for was seeing her childhood friend, Beth Everett. Beth had just relocated to the canyon with her family. Her aunt Lilly had died a year ago and left her Spirit Canyon Lodge, a premier hotel in the canyon. This weekend would be their first chance to spend time together since the funeral, and Zo couldn't wait. She'd spent lots of summers with Beth at the lodge. Now, twenty years later, she would spend another.

But she wouldn't be able to survive the holiday weekend without coffee, and she was completely out. She put on her black Ray-Ban Wayfarer sunglasses, tossed a leg over the bike, and sailed down the hill, the crisp pine-scented air providing the wakeup call that caffeine hadn't.

She applied the brake as she approached downtown Spirit Canyon, a mere block away. It was the prettiest little mountain town she'd ever seen, and now, one of the trendiest. Nature lovers of all ages flocked to Spirit Canyon for its granola vibe. Although small, the town had all the amenities of a larger city: three coffee shops, two bookstores, several restaurants, a wine bar, and even an opera house with a thriving theater company.

Parking her bike at Green Market, the downtown grocery store, she took a moment to peruse the fresh produce outside. The enormous watermelons would entice more than a few weekend shoppers, but not Zo, who only bought for one person. She selected a bunch of grapes and a ripe, red apple before entering the store.

"Good morning, Zo," said a woman standing behind one of the three checkouts. It was the owner, Virginia Palmer, whose store aisles were well stocked and her employees well versed on healthy food.

"Good morning." Zo pushed up her sunglasses. "Outta coffee."

"How's business?"

"Good," said Zo. "You?"

"Can't complain." Virginia shrugged.

Zo nodded and kept walking to the organic pasta aisle. Virginia was a smart woman; she knew her customers appreciated organic, GMO-free options. There wasn't a noodle, lo mein, or vegan alternative she wasn't willing to order. Zo counted five pasta varieties just passing through.

Since it was early, shoppers were sparse but filled in quickly as the minutes passed. Memorial Day weekend was fast approaching, and that meant picking up supplies for weekend barbeques and events. Zo stopped at the meat counter, which was running a special on hamburger, and requested a single patty. It was only slightly humiliating, she decided. She was thirty-three and temporarily out of boyfriends. Chances were, she'd be eating alone this holiday.

She put the hamburger in the cart and kept walking. She might not even need it. Beth had invited her to the lodge for the grand opening. They might grab something to eat on the holiday. Still, it'd been five years since the lodge was open to guests. Even with the renovations completed, Beth might have her hands full.

A woman with chestnut brown hair rummaged through the low bins in the spice aisle, and Zo stopped, wondering if it was Beth, or if she'd been thinking about her so much that she imagined it was. As if feeling Zo's eyes on her, the woman looked up, and Zo knew it wasn't her imagination.

"Beth!" Zo rushed to greet her, practically bowling her over in excitement. "I didn't think I'd see you until tomorrow."

Beth stood, and they hugged for a full minute. Beth was tall and slim with a pretty style, simple but chic. And flowers! She'd loved flowers since they were kids. She always wore something floral—a scarf, a barrette, or earrings. Today it was her Vera Bradley handbag covered in purple wildflowers.

"Oh, my gosh," said Beth. "It's great to see you. I've been thinking about you for days, and here you are."

Zo laughed. "Same. It's like I pulled you out of my imagination."

"You're planning on coming to the grand opening on Saturday, right?"

"Of course," said Zo. "I'm going to write about it in my column." The *Curious Camper*, which ran every week in the *Canyon Views* newspaper, was a short column related to all things in the area. Since Zo had been a writer for the Black Hills *Star* before opening her store, it was a natural fit. Plus her shop kept her up-to-date with area trends. Zo indicated out the window. "Do you have time to grab a quick cup of coffee across the street? I open at ten."

"If it's quick. I have guests coming this afternoon. Let me just check one thing." Beth scanned the spices one last time. "Dang. No turmeric."

"Don't worry," said Zo. "The bike shop up the street probably sells it. Spokes and Stuff. They have an entire section of spices."

"Really? The bike shop? I wouldn't have guessed. Thanks."

Zo nodded. Spirit Canyon was unique, modern, and diverse.

They approached the cashier, and Zo paid for her groceries, then waited as Beth checked out. "You haven't changed," said Zo. Even as a girl, Beth wore leggings and flats, the same attire she had on today.

"You haven't either."

Zo chuckled. "My hair is way different. I cut it off a few months ago." It was the day she broke up with Hunter, who used to say how much he loved her long blond hair. Turned out, he loved it more than she did.

"I noticed," said Beth. "I love it." She paid the cashier, and they walked out the door with their grocery sacks. Zo gave Virginia a wave good-bye.

"This is me," Beth said as they approached a red SUV, where she placed their perishables in the cooler. Zo noted the items in the trunk were arranged by size and purpose. No wonder she'd been an event planner at a famous Chicago hotel. She was meticulously organized.

"Have you been to Honey Buns?" asked Zo.

Beth shook her head and relocked the SUV.

"It's new." Zo gestured to the store. "It has great coffee and a bakery."

"Perfect," Beth agreed. "I'll need all the carbs I can get to finish my shopping list."

Zo led her across the two-way street. She pulled open the door, and the bell buzzed like a bee.

Beth grinned. "How fun!"

It really was a fun new store. The croissants, scones, and muffins tasted as good as they smelled. Zo should know; she'd tried them all. Behind the display case were buns, bagels, and specialty breads. Pumpernickel was her favorite, this week anyway.

The shelves on the opposite wall were filled with jars of chokecherry, blackberry, and rhubarb jams, as well as several variations of South Dakota's state product, honey. Looking like a tourist, Beth browsed the shelves, and after a few minutes, approached the register with an armload of merchandise. A few items spilled onto the counter as she ordered *pain au chocolate* and espresso. Zo ordered the same, and they selected a table as they waited for their drinks.

Beth picked up her pastry. "I don't know if chocolate is the best choice for breakfast."

Zo waved away her concern. "It's the *perfect* choice for breakfast, lunch, or dinner. Trust me. You'll love it."

Beth took a bite. "You're right. It's heavenly."

The barista brought out their espressos, served in tiny cups decorated with pictures of beehives. Zo took a sip, letting the brew awaken her senses. No matter how many healthy smoothies she tried, they couldn't replace good old-fashioned caffeine.

"So what have you been up to?" asked Beth.

"Mostly working—and looking for my cat, George. I see him stalk by the window late at night sometimes." She took another sip of her coffee. "It's pathetic."

Beth frowned. "He won't come in?"

"Every time I try to grab him, he dodges me. He's as quick as lightning for a fat guy. He still comes home to eat." She shrugged. "I guess that's something."

"You know how cats get in the spring," said Beth. "They want outside, constantly."

"Do you have a cat?" Zo tried to imagine Beth rolling her clothes with a lint roller. Nope, she couldn't picture her dealing with cat fur.

Beth shook her head. "How is the store?"

"The store is great," said Zo. "I have a full-time employee in the summer, Harley Stiles. You have to meet her. She's been with me since the beginning."

"It looks adorable," said Beth. "I've been meaning to stop in, but getting the lodge ready for this weekend has taken all of my time."

"Don't worry," said Zo. "I understand how hard it is opening a business." A shot of anger pulsed through her as she remembered how she had to start her business—twice. After her year lease was up, old man Merrigan decided to use her previous space himself. That's when she moved to her new location, a block from downtown. Moving was a painful subject for her, so she tamped down the bad feelings and refocused on Beth. "Are you ready for this weekend?"

Beth wrinkled her nose, finishing her sweet. "I think so. I worked at the Waldorf Astoria for ten years coordinating weddings. A lodge in the Black Hills should be a breeze, right?"

Zo nodded, but her friend didn't sound as confident as she looked.

"My mom's been great with social media, and Jack has been better at repairs than I thought he would be. The girls love the place. But it's still hard."

Zo understood. "You miss Lilly?"

"I do." Beth offered a small smile. "Coming back here has brought back so many memories. Good memories—but sad at the same time. I'm starting to go through her things."

"I miss her, too." Abandoned at birth, Zo used to think of Spirit Canyon Lodge as home. Foster homes came and went, but the lodge never changed. The people, the food, the friendship—they were what she imagined family felt like. When Beth told her she was coming back to reopen the lodge, Zo felt like a piece of herself was returning.

"She loved you, you know," said Beth. "Loved the way you used to ride your bike through the canyon like the devil was chasing you." She chuckled. "Remember that old ten-speed?"

"How could I forget?" Zo laughed. The blue bike had taken her everywhere.

A man in a green forest ranger uniform tapped on the window, startling them.

"Great," said Zo. "It's Smokey the Bear."

"Who's that?"

"Max Harrington. He's a forest ranger."

Max entered the bakery and strode over to their table in two large steps. His light brown hair was clean-cut, and the creases on his shirtsleeves framed his muscular arms. Everything about him said wholesome, except his eyes. They were blue, dead serious, and directed at her.

"I'm not going to tell you again that you need to get registration decals on your kayaks, Zo," Max said. "If you don't, I'm reporting you myself."

Zo ignored him, speaking to Beth. "Max thinks he's the official law and order around here. He's always busting my chops over some sticker or another."

"I'm a Law Enforcement Officer for the National Forest Service," Max snapped. "I *am* the official law and order around here."

Zo rolled her eyes. "Please."

Beth gave him a sunny smile. "Hi. I'm Elizabeth Everett, but everyone calls me Beth. My family and I just moved into Spirit Canyon Lodge. We're the new owners."

Max held out his hand. Zo decided it looked like a large paw. "You have a gorgeous place up there. I'm glad to see it reopening."

"Thank you," said Beth. "I spent lots of summers here as a kid—that's how I know Zo."

Max turned his attention back to Zo. "Look. I know you think I'm picking on you, but I'm not. It's the law, and I don't want to see you get in trouble. Just get them on there, all right?"

Zo gave him the okay sign.

"It was nice meeting you, Beth," Max said.

Beth nodded, and he was gone.

"Bear or not, he's cute," said Beth.

Zo shook her head. She was not having this conversation.

"So what's this about decals?" asked Beth.

"He's right." Zo reached for her sweater, which she'd hung on the back of her chair, and tied it around her waist. The decals needed to be on the kayaks before the busy weekend. "I have to get them on there. I meant to do it yesterday."

"I'll see you tomorrow?" Beth pushed back her chair. "I've told the kids all about you."

"I wouldn't miss it." Zo hadn't met Jack or the children at Lilly's funeral. They'd stayed behind because Beth's daughter had just started middle school. "Did you tell them it's haunted?"

"What? The lodge?" Beth adjusted her purse on her shoulder. "I stayed there for years and never saw a thing."

Zo smiled. "No, you city slicker. Spirit Canyon."

Chapter Two

Saturday was always Zo's busiest day at Happy Camper, when weekend travelers did most of their shopping. Today was no exception. The moment she flipped the sign to OPEN at ten o'clock, she had a steady stream of customers. It took both her and Harley to answer questions and ring up sales. It wasn't until the afternoon lull that she was able to restock her Happy Camper line of merchandise.

Designed with fun colors, fonts, and flowers, it was incredibly popular because of its positive messages like HAPPY CAMPER, DAY DREAM BELIEVER, and FLOWER SNIFFER. She'd just received new stoneware mugs from Demarco, the artist who designed the line for her, and they read, HALF FULL. She put them next to the coasters and tea towels. Then she grabbed the s'more-shaped sugar cubes, added them to the display, and stood back to admire her work. *Nice!* Everybody needed a little more happiness in their day.

That was the idea, to surround herself and others with things that inspired happiness, and so far it had worked. It made her day when she saw someone standing next to the greeting cards, smiling and picking one out for a friend. With Paul Simon's *Graceland* album playing in the background, the afternoon sun streaming in the large storefront windows, and her upcoming visit to Spirit Canyon Lodge, she decided this was her Cloud Nine.

"You're doing that thing again, aren't you?" Harley crossed her arms in front of her. At twenty, she had all the spark and fire Zo had at her age—plus math skills. She balanced Zo's books with pinpoint accuracy and was incredibly kind. If she was the future, Zo was investing in her.

"What thing?" said Zo, but a smile touched the corners of her lips.

"The embracing-your-happiness thing." It was a technique they'd learned in a gratitude journaling class. The speaker said to take one minute every hour to embrace the happiness in your life right now. Zo was convinced it was working.

"Okay, I am, but these are so darn cute," said Zo. "Don't you think?"

Harley sauntered over to the display. Willowy and tall, she was dressed in a camouflage shirt and black jeans. "They're adorable. What about the honey sticks?"

"Right," Zo said. "I should order some more."

Harley walked toward the counter. "I'll do it. You've got that thing to go to."

Zo checked the wall clock. It was after four, and she wanted to get to the lodge early. Beth was having a chuck wagon supper. "Are you sure?"

"Yep," said Harley. "Positive."

"Okay." Zo grabbed her backpack from under the counter. "I'll get George. It's supposed to storm tonight, so I want him inside."

"Good luck with that."

Zo started toward the door, noting how homey the store felt. When she first moved to this location, she worried it wouldn't be the same, that she wouldn't like it as much as her downtown storefront. As it turned out, she liked it even better. It was the home she'd always dreamed of. It *looked* happy, and nothing said camper like a cedar cabin. With its corner location, she decided it was the best of both worlds. Downtown was a block away, and home was just upstairs.

Something furry brushed against the back of her legs as she pulled the door shut. She froze, knowing in an instant it was George. This was as close as he'd come in a long time, except to visit his food dish, which he emptied sometime after she went to bed. Carefully, she turned around. He rolled to his back, scratching on the gravel parking lot.

"Hey, George."

He meowed a response.

She bent down slowly and rubbed his chin. "I see your ears still look good."

He answered by rolling to his other side, his white stripes of fur brown from the dirt.

She petted him a long time before making her move. It was now or never. A thunderstorm was predicted for the area, so he couldn't stay outside tonight. Spring storms could be dangerous.

She stood and slowly reopened the door of Happy Camper. He didn't bolt. He was watching her. Putting her finger to her lips, she warned Harley not to make a sound. She tiptoed to the cash register, where she had a can of whitefish tuna stashed below the counter. She pulled back the metal tab. The smell of fish filled the small shop, and George stepped one orange paw over the threshold. She placed the container on the counter and stared at the computer screen. If George saw the glint of hope in her eyes, he would be gone.

Slowly he sauntered inside, stopping once to lick a spot on his leg. Zo's heartbeat picked up as she noticed him turn and look back at the door. But then he surprised her by leaping to the counter with a meow. When he was fully engaged with the tuna fish, Harley nodded, and Zo stepped toward the door, first slowly, then quickly before he could change his mind. As she scooted out the door for a second time, she congratulated herself on successfully capturing a domestic animal—and also keeping his litter box. There were a few times she'd thought about throwing it away when he didn't come home night after night.

She glanced down at her jean capris and flip-flops, deciding she didn't need to change. Chuck wagons didn't require fancy attire—at least the ones she'd attended. She untied the green sweatshirt from her waist and put it on. She liked the color because it matched her eyes. Cunningham said they reminded him of a cat's, but obviously George didn't see the resemblance. If he did, he might have treated her better. She repositioned the silver moon necklace she always wore. Engraved with the name *Zo*, it was the only delicate piece of jewelry she owned. It was with her when she was found at the police station as a baby. She hadn't taken it off since she was old enough to fasten the clasp.

Despite the storm warning, the night was calm, and as Zo drove into the canyon, she rolled down her window to let in the fresh air. She loved Spirit Canyon, and not just because of the spooky lore surrounding it. Well, actually, the lore had a lot to do with it. Passing under a rock archway, she imagined she was entering another world. In the cold months, Spirit Canyon remained a frosty wonderland, and in the spring and summer, the weather was unpredictable. On sunny days, for instance, the sun didn't always reach deep crevices of the ravine. Sometimes it just brushed the tree branches on the skyline, leaving the canyon dark and mysterious. There was a narrow crack called 11th Hour Gulch because it received a single hour of sunlight. Where else in the area could you find a place that boasted just one hour of light per day?

When Zo arrived at the lodge, it was decked out in a GRAND OPENING ribbon and two pillars of colorful balloons. It was a log A-frame with a wraparound porch situated near a creek in the meadow. She remembered the many days and nights she and Beth sat on the oversized porch, playing Barbies, making forts, and eating popcorn. It'd been such a long time ago. She'd forgotten how important the lodge was and what a good friend Beth had been.

As she put her Subaru Outback in park, she noticed the KRSO news van in the lot. They must have been covering the grand opening. She also noticed the updates to the lodge. The Adirondack chairs and hanging lanterns were new, as were the purple and blue impatiens, which added a perfect pop of color. Beth always did have an eye for details. If anyone could modernize this 1960s lodge, she could.

Zo walked up the cobblestone path, lingering a moment before approaching the front door. The updates, although pretty, didn't change the rugged beauty of the place. The ponderosa pines, which gave the Black Hills their dark appearance, stood like stewards in the distance, and wild sagebrush gave way to their natural splendor. Despite modern conveniences, the lodge would always be a long road from the rest of civilization.

"Zo!" said Beth as Zo opened the door. "You made it."

Like the outside, the inside was familiar but new—and buzzing with activity. The floor-to-ceiling stone fireplace hadn't changed. It was flanked by long windows that overlooked Spirit Canyon. On the mantel were tiny vases of purple pasqueflower, the state blossom and first sign of spring. The large buffalo head from Zo's childhood no longer hung above the hearth. Replacing it was a gorgeous photo of the animal. Surrounded by snow, the buffalo puffed two streams of frosty breath from his nostrils. The striking contrast between the buffalo's dark tawny fur and the all-white background provided the perfect focal point for the room.

"Can you believe it?" Beth met her near the entrance. Wearing a sleeveless flowered tunic over leggings, she looked much more feminine than her surroundings. "My mom contacted KRSO's media department, and here they are. I insisted they stay for the chuck wagon."

Zo would have recognized the KRSO reporter Justin Castle anywhere. Although young, he was polished like a shiny...rock, Zo thought with a smile, and as slick as one, too. The cameraman she didn't recall. He wore a cap that hid most of his face, except the red-brown stubble on his chin. They were set up opposite the fireplace, near the six enormous bookshelves. It looked as if they were interviewing Beth's guests.

"That's amazing," said Zo. "*This* is amazing." She took in the room a second time. "Really, Beth, it's gorgeous."

Beth took her arm and led her to the reception desk. "Thank you. I hoped you'd like it."

"And the staircase?" Zo pointed to stairs that angled up to the second floor like an L. "How many times did Lilly tell us not to play on the steps?" "A million?" Beth grinned.

"She thought we would fall and break our necks," Zo reminisced. "Then your mom wouldn't let you come back."

"I never wanted her here in the first place," called a woman from the hallway. She stepped into the great room, and Zo recognized her as Beth's mother. Although her hair was short and spiked, she had the same wide, blue-gray eyes as Beth.

"You remember my mom, Violet." Beth raised an eyebrow.

Zo remembered. She also remembered that Vi Degen and her sister, Lilly, didn't get along. Vi claimed that Lilly, ten years her elder, tarnished the family name when she ran off and married a cowboy from South Dakota. It caused a huge family rift, and Vi said she never recovered.

"Hi, Vi." Zo shook her hand.

"It's good to see you again, Zo," said Vi. She turned to Beth. "What I came in here to say is we're booked until Labor Day. My Facebook post went viral, thank you very much."

"My mom is a social media doyenne," Beth said to Zo. "She tried to get me to rent out our cottage when the ad took off, but I had to draw the line somewhere."

The cottage was the small house behind the lodge. Pete and Lilly had built it years after the hotel became successful. It was their home, and now it belonged to Beth and her family.

"The chuck wagon is also Mom's idea," Beth continued, nodding at her mother.

"People really go for these dude ranches and chuck wagons," Vi whispered. "I've been doing some research. Beth is going to make a fortune."

Beth took a breath. "That's not what this is about, Mom."

"I know, I know," said Vi. "It's about 'recreating the past with a touch of class.' Doesn't exactly roll off the tongue, does it? But I found recipes for cowboy burgers and cowboy cookies—heck, cowboy everything. It's going to be delicious."

"I love cowboys." Zo chuckled. "I can't wait."

"Where are Molly and Megan?" asked Beth. "Zo should meet them."

"Outside with Jack. They're helping with setup." Vi pulled her iPhone out of her pocket. "Dang. Still not working. I need to access Pandora, and the WiFi has been sketchy all day."

"It always is in the canyon," said Zo. "You might go hours without cell service and no explanation."

"Nature," Vi grumbled, rechecking the signal as she walked away.

The thought of being disconnected was disconcerting to some people, and Vi was obviously one of them. Zo liked the idea of disappearing into the deep of the canyon, the tall trees acting as a barrier from the rest of the world. Seclusion brought her peace, and even a certain clarity, but she realized its danger. Isolation had risks, risks that tourists didn't always recognize.

Chapter Three

After Vi left, Beth filled Zo in on the guests. The women talking to KRSO were attending their ten-year college reunion, which had been coordinated with the Poker Alice festival in Deadwood. Zo knew the legend of Poker Alice, whose real name was Alice Ivers. She'd owned a saloon called Poker's Palace in Deadwood, South Dakota, about twenty minutes from Spirit Canyon Lodge. Although she wasn't as lucky in love as she was in poker—Zo could totally relate—she enjoyed her cards, her ranch near Sturgis, and of course, her famous cigars. Unfortunately, all three husbands died soon after their marriage to her, and she lived most of her life alone.

"So, they checked in yesterday, another couple checked in last night, and a woman checked in this afternoon." Beth was breathless. "I'm almost at full capacity!"

"I'm not surprised," said Zo. "Remember when we were kids? This place was always packed." It was true. The lodge had a reputation that lasted long after Lilly closed it. When her husband, Pete, died, Lilly couldn't deal with the upkeep, or the memories, and moved into an independent living facility in town. When Zo saw her once in a while, before she got ill, Lilly always remembered her. It meant a lot to Zo.

Beth nodded. "That was years ago, though. I didn't know if it would still be popular." She glanced in the direction of the recording equipment. "It looks like they're finished with the interviews. Come on."

The cameraman, whom Justin called A.J., closed the lighting shade, and Justin packed away the microphone while Beth introduced Zo to the group. The women's matching t-shirts had their sorority sigma on them. That must've been how they were connected.

"So, let me see if I remember," said Beth. "This is Kaya Cantrell." She motioned to the woman with tan skin and a scar near her eye. "The one on the phone is Jennifer Greene, and you're Allison Scott and Sarah Johnson, right? This is my friend Zo." Sarah wore baggy mom jeans with her t-shirt. Allison wore a Patagonia fleece over hers.

"Good memory," said Kaya as she shook Zo's hand. "Nice to meet you."

"Beth says you're here for a college reunion."

"Yep," said Kaya. "The t-shirts were Jennifer's idea. A little pink for my taste, but Sandy will love them."

"Sandy's our house mother," Sarah explained. She had short brown hair and a round face. "Or she *was*, I should say. She lives in Deadwood."

"For now, anyway." Allison frowned.

"How about a drink?" Jennifer had ended her call.

"Feel free to help yourselves." Beth motioned to the sideboard, stocked with liquor.

Jennifer didn't need a second invitation. She poured herself a hefty glass of sherry. Instead of sipping the aperitif, she downed it as if it were a shot.

"I hope what happens in South Dakota, stays in South Dakota," whispered Jennifer, winking at her friends. After pouring another glass, she strode toward the reporters, who had moved to the other side of the room to collect the rest of their equipment.

Allison's eyebrows formed two triangles. "I don't think she has to worry about that. I've found most things that happen in South Dakota stay in South Dakota."

"Agreed," said Zo with a laugh. "I live in Spirit Canyon. Do you live in the area?" Zo noticed she had a slight lisp, which made listening to her interesting.

"I live about thirty miles from here." Allison tucked a curl behind her ear. Her natural golden waves made her shoulder-length cut less plain. "I teach geoscience at Black Mountain College."

"It's great to meet another local," said Beth. "You'll have to keep in touch after you check out."

"How about you guys?" asked Zo. "Do you live near here?"

Kaya answered for her and Sarah. "I live in Wyoming, Sarah lives in Iowa, and Jennifer lives in Colorado. But we've all stayed close since college."

Jennifer returned, discreetly pointing to Justin and A.J. "Single, both of them. Thank you very much."

"They're cute," said Sarah.

"They're staying for dinner." Jennifer refilled her glass again. "Man I need this after the day I've had."

"How much money did you lose?" asked Kaya.

Jennifer raised an eyebrow. "A lady never tells."

A couple walked down the stairs, and Beth excused herself and Zo from the group, saying Zo should meet them. The woman had straight hair, pulled into a low ponytail, and an angular face. Her clothes were expensive and fit her jaunty frame—and confident attitude. Her boyfriend was tall, especially standing next to Zo, who was on the short side. He had wavy hair smoothed by pomade, going for the slick look she saw some younger guys wearing. He was older than Zo, though, somewhere around forty.

"Nice to meet you," he said. "I'm Griffin, and this is my fiancée, Robyn."

Griffin seemed vaguely familiar, but Zo couldn't place his face. It was the kind, friendly face she met every day. "I'm Zo. I own a shop in Spirit Canyon, Happy Camper."

Griffin nodded distractedly. Robyn made up for his lack of conversation. "I like this place," Robyn said, admiring the great room. "Normally, I'm not a big fan of lodges. But this is rustic chic. Very mod."

"I like that description," said Beth. "Mind if I use it in the brochure?"

"Not at all." Robyn's smile turned to a frown. "What's with the news crew? What are they doing here?"

Beth followed Robyn's gaze in the direction of Justin and A.J. "Oh, they won't be bothering you. They're done. They covered the grand opening, so I invited them for dinner."

"Good." Robyn looked relieved. "I don't want to be on TV."

"Me neither," Griffin agreed.

"Help yourself to a drink." Beth indicated the sideboard with a short wave. "We'll walk to the chuck wagon in just a few minutes."

They left, and Beth crossed her hands over her heart. "*Lovebirds.* He just popped the question last night. I told you my love bug is contagious."

Zo laughed, remembering the reason why Beth got into wedding planning in the first place. She was right. People around her did seem to marry quite often.

"Come on," said Beth. "Help me grab some supplies."

Zo followed her to the supply closet under the stairs, which was filled with flashlights, water, bandages, sleeping bags, umbrellas, and first-aid equipment, all organized alphabetically.

Beth handed Zo two oversized umbrellas. "Would you carry these? In case it rains."

"It's going to rain," Zo predicted. "I spotted thunderheads earlier."

Beth didn't pay much attention, and Zo got the feeling she didn't realize how dangerous storms could be out here. Lightning storms occurred twice as often in the canyon than the surrounding areas. It would take more than a golf umbrella to protect guests from a downpour.

When they reentered the great room, the noise decibel had increased with everyone talking amicably. Beth mentioned her relief. She was thankful that, despite the different personalities, they all were getting along. If this kept up, dinner would be a cinch.

A couple guests looked in their direction, and Zo wondered if Beth's comment had been audible above the conversations. More heads twisted, and confused, Beth blinked. Zo realized they weren't looking at Beth, however, but someone on the stairwell. She glanced behind her and saw Enid Barrett, the owner of Serenity Hills, a nearby resort. Enid was dressed in a cashmere cape, gray leggings, and dark leather riding boots. Wealthy and sophisticated, Enid paused on the landing and surveyed the group, her brown eyes stopping on someone. Zo didn't know why she'd be here with a perfectly good resort of her own and a mansion outside of town besides.

"I'm so glad you decided to join us," said Beth. "Welcome." She turned to the rest of the group to explain the new arrival. "Ms. Barrett checked in this afternoon."

Beth might not know Enid, but Zo did—at least by reputation. If Beth had, she wouldn't have been so welcoming. Enid Barrett was unpleasant and becoming even more so as she aged. Zo had tangled with her a few times when tourists complained to her about double-booked rooms at Serenity Hills. Without rooms, they were left scrambling for a tent. When it happened a second time, Zo called Enid as a courtesy. All she got was an earful from Enid telling her to mind her own business.

Fashionable cane in hand, Enid gripped the handrail as she descended the remaining steps. "I won't be eating. A glass of sherry, please."

"Of course," said Beth. The group parted like the Red Sea as Beth approached the sideboard. She filled the tiny glass and gave it to Enid. As Enid sipped, the room waited on her approval.

Enid studied Beth. "You remind me of Lilly."

Beth's face lit up at the compliment. "You knew my aunt?"

"She spent money foolishly, just like you." She pointed to her glass. "This has to be a hundred dollars a bottle."

Beth deflected the comment. "I want my guests to enjoy themselves. Some are celebrating special occasions." She looked at Griffin and Robyn and smiled. "And this is my grand opening. I don't mind the expense."

"You will when it sends you into bankruptcy court," said Enid. "It looks like this one's already had several glasses." She pointed her cane toward Jennifer, who scowled in response.

"I'm on vacation, if you don't mind," said Jennifer.

"And a vacation to the Wild West wouldn't be complete without a chuck wagon." Beth changed the topic. "Let's get started."

Zo wanted to warn Beth about Enid, but she was already leading guests out the deck door toward the event, so Zo silently followed. Enid had no right to say what she did about Lilly. Zo couldn't imagine how Beth felt. Beth was used to dealing with difficult people, Zo reminded herself. She wasn't the same young girl she used to be. She must have worked with more than a few bridezillas because she had no problem asserting herself. But Enid would test her resilience. She'd already subdued the party by walking down the steps. Having her join them for dinner might squelch conversation altogether. And why was she here in the first place? Zo couldn't think of a reason, unless she was snooping on Beth's lodge. That was probably it. Enid was a cutthroat businesswoman. She had another spa besides the one in Spirit Canyon; she might be looking for more property. If she had an interest in Spirit Canyon Lodge, competitive or otherwise, she would do whatever it took to gather information.

Unfortunately, there was no catching up with Beth, so Zo decided to hang back and talk to Enid herself. No way was she going to let her friend get blindsided by the cantankerous old woman. She'd seen the way Beth, and everybody else, shrunk when she entered the room. But Zo had no reason to fear her. She'd dealt with her fair share of difficult people at the *Star*. She wasn't afraid of Enid Barrett.

As everyone else descended the deck steps, oohing and aahing over the illuminated cobblestone path, Zo waited. Just as she thought, Enid took the steps slowly, giving Zo an opportunity to ask her if she needed assistance.

"No," said Enid, clumping down the steps with her ivory cane. "I might use a walking stick, but I'm not disabled."

"I'm Zo, by the way. I own Happy Camper. You own Serenity Hills, right?"

"I know who you are," Enid snapped. "We spoke on the telephone a year ago. You had some advice for me as I recall."

"Not really advice," said Zo, admiring the campsite coming into view. A canopy draped in white lights covered three picnic tables, each with its own candle in a glass Mason jar. "I wanted you to know that a couple tourists complained about not getting rooms even though they'd booked them in advance. I thought it might be a computer glitch or something."

Enid stopped short, taking in the scene for a moment, then continued walking. "I don't have computer glitches. I run a high-functioning and highly profitable business. It was probably a matter of paying." Just then, her cane caught between stones, and she stumbled.

Zo reached for her free hand.

Enid coughed and resituated her cane. "Thank you."

"So, you knew Lilly?" asked Zo. Maybe that's why she was here.

"And her husband."

Zo thought back to the couple. "They were a cool pair, weren't they? When I come across the words young love, I always think of them, even though they'd been married for years when I met them."

Enid gave her a glance. "*Young love.* Silly Americans is more like it. Lilly ran off with him when she was just a girl. Her parents thought it was a bad match from the get-go. But that was Lilly, always thinking with her heart instead of her head. Her niece is just like her."

This was the other thing that irritated Zo about Enid Barrett. She was from Wales but raised in America. Yet she acted as if the United States was second-rate, always talking about her travels overseas. Zo wished she'd go back to the UK permanently—or anyplace else that would take her.

"Thinking with your heart isn't a bad thing," said Zo with a smile. She silently repeated a line she remembered from one of her books on the power of positive thinking: *Try to open up the channels of communication again.*

"If that's what you believe, you won't be in business long either," Enid declared.

Channel officially closed.

Some people's negativity was too powerful to combat. Zo picked up the pace, putting some distance between herself and Enid. Her temper could get the best of her, and she was about to say something she shouldn't, which might make matters worse.

She focused on the towering ponderosa pines instead, listening to the wind as it bent through the treetops, the narrow trunks swaying back and forth. It made a whishing sound, like a breath, inhaling and exhaling. Three hoots broke through the air, and Zo glanced toward the creek, where she saw a great horned owl perched in a tree, his distinctive ear tufts giving him the appearance of having horns. As if sensing her watching, his yellow eyes turned toward her, and she turned away, focusing on the domestic illusion created by the canopy. For Zo knew that's really what it was: an illusion of civilization. Owls, mountain lions, and pronghorn antelope owned the canyon. Everyone else was on borrowed space.

Chapter Four

Zo had been to enough Wild West shows, museums, and reenactments to know that a chuck wagon was essentially a cowboy's kitchen. The cook did all his prepping and cooking in the mobile kitchen. After a long day of driving longhorn cattle, cowboys huddled outside the wagon or under a canopy for a hot meal, usually beans and biscuits. Beth's chuck wagon was pretty much the opposite. It was a dining experience.

The canopy, the candles, and the tinkling creek made a perfect backdrop for a magical evening. Well, almost magical, thought Zo with a snicker. The cowboy music might not be exactly what Beth had in mind. Vi had Country Classics cued up on Pandora next to her large cast-iron pot of beans. Behind her, Beth's husband, Jack, was grilling cowboy burgers.

"When she said chuck wagon, I thought we'd be eating in a wagon," murmured Sarah, whom Zo had caught up with. "This is so much nicer."

"It's incredible," said Zo. From the vintage-looking graniteware dishes to the wooden condiment crates, Beth had thought of everything.

Beth told guests to help themselves, and as they started gathering plates, she and a little girl approached Zo. She had thick brown ringlets and a perfect button nose.

"This is my youngest daughter, Molly," said Beth. "Molly, this is Zo."

"Dad says it's going to rain," said Molly. "Grandma Vi's tracking the storm on WeatherBug. She says it's going to be a humdinger!"

Zo smiled at the girl's enthusiasm, despite her grim news. "It's good to meet you, Molly. Is that your sister?" She motioned to the older girl, who was standing behind three tiers of mouth-watering buttermilk biscuits, spice cakes, and brownies.

Molly nodded. "Yes, that's her. The weather's making her hair frizzy."

"Molly," scolded Beth. "What have I told you about sharing everything?" "Not to." Molly rolled her eyes. "Bye." The young girl bounded off to chat with other guests.

"She's adorable," said Zo.

"She's seven." Beth brushed back a piece of stray hair.

Zo motioned to the dining accommodations. "This is perfect, by the way." "Do you think so?" Beth asked. "It's not like when we were kids, but I wanted an event that would appeal to children *and* adults."

When they were young, Beth's uncle Pete had a cookout almost every weekend. After eating, they'd sit around the campfire on blankets and tell stories or sing songs. "A chuck wagon is a great idea," said Zo. "I can't think of anyone around here doing something like this, and I've been to my fair share of dinner shows. They're over-the-top western. This is…classy."

"I would like coffee," Enid interrupted. She'd finally caught up and stomped her cane three times to emphasize her arrival.

Zo wondered if she'd overheard their discussion. She was probably upset she hadn't thought of the chuck wagon idea herself. But Enid's inn wasn't a lodge; it was more of a Victorian bed and breakfast. Zo couldn't imagine a cookout there.

Beth walked toward the buffet. "No problem."

Zo followed, grabbing a plate.

"Decaf," added Enid. "I have a heart condition."

"Still no problem," Beth called back. From beneath a serving table, she pulled out a cooler holding two thermoses, one marked with a bright orange lid.

Zo proceeded through the line, deciding she was too impatient to be any good at the hospitality industry. One more remark out of Enid and she would have knocked her into cowboy heaven. Vi must have felt the same way. Zo sensed a simpatico relationship forming with the older woman. They exchanged eye rolls as Vi scooped beans onto her plate.

Zo introduced herself to Jack. A short man with a slight build, Jack wore Dockers and a button-down checkered shirt. Zo remembered he was an accountant, but he was doing a pretty good job on the grill. She also introduced herself to Megan, who was a picture of young Beth, elegant and inquisitive. She had the same straight hair, albeit—like her sister said—a little frizzy.

Zo had just sat down with her loaded plate when she heard the first rumble of thunder, low and angry, like the growl of a dog. If anyone else heard it, they didn't react. They were too busy eating and talking. Justin from KRSO was flirting with Jennifer, and his cameraman had just joined them. Sarah was trying to get a signal on her phone and had left the tent to move closer to the lodge. Munching her hamburger silently, Zo watched her, wondering what was so important.

"Where's she going?" Kaya asked. She'd been talking to Allison and hadn't noticed Sarah leave.

"She said she missed a call from her mom," said Zo. "Is everything okay?"

"Her mom is watching her daughter, who's two. Sarah worries about her constantly," Kaya said. "I would, too."

Zo nodded but didn't reply. Maybe something was wrong with Sarah's daughter, or maybe it was new-mom jitters. She didn't feel as if she knew her well enough to ask.

Zo glanced around the tent. The guests were enjoying themselves—except Enid. She was having a heated conversation with Griffin near the cooler. Well, it wasn't really a conversation. Griffin wasn't saying anything. He was opening a bottle of lemonade, and Enid had him cornered. Robyn, Griffin's fiancée, watched with her arms crossed. The cameraman watched, too.

Zo looked for Beth, but she was talking to Jack near the fire pit. Jack was stacking firewood like a teepee in the large iron grate. He was hesitant handling the wood, stopping when the sky rumbled. This time, the whole group noticed the noise.

Beth approached, probably to address the impending storm, but another boom shook the table, and a few guests cried out. Before Beth could quell their concerns, Vi's cordless speaker began to play the Oak Ridge Boys' ever-popular "Elvira." Country twang filled the void left by the hushed group. Beth threw her mom a look, and Vi turned down the volume. Zo bit her lip to keep from laughing.

"It sounds as if we have an uninvited guest," Beth observed, pointing at the clouds. "We may need to continue the festivities indoors."

"It's Thunderbird, one of the great Thunder Beings." Allison searched the darkening sky as she spoke. "The Lakota say he returns to the area in the spring and brings powerful electrical storms."

Zo noticed that Allison joined conversations when she had something intellectual to contribute. She was smart, though. Zo enjoyed listening to what she had to say—and not just because of her lisp.

"So, is he good or bad?" asked Sarah. The new mom, who'd rejoined the table, wanted the short version of the young professor's lecture.

Allison smiled. "Both. He can give life—and take it away." A sudden flash illuminated the sky. "The Lakota would say he's glaring at us."

Molly rushed to Beth's side. "Don't let him get me, Mom!"

Enid snorted. "Thunderbird. That's folklore—a myth."

"I'm not sure what you're getting at," said Kaya. "Native American beliefs are no more mythical than yours." Perhaps Native American herself, she wasn't about to let the comment go unchallenged.

"Kaya's right." Allison might have been quiet, but she was also passionate. Her neck was growing red with irritation. "All origin tales use stories to relay their message."

"Well my origin tale, as you call it, is over two thousand years old," said Enid. "No one was even here back then."

Zo didn't want to add more disagreement to the conversation but had a hard time holding her tongue. Native Americans had been here a long time, and she was just about to say so when Allison piped up again.

"Not true," said Allison. The blotchiness was spreading up to her face. "Scholars suggest the first humans were here thirteen thousand years ago. The Lakota believe they emerged from Wind Cave, coming to earth through its narrow opening."

Enid let out a noise that might have been a laugh.

"Because coming out of a garden is so much more believable, *right?*" Kaya said. Her scar grew sharper with the narrowing of her eyes.

"Any religion becomes suspect when looked at from a nonbeliever's viewpoint," said Allison. "You must realize that."

Zo was impressed with the way Allison had her friend's back. Even though Enid was older and opinionated, Allison didn't retreat from the argument.

Enid turned her gray head to one side. She reminded Zo of a bird. "Are you from here? Do I know you?"

Allison lifted her chin. "I'm a professor at Black Mountain College."

A few hard drops of rain hit the canopy. They multiplied quickly.

"I think we'd better take cover inside," said Beth, "before we get caught in a downpour."

Vi, Megan, and Molly had already started for the cottage. Meg carried the baked goods, Vi carried the beans, and Molly carried the sarsaparilla.

Beth looked at Jack for confirmation.

"You go ahead," Jack called, throwing on a windbreaker. "I'll get the rest of this."

Huddled under Justin's jacket, Jennifer let out a squeal as she and the rest of the group raced back to the lodge. Zo waited for Beth, but Beth had the situation, and Enid, under control. She opened her large golf umbrella and insisted Enid join her. Zo pulled up the hood of her sweatshirt and walked behind them, carrying the coffee thermoses. She could hear Enid complaining all the way to the lodge.

"A terrible idea," grumbled Enid. "These are Chanel."

Beth glanced at Enid's boots. "I'm sorry. I'd be happy to clean them up once we get inside."

"You have no idea what you're doing." Enid clumped up the deck stairs to the back door. "You don't know how to run a hotel. You'll be out of business before Labor Day if this keeps up. But I'm willing to help you."

Beth held open the door as they passed inside to the large dining area. "I'm not sure what you mean."

Griffin met them with two large towels. He handed one to Enid, who kept her hands stiffly at her sides. Water dripped from her shawl onto the pine floor.

"Thank you, Griffin," said Beth, reaching for a towel. "That's very kind of you."

Zo took one as well.

"*You* are a great disappointment," Enid said to Griffin. "You've been swindled by this…this snake."

Zo's jaw dropped. *Did she just say snake?* She couldn't have. Robyn was his girlfriend and a mere step away.

"She's not a snake, Mom." Griffin's voice was whiny but deferential. "She's my fiancée, so you'd better get used to it. I'm almost forty years old and can do what I want."

Robyn held up her ring finger. The diamond was at least one carat.

Enid didn't acknowledge Griffin's announcement or Robyn's ring. Instead, she turned away, saying, "It's like I've always said. If I want something done right, I have to do it myself."

A crack of thunder shook the room, underlining her dramatic exit.

Chapter Five

Everyone stared at Griffin and Robyn, Zo included. It seemed obvious now that Enid was his mother; they were both tall and had dark brown eyes and wavy hair. But they'd barely spoken during dinner, and the one exchange they'd had by the cooler seemed heated. Maybe Griffin was trying to hint about his engagement to Robyn but wasn't having any success.

"So, that went well," Robyn observed wryly. "It provided tonight's entertainment, if nothing else."

"I'm sorry, honey," said Griffin. "You know how she is."

"You're Griffin Barrett," Justin Castle said. "I *knew* I recognized you."

Jennifer looped her arm through Justin's. "Let's give these guys some privacy. I hear a glass of wine calling my name."

Zo was glad Jennifer was more interested in flirting than gossip. Zo didn't want the spat causing any bad publicity for Beth, and Justin was hanging on every word like a troll.

"Come on," Jennifer said, and Justin reluctantly turned away. The rest of the group trailed behind them.

"I didn't realize Enid was your mother," said Beth. "Why didn't you or Robyn say so?"

"Do you want the long or short version of that answer?" If Robyn was bothered by the outburst, she didn't act like it. Her face was as placid as a pond. If anything, she was bothered by Griffin's meek response. Enid obviously had a lot of control over him.

"Short version." Zo wanted the story as quickly as possible.

"Enid owns Serenity Hills. I gave it a bad rating in *Western Traveler*, and now she hates my guts," Robyn said. "She tried to get the editor to recall my review."

Beth's eyes narrowed. "You're with *Western Traveler*?"

Western Traveler was a magazine that included several destinations in the West, including the Black Hills. Zo had placed some ads in the magazine when she first opened Happy Camper. It was an incredibly popular magazine.

Robyn tipped her chin. "Not on this occasion, but yes, I am. I've been with them for five years." She looked at Griffin. "I thought this trip was about asking me to marry you, but maybe I was wrong."

"You're not wrong." Griffin grabbed for her hand. His shoulders softened, making him look older and less hip than his clothes. "I wanted to give you a weekend to remember."

"Then why is Enid here?" asked Robyn.

Zo had been wondering the same thing.

"I...my mom..." Griffin clearly didn't want to answer the question. "What does it matter? I wanted to ask you to marry me at a beautiful place in the Black Hills because I know you love it here. And this is a beautiful place, isn't it? You said yourself how much you liked it."

"And your mom, who hates your fiancée, just *happened* to be here at the same time?" Zo pressed. Something was off about this situation, and Beth was too polite to push. Zo had no such reservations.

Robyn crossed her arms, waiting for an answer.

"Look, I'll be honest with you. She wanted me to get some dirt on the place. She's worried the lodge will affect business." Griffin rubbed his hands together. "I guess she didn't trust me to get the job done. I never thought she'd check up on me."

Despite his weasely actions, Zo felt kind of bad for him. He looked like an overgrown schoolboy who'd been reprimanded by his teacher. If only he could get out from underneath his mom's thumb, he might be a decent guy.

"I can't believe this." Robyn's jaw was set in an angry square. "You take a marriage proposal as an opportunity to spy on the competition? You're just like her, aren't you?" She turned toward the staircase.

"I didn't find anything." Desperation crept into his voice. He loped after her. "Come on, Robyn. I know a way to fix this."

Beth stood there blinking, perhaps stunned by Griffin's admission. Her normally smooth hair was starting to frizz like her daughter Meg's. "Could the night get any worse?"

Just then the lights went out.

"I guess that answers that," Zo said.

From her oversized tote, Beth rummaged beneath a blanket and found the miniature flashlights. She handed one to Zo. "At least I'm prepared, right? I need to hand these out."

Beth walked to the great room, a small circle of light leading the way, and Zo followed.

She admired the way her friend remained calm despite the turn of events. The storm, the argument, and the news that a guest was collecting dirt on her lodge hadn't shaken her resolve. If it were her place, Zo would have sent the Barretts packing by now.

"I have flashlights." Beth began passing them out to the guests. "I'll see to the fuse box."

"Don't bother," said Justin. "I just got an alert from KRSO. A tree struck by lightning fell on a power line across Canyon Road. They'll need to remove it before we can get through."

"It looks like you'll have to stay overnight," said Jennifer, tossing her blond hair. She was cuddled next to Justin on the couch. "Oh, darn."

"I'm sure there's another way." A.J. took off his cap and smoothed his red-brown hair, which had curled in the rain. "You've got the station's van. It's good in the rain, and I need to be somewhere early tomorrow."

Zo realized it was the first time she'd heard him speak.

"There's not another way," said Justin. "I checked."

Justin's comment didn't leave A.J. much choice in the matter. They were driving together, and Justin was his boss. Zo thought A.J. looked annoyed at being told what to do. He was older than Justin and capable of making his own decisions. But his reticence made him seem younger.

"You're welcome to stay overnight for free." Beth's peppy voice lightened the mood. "You, too, Zo. I don't want anyone having an accident. And speaking of accidents, I need to see about the guests upstairs. They don't have flashlights yet." She hurried up the steps.

Zo was sure Beth didn't want Enid falling and breaking a hip during her stay. A mishap like that would give her the dirt she needed to smear the lodge's reputation.

From the deck, Jack entered the dining area, soaked from head to foot. His checkered shirt clung to his neck. The windbreaker hadn't been able to protect him from the violent storm. "The electricity's out," he said.

Zo held up her flashlight. "I know. Beth went upstairs to hand out flashlights. Justin said a tree fell. The power might be out all night."

"I'll get the lanterns," Jack offered. "Vi is staying with the kids in the cottage. I'm making up the innkeeper's suite down here for Beth and me."

Zo knew they normally stayed in the cottage, too. Jack must have wanted to remain close to the guests during the storm. "The innkeeper's suite sounds lovely."

"It *sounds* lovely, but it's in desperate need of TLC." Jack wiped his face with a towel. "Lilly and Pete hadn't stayed in the room for years. It was being used for storage. We're going to renovate though, so we'll have a handicap-accessible room. You can take the open room upstairs."

"Thanks," said Zo. "I don't want to drive back in this weather."

"And we don't want you driving back," he said. "It's really bad out there."

Jack left and returned with a couple lanterns. Zo asked if she could help, and he handed her a lantern. After they placed the lights around the great room, he hurried off to find a few more.

Zo glanced up the stairs, wondering what was taking Beth so long. She didn't like the idea of her being upstairs with Enid, Griffin, and Robyn. Who knew when another fight would break out? She decided to check on her, making her way up the stairs with the flashlight. When she got to the top of the steps and turned into the hallway, she heard Beth talking in a raised voice. Sarah, who had opened her room door, must have heard too because she gave Zo a worried look. Zo managed a shrug and a smile, hoping Sarah would blame the argument on Enid's bad behavior. Everyone had witnessed her exchange with Kaya and Allison at the cookout, not to mention her comments to Griffin and Robyn. But to be honest, Zo was surprised. She'd never heard Beth sound so forceful.

"*Keep your money.*" Beth's voice was angry. "The answer is no. You've insulted me and my family. Consider this your last night at Spirit Canyon Lodge."

Shutting Enid's door, Beth bumped into Sarah. "Sorry about that."

"No problem." Sarah's eyes were as round as her face. "It's so dark up here."

"I'll bring up a lantern." Beth's voice was still curt. She turned toward the stairs. "Zo! I didn't see you standing there."

"I thought you might need some help," said Zo. She could tell Beth was upset. Her soft blue-gray eyes were like icicles. Enid must have said something really awful.

"That's okay," said Sarah. Perhaps she sensed Beth's frustration, too. "I don't need a lantern. I'm going to bed anyway, and I have this." She held up the miniature flashlight Beth had given her.

"If you're sure you don't need one…" Beth took a deep breath. She looked more like herself.

Sarah nodded. "Positive. Goodnight."

Beth and Zo returned to the great room. The fireplace was ablaze with fresh firewood and candles. The mood was rustic and romantic, which Justin and Jennifer appreciated—and maybe A.J. and Allison, too. A.J. appeared more content with staying than he had earlier. He was seated close to Allison, discussing a book she was holding in her lap. With Sarah upstairs, Kaya was the only one without companionship, but she didn't seem to mind. She was reclining in a chair with her feet up, watching the fire.

Jack placed a lantern on the reception desk. "That's all of them."

"What about A.J. and Justin?" asked Beth, leaning toward Jack. "Where will they stay?"

"Already handled." Jack pointed to the rollaway cots, each topped with a stack of blankets. "If they stay, they'll stay in the great room. A.J.'s going to keep tabs on the weather. If it clears up, they plan on leaving."

"And how about the others?" Beth asked.

"They seem to be enjoying themselves," he said. "I don't know if I can say the same for my wife, though." He swept a piece of hair from her face. "Why don't you take a few minutes to relax and visit with Zo? You've hardly had time to talk to her. I've got this under control."

Beth turned to Zo. "He's right. I've been an awful friend."

"Nope," said Zo. "Just a busy hostess."

"Go have a glass of wine." Jack shooed them off. Then he added quietly, "The good stuff is in the pantry."

Zo followed Beth through the dining area into the kitchen, where she lighted a large lantern. Though tiny, the room was meticulous. See-through cupboard doors revealed stacked white dishes and crystal goblets in various shapes and sizes. Beth grabbed two red wine glasses and set them on the granite island. Then she vanished into the pantry, reappearing with a bottle of pinot noir.

"What a night." Beth heaved a sigh as she uncorked the bottle. "Can you believe this storm?"

"Bad timing, for sure," Zo agreed. She accepted a glass from Beth and swirled the ruby liquid.

"And that Enid woman." Beth took a slug of her wine. "What a menace. Can you believe she called her future daughter-in-law a snake?"

Zo smiled. Beth obviously needed something to take the edge off. "Actually, I can. I've talked to her a few times, and she's not the nicest person."

"I don't know how her husband puts up with her," said Beth, taking another drink of her wine.

"Being dead helps," said Zo. When Beth made a face, Zo continued. "He died several years ago and left her his hotel fortune. She not only owns Serenity Hills, she also has another spa out near Lead called Serenity Falls." Beth set down her wine glass with a *plunk.* "I wish I had your information. It makes sense now."

"What makes sense?" asked Zo.

Beth lowered her voice. "Enid offered me twenty thousand dollars to close the lodge. She told me I didn't have what it takes to make it in the hotel business. That's what we were arguing about upstairs."

"Was she serious?"

Beth nodded. "Completely serious. She has an envelope with cash in it. I spotted it earlier. I wanted to ask her to lock it in my safe, but I didn't want her to think I was snooping."

"The lodge must pose a real threat to her hotel," said Zo. "That's why she's checking up on Griffin."

Beth scrunched up her nose. "Do you really think she sees me as a threat?"

Zo nodded. "Even though it's not a resort, like hers, it's in a better location. There aren't many places to stay in the canyon. I can think of just one other, and it's a mom-and-pop shop. Totally run down."

"Good, I'm glad she's afraid. She should be. I hope I *do* run her out of business. She's not going to threaten me or my family. Good riddance, I say." Beth raised her glass.

Say it all you want—just don't say it too loud, Zo thought, for she knew how voices carried in the canyon.

Chapter Six

That night, Zo slept the peaceful sleep of her childhood, the feeling of home cocooning her in blithe happiness. In the morning, she lay perfectly still under the fluffy down comforter, wishing she could stay in bed all day. But the hope was quickly erased by a woman's scream. Zo blinked, wondering if she had dreamed the sound. When she heard loud voices, she knew it wasn't her imagination.

She jumped out of bed and flung open the door, looking up and down the hallway. Robyn and Griffin stood outside Enid's room, and when Robyn glanced in her direction, Zo knew something was wrong. Her plain face was changed with shock, and tears moistened Griffin's cheeks. Zo hustled to join them, stopping outside Enid's room. Inside, on the floor, Enid Barrett lay tangled in a crumpled heap of sheets. Zo wasn't a medical expert, but she didn't have to be. Enid was dead. Her face appeared distorted, unnatural. No wonder they'd hollered out. Seeing a dead body was scary.

"Something's wrong," Griffin said. "She's not breathing. I've called 911."

Robyn stood next to him, silent as stone.

Wearing a zip-up robe, Sarah opened her door. She rubbed her eyes. It didn't look as if she had slept well. "What's going on? I heard a scream."

"It's Enid Barrett," said Zo.

A.J. and Justin heard the commotion and joined them upstairs. Unprepared for the overnight stay, they were still dressed in their clothes from the night before. They might have been on their way out.

"Whatever happened to *Do Not Disturb?*" Jennifer padded out of her room in glitter slippers and a Victoria Secret's Pink nightshirt. "Hey Justin."

They shared a secret smile that told Zo they enjoyed a lot more than a glass of wine the previous night. But Justin was more interested in Enid's fall than Jennifer's greeting. He'd gone into reporter mode, excited about the trouble. He edged close to the door. "What's going on in there?"

Kaya stumbled into the hallway at the same time as Allison. Allison, clad in a knit pajama set, prompted, "Well?"

Since Griffin and Robyn seemed unable to state the obvious, Zo supplied the answer. "Enid's on the floor. We think she's...dead."

"No!" Sarah covered her mouth with her hands. "That can't be."

"Let me through." Allison nudged her way through the crowd at Enid's door. "I'm a doctor."

Although Zo didn't think Allison was a medical doctor, she moved out of the way so that Allison could enter the room. She was the closest thing they had to a doctor right now. Besides, she looked like she knew what she was doing. She examined Enid's body like doctors did on television. The group waited for her assessment.

"Was she on medication?" Allison asked. "Does anybody know?"

"Heart medicine," said Griffin.

Allison was unimpressed with his answer. "Do you know the name?"

"I...uh...yes, digoxin," Griffin stuttered. "She has heart disease."

"She's dead." Allison stood. "She's been dead several hours. If I had to guess what happened, I'd say she had a heart attack. It looks as if she tried to get out of bed and fell."

I wouldn't want her as my doctor, Zo thought. *She has a terrible bedside manner*. She didn't consider Griffin's feelings at all when she broke the news. *Poor guy*. Obviously, she was better with rocks than people. "I think we'd better get Beth."

"Yes..." Griffin choked on the word, and Robyn put her hand on his shoulder. "Go get Beth."

Zo hurried downstairs. She noticed Justin was on his cell phone, probably calling the station. *What a piece of work*, thought Zo as she knocked on the innkeeper's suite. Enid's body was still warm and he was gathering fodder for the evening news.

Beth opened the door. She was already showered and dressed. "You're up early. I was just on my way to put out the continental breakfast. What's the matter?"

The distress must have shown on Zo's face, and she quickly filled in Beth and Jack on the happenings upstairs. It took a few moments for them to grasp the problem. They kept interrupting with questions.

"Are you sure she's dead?" asked Beth. "She seemed like one of those women who would live to be a hundred."

Jack was sitting on the edge of the bed putting on his tennis shoes. "And yet she made her timely departure at our lodge. How convenient for us."

"She *looks* dead, and Allison says she's dead, but Griffin called the police when he found her." The welcome chime rang out. Someone entered the lodge. "That must be them now," said Zo.

They rushed into the great room and were greeted by Max Harrington. In his green uniform and forest ranger badge, he looked official but hardly qualified to deal with a corpse.

"Seriously?" Zo sighed. "We need *real* help. A woman might be dead."

"We got a call about an unconscious female, elderly, with a heart condition," said Max. Another ranger with a medical bag was with him. "We're the closest help available."

"She's upstairs." Zo hurried up the stairway with Beth on her heels. Everyone else was half in their rooms and half in the hallway. It was as if they were afraid of getting too close to a dead body. Only Justin inched closer with his phone. *Is he thinking about taking a picture?* Zo thought. Ignoring him, she led the charge into Enid's room with Max, the medic, Beth, and Griffin following. Griffin informed Max that the woman on the floor was his mother.

It didn't take Max long to determine Enid was dead. He must have agreed with Allison's assessment because neither he nor the medic attempted resuscitation.

"This is Enid Barrett," said Max. "What was she doing staying here? She lives in Spirit Canyon."

"I know," said Zo. "She was getting dirt on Beth's lodge. She wanted to shut her down."

Max looked to Griffin for confirmation; he nodded silently.

"Tom, would you take Griffin downstairs?" said Max to the medic. "Get him a drink of water while we wait for the police to arrive."

Griffin nodded again even though Max wasn't talking to him. Griffin didn't look well; he was pale and leaning against the door. Maybe he was faint or in a state of shock. Robyn followed them down the stairs.

When they left, Max turned to Zo, glancing at her pajamas. She was wearing a pair of Beth's heart lounge pants, which were too long in the legs, so she'd rolled the waistband to hike them up.

"You stayed overnight," said Max. "Was Enid having any troubles? Complaining of chest pain?"

"No, but she was on heart medication," said Zo. "Griffin said diga-something…"

Max glanced around the room looking for the medication. Finding none, he continued. "You said Enid was trying to get dirt on the lodge, to shut it down?"

"She was," said Beth. "She offered me twenty thousand dollars to close it. She had the cash in an envelope."

"This envelope?" Max pointed to a large manila envelope on the nightstand.

Beth nodded.

After slipping on a pair of disposable gloves, he opened it. But the money was gone. It had been replaced by dozens of folded sheets of Spirit Canyon Lodge stationery.

* * * *

Zo and Beth sat across from Max in the lodge's knotty pine dining nook. They'd come in here to avoid Justin, who looked as if he was mentally recording the event from the great room. Beth was recounting her strange interactions with Enid, and Zo was studying Max's reactions. He was a good listener; Zo gave him that. He hadn't interrupted Beth once since she began. Sometimes his blue eyes narrowed or his brow furrowed, but he remained silent, giving Zo the feeling he was tucking away each word in a safe somewhere.

A loud noise broke up the subdued atmosphere, and Zo's attention turned to the door. An officer from Spirit Canyon police arrived. She knew who he was before he introduced himself. He had black hair, green eyes, and was well over six feet tall—all telltale signs. It was Brady Merrigan, the cop she'd tangled with a few times in her youth. Growing up in different foster homes meant changing rules—and curfews. Unfortunately for her, Officer Merrigan was always consistent in his reprimands. But that'd been a long time ago. Maybe he'd forgotten who she was.

"Thanks for your quick response, Maxwell," he said as Max pulled over a chair from another table. "Brady Merrigan, Chief of Police." His eyes landed on Zo. "Fancy seeing you here. I thought you were keeping out of trouble these days."

Of course he remembered. Merrigans were like elephants: they never forgot. "I do my best."

His chair creaked as he sat down. "You must be the new owner of the lodge, Lilly's niece. You and Zo were friends, if my memory serves me correctly."

Beth nodded. "Yes, I'm Beth, and that's my husband, Jack." She pointed to Jack, who was putting out muffins on the breakfast bar.

Jack set down the tray and shook Brady's hand. "Muffin?"

Brady smiled. "Thank you."

Jack offered him the tray.

"Why don't you tell me what happened this morning, Beth, from the beginning." Brady removed the muffin wrapper. "It will help me determine how to proceed."

Unlike Max, Brady looked impatient as Beth recounted the story. He took notes, clicking his pen whenever she paused. Once she was finished, he leaned back and crossed his arms. "Where are you guys from again?"

Beth glanced at Jack. "Chicago."

"Why?" Jack asked.

"Nothing." Brady shrugged. "I thought I heard an accent, that's all."

Zo shook her head. Brady was acting as if Chicago was the other side of the world. It was so embarrassing. If she had to guess, he was thinking *gangs* right now.

"Twenty thousand dollars is a lot of money," continued Beth. "Who filled the envelope with stationery?"

"Spirit Canyon isn't Chicago, Mrs. Everett. We've got our own way of doing things, so why don't you leave the questions to me," said Brady. "In fact, I have one for you."

The group waited. Zo tapped the table with her stubby fingernails, frustrated by the direction of the conversation.

Brady wasn't in a hurry now. He glanced around the dining room and into the great room. "You've made a lot of changes to this place since I was here last. They must have cost a pretty penny." He pointed to the kitchen. "Like subway tile. It's trendy and expensive."

Beth frowned. "The renovation did cost quite a bit, but I'm sorry. I don't understand the question."

"Let me be clear," said Brady. "How would you describe your financial situation?"

"That's none of your business," Jack shot back.

Beth stood and put a hand on Jack's shoulder. "I didn't take the money if that's what you're insinuating. We would never close the lodge for twenty thousand dollars."

"So, where is it?" Brady asked.

"I don't know." He hadn't shaken Beth's resolve. "That's why I'm asking you."

"It'd be nice to have twenty thousand dollars *and* the lodge, wouldn't it?" said Brady. "With Enid gone, you wouldn't have to worry about fulfilling your end of the bargain."

"She didn't have to tell you about the money, you know," said Zo. "Ever think of that?"

"Except for one thing, dear. Her son knew about the offer." Brady laced his hands behind his head. "If Beth didn't tell me about the money, Griffin would have."

"Beth didn't do anything to Enid or her money," said Zo. "And don't call me *dear*."

"Okay, *Zo*," said Brady. "You're Beth's friend, right? You're trying to help her out. I understand. I'd do the same for my friend. But I wouldn't help cover up a crime."

"I'm not!" Zo denied. She couldn't listen to him make up stories about what had just happened. Jack couldn't either. He was clenching his jaw to keep silent.

Max jumped into the conversation. "Listen, Enid probably had a heart attack. She was older and on medication. The autopsy will tell us for sure. As for her money, it will turn up. Like Beth said, it's a lot of cash. Maybe Enid stashed it somewhere."

"Yes!" said Beth. "Maybe she hid it."

"I appreciate your opinion, Max, but this is official police business. You stick to what you do best—nature stuff." He looked out the window. "There's probably a poacher going over the limit right now."

Max's blue eyes darkened with anger. "I was the first one on the scene, Brady. I've got just as much right to be here as you do. Besides, we're in Black Hills National Forest—like you said, *my* territory."

Brady laughed. "You're determined. I'll say that. Okay, kid. You go ahead and stay." He patted Max on the back. "Just be smart. With the money missing, we can't assume Enid died of natural causes." Just then, crime scene investigators arrived with cameras and equipment. Brady stood to direct them. "I'm ruling it a suspicious death until further notice."

Chapter Seven

Even though electricity had been restored, the lodge was still shrouded by the dark clouds hovering over the canyon—and dark secrets. As Zo entered the great room, now dotted with police personnel, she considered the murkier aspects surrounding Enid's death. Had Enid died under suspicious circumstances, like Brady said?

First was the cash in her room; it was missing. Money could be a motive for murder, and Jennifer herself admitted to losing a lot of it in Deadwood yesterday. Sarah was a struggling single mother, and Allison, a new professor, probably wasn't any better off financially. But none of them knew about the money, did they?

Griffin definitely knew about it. He and Robyn were celebrating their engagement, but Enid had denounced the decision right to their faces. Over the course of dinner, she'd also denounced Native American practices, offending Kaya and everyone else. Justin and A.J. were locals, so a past offense might be possible there. Plus Justin was just a little too excited about the turn of events. When Zo thought about it, Brady was right. Any one of them might have sent Enid to her final resting place.

"What did the ranger say? Does he know what happened to Enid?" Allison asked when Zo joined the group. Allison had been thumbing through a copy of *Scientific American*. The rest of the group, coming down from the upsetting moment, relaxed on the sofa. Jennifer, perhaps hung over, had her slippers on the coffee table and her eyes closed. Next to her, Kaya had her arms crossed and her legs extended. Sarah gingerly sipped a cup of coffee. They glanced at Zo, waiting for her response.

Zo shook her head. "No, he doesn't. I think it was a heart attack."

"Serves the old biddy right," said Jennifer, closing her eyes again.

"Jennifer!" said Sarah. "You shouldn't say that."

Jennifer gave Sarah a look. "Come on. She was mean to everyone, even her own kid. Would you ever treat Lexy like that?"

"Of course not," said Sarah. "I would love to see her get married and—" She broke off abruptly, tears filling her eyes.

Maybe Enid's death had shaken her more than Zo realized. Her eyes had not only tears but dark circles under them. They made her appear older than her friends.

"You *will* see her get married," said Allison. "She's going to grow into a beautiful young woman. She's getting stronger every day."

Sarah seemed reassured by the statement. She must have trusted Allison's intelligence because her face brightened. She turned to Zo, who was hoping, but not asking, for an explanation. "My daughter—she's two— was diagnosed with leukemia. Things have been pretty hard since then."

"I'm so sorry." Zo's heart went out to the young mother.

"She's better," she was quick to add. "Otherwise I wouldn't be here. My mom has been great. She's watching her right now. God knows I couldn't count on Lexy's father to do anything."

Kaya looked up from her phone, her high cheekbones becoming more prominent. "Damon's a jerk."

"World-class," agreed Jennifer.

"We divorced last year," Sarah explained.

"It's said that many families split after a traumatic illness," said Allison. "That doesn't make it any easier, though," she added when Kaya and Jennifer turned icy stares on her.

"It's okay," said Sarah, forgiving her friend's awkwardness with a smile. "I know what Allison says is true. It wouldn't even be that bad if Damon had agreed to pay alimony. I mean, how am I supposed to take care of a sick child and work full time?" She shook her head. "It's crazy."

Jennifer took her glitter slippers off the coffee table and sat up. "Come with me to Deadwood. I've got a feeling today's your lucky day."

"Like yesterday was your lucky day?" asked Kaya. "Besides, we're going to see the heads."

Zo knew Kaya was referencing Mount Rushmore, one of the most visited tourist attractions in the Black Hills. Carved out of granite, the sixty-foot faces of Washington, Jefferson, Roosevelt, and Lincoln greeted over three million visitors a year. Another popular face was that of Crazy Horse, a Lakota warrior. It would be even bigger when it was finished. Zo had seen both monuments about five thousand times, but that didn't make them any less impressive. "If it gets late, don't miss the lighting ceremony. It starts at nine with a short film and lasts about forty-five minutes."

Allison motioned toward the dining area. "From the looks of it, it *will* be late. They're not even finished with Justin."

Zo gave her an encouraging look. "It won't take long. Mine didn't. Justin is a reporter. I think he's asking them more questions than they're asking him."

"I don't see why we have to talk to them anyway," said Kaya. "It's sad and all, but old people die every day."

"Right?" Jennifer reclined again, her blond hair splayed over the couch cushions. "Even by dying, the old hag is causing problems."

Zo agreed but kept quiet. Jennifer had no problem sharing her opinions. She might, however, after she talked to Brady Merrigan.

Across the room, Beth put another log on the fire. She dusted off her hands and gave Zo a wave. Zo excused herself from the group.

"You need help?" Zo asked.

"Vi has the kids, and Jack is doing cleanup," Beth said. "As long as that log catches fire, I think I'm good."

A murmur caught Zo's attention, and she turned around. Griffin and Robyn were engaged in a conversation on the couch. Griffin rested his head on Robyn's chest, looking as if he enjoyed the touch of her hand. Robyn was less content with her role as consoler. Death or not, she didn't seem like the type who played the supportive role. She would want Griffin to take charge of his destiny now—and the family business as well.

Beth followed Zo's gaze. "Does Griffin have any siblings? I know you said Enid was a widow."

Zo shook her head. "None that I know of. I didn't even realize *he* was Enid's son. That has to make him Spirit Canyon's most eligible bachelor— or *did* make him the most eligible bachelor," Zo added. "I can't believe he's engaged to the same woman who nearly brought down Enid's resort with a bad review."

"Was it really that bad?" said Beth.

Zo nodded. "I remember it now. It was last fall. That's probably how Griffin met her. Enid did all sorts of damage control afterward. At a town meeting, she handed out postcards of the resort and asked businesses to place them near their registers. She also placed ads quoting sparkling reviews in *Canyon Views* and put up that hideous billboard outside of town. It's gigantic."

Beth's blue-gray eyes grew wide with curiosity. "I've seen it, and you're right. It's hideous. Why did townspeople go along with it?"

"They didn't have a lot of choice." Zo shrugged. "She had a ton of money. Besides, she wasn't the type of person people confronted. Her own son seemed afraid of her."

Beth walked to the reception desk, near the dining area. Zo followed. The area was more private, but Beth spoke in a hushed voice. "Do you think Brady is right? Do you think someone could have killed her for the twenty thousand dollars?"

"It's a definite possibility," said Zo.

"Like who?"

"It could have been anybody," whispered Zo.

"Brady thinks it was me," said Beth. "Why?"

"You went to her room late last night. You had motive *and* means to kill her."

"But I didn't do it!" said Beth, a little too loudly.

Finished talking to Justin, Brady Merrigan stood and crossed his arms, his police uniform stretching tightly across his chest. He blocked the little bit of light streaming in from the dining area.

Zo nodded toward the doorway. "Try convincing Brady Merrigan."

* * * *

Happy Camper didn't open until noon on Sundays, so Zo returned to Spirit Canyon in plenty of time to change before opening the store. She felt grubby driving home in last night's capris and t-shirt and longed for a hot shower. It would help clear her mind, still whirling from the early morning events. A dead guest wasn't the kind of publicity Beth had wanted for her grand opening, and Brady suspected foul play. Zo climbed the steps to her house. The lodge was open all right—*open for murder.*

She hung her backpack on the hook and tossed her keys on the small kitchen table, glad to be home. She loved her story-and-a-half. It was older, built in the 1970s, but it suited her business and complemented its surroundings. The living room was decorated with odds and ends from the auctions she attended. Like the store, it was cozy and inviting. She thought of her cedar deck as an extension of her living space and arranged it with just as much care, investing in an outdoor fireplace and cushioned furniture. Enjoying a cup of tea or hot cocoa under the stars was the best part of her day.

After showering and towel-drying her hair, she pulled on a pair of jeans and LIFE IS GOOD t-shirt. Donning her flower flip-flops, she grabbed her purse and store key. If she hurried, she could grab a sandwich to-go at

O.K. Coffee Corral, a walk-up restaurant with a large outdoor dining area that, with imagination, looked like a livestock corral. Although the food options were limited, it was popular with tourists because it was fast and had a great view of the Black Hills. Even on days like today, with the sun just breaking through, everyone wanted to be outside enjoying the low humidity and clear mountain air.

Cunningham was in his garden again, and as she locked up, she remembered what she wanted to ask him. Like Cunningham, Allison was a professor at Black Mountain College. She wondered if he knew Allison or anything of her work there.

"Hey Cunningham," she said from her deck. He glanced up in her direction, his straw hat tilting to one side. She waved and walked down the steps to where their lawns met. "I found my cat."

"It's not the finding part you have trouble with," he said, returning to the new shoots. "It's the keeping."

She ignored the remark. George's disappearances bothered her more than she liked to admit. Some days she worried she'd never have a significant relationship in her life, even with a cat. "Do you know Allison Scott? I met her last night. She said she teaches science at Black Mountain."

"Science." He put down his trowel. "That clarifies a good deal."

"Come on, Russell," she said. She didn't have time for his word games today. She needed to open Happy Camper in forty-five minutes. "Do you know her or not?"

"Yes, I do."

Zo took a breath. The man could be so trying sometimes. "Well, what's she like?"

"She's young and passionate, like you, but more level-headed," said Cunningham. "A geoscientist, I believe. She's quiet, perhaps still finding her way in academia. She has something to do with the research out at Homestake Mine."

That reminded Zo of a thought. "What would a new professor make, approximately? In terms of money? It can't be much."

He set his straw hat on the ground, and ran his fingers through his snow-white hair. Despite his hat, his scalp was pinkening. "Certainly, she would be at the lower end of the spectrum as a new professor, but her work at the lab might compensate for her lack of tenure. Why do you ask?"

Zo explained Enid's death and the missing money. Cunningham listened intently, which was why she liked him. Everything she said was a matter to be taken seriously—cats, cocktails, murder. All were equally worthy of his time.

"People have killed for less, certainly," he said when she was finished. "One need only skim the surface of literature to find examples—"

"I'd love to hear them, but I've gotta run. Drinks tonight?"

"You bring the rum," he said.

She laughed, gave him a wave, and started for downtown.

Chapter Eight

When Zo opened Happy Camper thirty minutes later, breakfast sandwich in hand, George ran out of the store before she could say hi or good-bye. Like an orange streak, he ran up the hill and disappeared into the tree that hung over her deck. Cunningham was right. It wasn't the finding; it was the keeping that evaded her. Boyfriends, money, cats. But wasn't the adventure in the pursuit? She flipped the door sign to OPEN. She hoped so.

The store had certainly been an adventure, a labor of love now filled with the things she loved. She turned on the Zenith radio, circa 1941, purchased at a recent auction. Bob Dylan's "Tangled up in Blue" played on the local station. She liked antiques but didn't always like selling them. She missed them when they were gone. They gave the store a vintage feel. So did the books. From birding how-tos to stargazing guides, she carried a little bit of everything. People loved to indulge when they were on vacation, buying things they wouldn't otherwise. Why not brush up on the constellations while staking a tent?

After counting out money for the register, she turned on her computer and waited. She noticed the sun was starting to peek through the clouds, creating a rainbow and signaling the passing of last night's storm. If Enid's death wasn't plaguing her thoughts, it would have been the perfect start to a Sunday morning. Even so, it was pretty darn good.

She unwrapped her breakfast, a flatbread sandwich with egg, veggies, and pepper jack cheese. It smelled spicy and delicious. She'd only taken one bite, however, when the first customer arrived. A mom in her late forties with two teenagers in tow needed a new tent.

"My tent didn't hold up under last night's rain," she said. Her eyeliner was smudged, and her sweatshirt hung off one shoulder.

"We slept in the car," said her son, who was at least five inches taller than his mother. He seemed to enjoy making the comment.

Since hers wasn't an outdoor store, Zo only had one tent, but it was good quality and would fit a family of four. A floor model was set up in the corner, with a pretend campfire, cookware, and skewering sticks. She led the family to it.

"It's not large, but it will work," she explained. "And most importantly, it will keep you dry."

"It's two hundred dollars!" said the woman.

"You saw what ninety-nine dollars got us, Mom," said the girl, not looking up from her cell phone, where she texted busily with both thumbs. "Come on."

"I do have a Memorial Day sale going on right now," said Zo. "Ten percent off all camping gear." She heard another customer enter the store. "I'll let you think it over."

Seeing the person, she realized it wasn't a customer; it was Melissa Morris from across the street. She worked at the visitor center, handing out maps, brochures, and information to tourists. A few years older than Zo, Melissa had grown up here, too. They'd attended school together and worked the odd jobs of a tourist town: funnel cake maker, balloon blower, and face painter. Now Melissa was a mom of three girls and worked part-time at the center. She said she didn't care where she worked, as long as it got her out of the house for a few hours a day. But the job was a good fit. She knew everyone in town.

"Did you hear?" said Melissa. "Enid Barrett died. It was on KRSO news."

Zo nodded and walked to the register to finish her breakfast. "I did. I was there."

"What?" Melissa followed her. "You were there?"

"Uh huh. My friend owns Spirit Canyon Lodge." She took a bite of her sandwich.

Melissa swiped at her straight bangs. The rest of her hair was curly, and the cut framed her face nicely. Most days she wore a high ponytail. She was a busy mom and liked it out of her eyes. But today she wore it down. "Why was she staying there anyway? She lives up the hill."

"To get information on the lodge," said Zo.

"Dirt, you mean?" Melissa, who was a gossip herself, rolled her eyes. "It doesn't surprise me. Tell me everything."

Zo relayed as many details as she was comfortable sharing.

"I wonder what will happen to the business now," Melissa mused after Zo finished.

"*Businesses*, right?" asked Zo. "She had another resort."

Melissa nodded. "One here and one by Lead—Serenity Falls. I'm sure Griffin will take charge of them, as much as he can take charge of anything." She picked up a few of the business cards Zo had on the counter. Multicolored, they had the Happy Camper logo on them. "We're out of these at the visitor center."

"I only met him this weekend, but I can't see him running two resorts," said Zo. "There's nobody else?"

"Nope," said Melissa. "Enid had a good manager, though. He's been there for years. He's probably the reason why Serenity Hills has done as well as it has. I'm sure he'll continue doing everything."

Melissa had info on everyone. She was a mom and volunteered—a lot. Zo couldn't think of a person or business that she hadn't baked for, donated to, or raffled on behalf of.

"Do you know him, Henry Miller?" Melissa continued.

"The name sounds familiar." Zo took the last bite of her sandwich.

"You've probably seen him at town meetings. He did a lot of legwork for Enid."

"Oh, I know who you're taking about," said Zo. "Tall guy, soft spoken, gray hair. Always wears a suit jacket?"

"Pretty much the exact opposite of Enid, and he's been there forever. Can you imagine?" Melissa shivered. "Working for her your whole life? Not this girl."

"When Harley punches in, I should take something out there," said Zo. "Offer my condolences."

"Like bake something?" said Melissa, raising her eyebrows. They disappeared under her bangs.

Zo nodded. Although she wasn't a baker, it would provide her a reason to get inside the resort. She hadn't been there in years and wanted to learn more about Enid and her businesses. It might prove helpful later. She knew how quickly a story could change.

"Well knock yourself out," said Melissa. "I wouldn't waste one chocolate chip on Enid Barrett's passing."

The mother and teens approached the register with the packaged tent, and Melissa said good-bye so that Zo could take care of her customers. Zo rang the item, but her mind wasn't on the tent or even the decent sale. It was on Henry. She wondered why Henry remained an employee at Serenity Hills for so many years. He always had a kind word for business owners at town meetings and was the first to volunteer. Maybe he was a good PR person. Or maybe he just needed a good job.

Enid was wealthy and might have paid well, and it wasn't easy to find employment in a trendy town like Spirit Canyon. Even college grads ended up working retail just to be close to the skiing, hiking, and the other outdoor activities in the area. Still Zo was curious enough about Henry to bake cookies. She perused her limited snack aisle: marshmallows, chocolate chips, and graham crackers. Or at least s'more bars.

* * * *

Serenity Hills was located on the last street in town, nestled into the foothills of Black Hills National Forest. A good location, it provided tourists with access to shopping and a buffer from street noise. The surrounding acres had lots of trees and even a nice view of Spirit Canyon's waterfall, pictured on many postcards. Though it was a lovely home and lovely location, Zo decided it looked more like a bed and breakfast than a spa or resort. Even the drive was gravel, and her Outback flung up rocks as she pulled into the lot.

Despite being Memorial Day weekend, plenty of open spots remained, and Zo wondered if the resort wasn't struggling more than she realized. She'd always assumed, probably because of the airs Enid put on, that the resort was the crème de la crème of lodging establishments, but glancing at it now, Zo decided it looked like a relic—almost out of place in the hip town of Spirit Canyon.

Grabbing the plate from the passenger seat, she noted the bars were still warm. The treats, which she'd baked between customers, made her car smell like a mixture of chocolate and marshmallows. She would be thinking of campfires for the next few days, which was okay with her. Nothing made her happier than a cozy fire and a sweet treat.

She hurried up the front steps, admiring the swing on the wraparound front porch. She could get used to spending time on the veranda, but the house was too formal to fit her style. It was a towering three-story Victorian, complete with ornate turret and a decorative front door. Inside was a small gift shop with all sorts of lotions and rubs that promised rest, relaxation, and rejuvenation. Zo glanced at a price tag: sixty-five dollars! She put down the bottle. For sixty-five dollars, it would have to make her aches—and her laundry—disappear.

No one was at the mahogany front desk, so Zo waited for a moment, listening to the sounds of a piccolo tinkling over the speakers. She took a deep breath, deciding the spa music had the desired effect. It was relaxing—for about thirty seconds. Then it got on her nerves. She was more of a classic-rock kind of girl.

"Hello?" she said and rang the service bell.

She heard footsteps somewhere within the oversized house. A moment later, Henry appeared, looking disheveled. Even though he wore a suit jacket, half of his button-up shirt was un-tucked, and his face was ashen.

"I apologize for the wait," said Henry. "How may I help you?"

"Hi Henry, I'm Zo Jones. I own Happy Camper." She placed her plate of s'more bars on the counter. "I wanted to offer my condolences to you and the staff. I understand you were close to Enid. I'm sorry for your loss."

His face relaxed, clearly glad for the friendly visit. "Oh…well, thank you," he said. "I'm sorry I didn't recognize you at first. I think I've seen you at a few town meetings. It's been a trying day."

"I understand," said Zo. "Businesses have to keep running as usual even when something goes wrong. You must be exhausted."

"I am," he admitted. "I could use a cup of tea. Would you like one? We always have hot water for our spa clientele."

"Yes, thank you." She joined him in the lobby and selected an orange-infused spice tea, the boiling water releasing the pungent aroma as it hit the teabag. Henry chose Earl Grey and added a sugar cube. He stirred the liquid as he sat across from her on the tufted couch, a gorgeous piece that must have cost a fortune. The entire lobby was decorated with antiques such as curvy wingback chairs and a fainting couch. The problem was they didn't really shout *spa*.

He removed the cellophane from the plate and took a s'more bar. Then he offered her one, but she shook her head. She'd had more than a few tastes as she prepared them.

"I haven't eaten all day," he said, setting the plate on a napkin.

As she watched him enjoy the dessert, she realized he wasn't as snappy of a dresser as Enid, but he was gracious. His manners were Old World and refined, the type Enid lacked but probably appreciated. Henry would grow better and more distinguished with age. In some ways, he was like the Victorian house he worked in, older but well made. Zo could see why Enid needed him at the resort.

"Did you know Enid was having heart trouble?" The old prickle of adrenaline rushed through her as she asked the question. She loved finding answers, getting to the truth behind a story. Maybe she'd liked working at the *Star* more than she admitted, but she liked Happy Camper even better. "The attack came as a surprise to me."

He dabbed his lips with his napkin. "Me, too. Of course I knew about Enid's heart condition, but she'd been on medication for years. In fact, she just had a checkup last week. The doctor didn't say anything about a problem."

"My friend, Beth, owns Spirit Canyon Lodge, and I was out there last night when Enid passed away," Zo said. "She seemed fine—except she did have a tense moment with Griffin. They had an argument."

Henry took a sip of his tea before continuing. He did nothing in haste. "To Griffin's credit, he mentioned it when he called this morning with the news. But Enid told me about the disagreement last night. We spoke on a daily basis, about the business."

About the business and what else, Zo wondered. It would have been late to call an ordinary employee. Maybe Enid demanded he be at her beck and call. "Did Griffin tell you about his engagement to his girlfriend, Robyn? Enid was pretty upset by the news."

"He did," Henry said.

He crossed his legs, and Zo noticed how worn his dress slacks were at the knees. Maybe Enid hadn't paid as well as she thought, or maybe Henry had an affinity for old houses and old clothes.

"Enid was naturally upset by the news. She couldn't believe Griffin would marry a woman who'd caused the family so much angst."

"Could one review really cause that many problems?" asked Zo.

He nodded. "It could and did. *The Western Traveler*, as you know, is well known in the area. It's hard to get into print these days; it's a shame the review was so damning. Robyn's column is incredibly popular with the younger crowd, one of our targeted demographics. We're trying to appeal to them."

Zo could see the predicament. Spas were trendy; old houses were not. Enid must have spent a fortune on the spa to appeal to hipsters. Robyn's review sounded like a stiff rebuke of her efforts. Zo needed to get ahold of that review and read it for herself.

"Honestly, I agreed with Enid. I don't know what Griffin sees in her," continued Henry. "She's a deceitful person. Mark my words, she'll hurt him if she gets the chance." He sipped his tea, perhaps to keep himself from saying any more.

Deceitful and snake—both words used to describe Robyn. Zo had a feeling there was more to Henry's and Enid's rebukes than Robyn's review. "Did something happen when she stayed here?"

"Despite appearances, I'm not a fuddy-duddy." He put down his teacup and laced his fingers. "I know what young people do. I see lots of things in the hospitality business."

Zo waited for the rest of the answer.

"She had a man in her room—overnight." Henry lowered his voice in clear disapproval. "It wasn't Griffin. And now she and Griffin are engaged."

Zo did the math in her head. Robyn stayed in the fall, which was nine months ago. Zo had a hard time keeping a cat that long, never mind a boyfriend. She wasn't about to judge Robyn for moving on if the night hadn't worked out.

Still, Robyn's tryst might be troubling to Griffin, and Enid would have had no problem telling him had she lived to see Sunday morning. Was it possible that Robyn murdered Enid to keep her secret safe? But what about the money? Judging from appearances, Zo didn't think Robyn had money problems, or if she did, they didn't prevent her from buying expensive clothes. Zo decided the money and the murder might not be connected. Two separate crimes could have been committed under one roof. The adrenaline *was* kicking in. She was getting way ahead of herself. Enid's death hadn't been determined a homicide—yet. But she was convinced it would be.

"It's a beautiful resort, Henry, no matter what the review said." Zo set down her empty teacup and stood. It felt good being one step closer to the truth. "If you need any help, please don't hesitate to ask. I'm just down the street, and I imagine Griffin will have his hands full running two hotels."

Henry rose, too. "He won't be running this one."

Zo stopped putting on her sweater.

"Enid left it to me."

Chapter Nine

Zo was stunned. She couldn't believe Enid would leave Serenity Hills to her manager instead of her son. Maybe it shouldn't have been so surprising, though, considering how she and Griffin had argued the night before her death. Perhaps they weren't close. A family business could complicate relationships. That might have been the case here.

Zo checked the dashboard clock; she had time to make it to the library. Robyn wrote a monthly column for *Western Traveler*, and Zo wanted to peruse the fall edition for the review of Serenity Hills. Hattie Fines, the librarian with a serendipitous last name and Zo's good friend, could easily help her locate it. She was a paragon of information. Google was pointless when Hattie was just down the street.

On the corner of Main and Juniper was the always-busy tiny brick building. Four book clubs met monthly at the library, and Zo's astrology group, the Zodiac Club, sometimes met here, too, during bad weather. Since it was late in the afternoon, and Memorial Day weekend, the parking lot was unusually bare. Zo zipped into a place near the front door and hurried in to find Hattie.

She spotted her pushing a book cart, reshelving the large print section. Barely five feet tall, Hattie toted a stool everywhere she went. Today she stood between authors with last names A and B, one Converse tennis shoe precipitously balanced on the middle shelf of the bookcase.

"Let me guess." Hattie gave Zo a glance before returning to call numbers. "You need me to interlibrary loan an astrology book from some exotic place like, oh, I don't know. San Diego."

"You'd better stick to reading books," said Zo, handing her another tome from the cart. "You don't have a psychic bone in your body."

"What then?" asked Hattie. "I'm at the end of my shift, so it must be about time for cocktails with Cunningham." Placing her red reading glasses on her head, she turned her eyes on Zo, the skin around them crinkling as she smiled. "You know he starts early."

Zo returned the smile. "It's a holiday. He'll be imbibing all weekend. Why don't you join us?"

"That man is a hopeless old flirt." Hattie stepped down from the stool.

Secretly, Zo thought they would make the perfect pair. They were both smart, fun, and in their sixties. But she kept that information to herself. She wasn't the matchmaking type. She couldn't find herself a steady boyfriend; she wouldn't presume to find one for someone else. "But first, I want you to help me find a review."

"What kind of review? A book review?"

"A review in *Western Traveler*," Zo said. "Do you have that magazine?"

Hattie gave her a look. "Do I have that magazine? Of course I have that magazine." She picked up her stool. "Follow me to periodicals."

Although short, Hattie was incredibly fast. She was already five steps ahead of Zo.

"What year?" she called out.

"Last year."

Hattie pulled a magazine tote from the shelf. "Do you know the issue?"

"Fall, I think," said Zo. "The reviewer's name is Robyn something-or-other."

"Robyn Reynolds?" asked Hattie. "She's writes 'Bird's Eye Reviews.'"

"Do you know her?"

"Not personally." Hattie thumbed through the fall issue. "But I follow her blog. She's spot on with her reviews. Refreshingly honest."

Hattie handed her the magazine, a glossy double-print issue highlighting the best scenic drives for viewing fall colors. Spirit Canyon, a dazzling array of brown, red, and gold, was featured on a two-page spread. Robyn's column and her review of Serenity Hills followed. Zo took it to a nearby table, bending her knee on the seat of a chair as she read.

"That's her column on Serenity Hills," said Hattie, leaning over her shoulder. "Enid was mad as a hatter after it came out. Poor thing. I saw on the news that she died last night."

Zo nodded but said nothing. She was too busy reading the review, which was just as damning as Henry said it was. It described the spa as "antiquated" and Enid as "combative." Robyn said tourists' money would be better spent at a Holiday Inn, which at least had modern plumbing. Zo cringed. Even she felt its sting.

"It's bad." Hattie joined her at the table. "I know. But Enid wasn't the pleasantest woman, and the inn isn't all it's promised to be. Guests pay a hefty price tag, you know. There's truth in her review."

Zo told her what happened at Spirit Canyon Lodge, including the fight between Enid and Griffin regarding his new fiancée.

"You mean Robyn was there?"

"And there's more." Zo checked her watch. "But your shift is over, and I don't want to keep you. Someone might wander in, and you'll be stuck here another hour. Come to my house, and I'll fill you in on the details. Cunningham *is* making cocktails."

"I have a few books left to shelve," said Hattie. "I'll meet you outside in five."

Zo snapped a picture of the article, shut the magazine, and pushed in her chair. "I'll be in my car."

She got as far as the front door when she ran into Max Harrington.

"What are you doing here?" asked Zo. "Picking up the latest installment of *Field and Stream*?"

His lips turned into a slight smile. Still in his uniform, he looked tired and a little wrinkled. "I've been too busy today for reading. Is Hattie still here?"

This was exactly what Zo didn't want to happen. She'd already kept Hattie past her shift; Max would keep her longer. "She's getting ready to leave. What do you need?"

"I need a review from *Western Traveler*," said Max. "Maybe I can look it up online..." He must have detected her hurriedness. He didn't move closer to the door.

"Robyn's?" Zo pulled her phone out of her pocket and touched the photo app. "Here. You can zoom in."

The library door opened, and Hattie walked out in the gray sweatshirt she always had resting on the back of her desk chair. It said, THAT'S WHAT I DO. I READ AND I KNOW THINGS. "Hi Max," she said. "Did you need something before I go?"

"Hey," Max said without looking up from the phone screen. "Is this Robyn's review on Serenity Hills?"

"Uh huh," said Zo. "I took pictures of it."

"We're on our way to Zo's for drinks," said Hattie. "Join us. We can talk about it there." She opened the door of Zo's Outback. "I've been on my feet all day."

Max gave Zo a glance, asking her the silent question.

"Sure, I don't care," Zo said. What else could she say? *No, you can't come over?* Besides, she wanted to talk to him about the rest of the interviews. This would be a good opportunity.

"I've got my truck," he said. "I'll follow you."

He got into his beat-up Ford, and she got into her Subaru. Hattie talked about the library's summer reading program as they drove to Zo's house. Zo had the feeling she didn't want to address the invitation she'd extended to Max. She knew Zo and Max had exchanged words about the tours at Happy Camper. But Hattie and Max were friends. Zo had seen them talking at the library. Maybe Max belonged to a book club. Probably a group of forest rangers reading *The Call of the Wild*.

Zo parked her car, and she and Hattie walked up the steps of her side deck, where they waved to Cunningham, already enjoying a cocktail on his deck. He held up his glass. "Hattie Fines. What a pleasant surprise. I hope this means you'll join us for a libation." He sat up straighter in his chair. "Is that Ranger Max? Well, it's going to be a party. I'll get the rum."

Zo opened the back door, telling Cunningham they'd be right over. She needed to find George, and the only way to do that was with food. She was digging in the lower kitchen cupboard and listening to Hattie complain about overdue videos when she heard Max on her deck. He was telling Cunningham to make his drink a double. *That's fine with me*, she thought as she grabbed the sack of gourmet cat food. The bigger the drink the more time she would have to question him about the interviews at the lodge. And Cunningham did make good cocktails.

She returned to the deck with the cat food and shook the bag. She thought the expensive brand might make him more willing to come home. As the minutes passed, though, she wondered if George knew the difference between ordinary kibble and brand name. "Kitty, kitty, kitty."

Hattie walked down the steps and across the yard to Cunningham's house, but Max waited with her, leaning against the deck railing. "Cunningham says you're having trouble with a tomcat."

"Yep," she said. "He has the same problem as all my boyfriends. He wants to come and go as he pleases."

He chuckled. "Sounds like you've got the wrong boyfriends."

"And the wrong cat," she muttered. "He was probably wandering the streets when they picked him up and shoved him into a cage at the Humane Society. I guess I missed the signs of wanderlust when I picked him out. He was incredibly cordial at the time, but looking back, I think he just wanted out of his crate."

"Don't be so hard on yourself," Max said. "Cats are independent creatures. They don't need a lot of human interaction."

She walked to the deck railing and peeked over, wondering if she was going to get a lesson on animals. He would be just the guy to give it. "George. Come on, kitty, kitty."

"Your deck is great, by the way," said Max. "I could sit out here all night." She turned around, admiring her new furniture. "I just redid it." Two padded chairs and a loveseat were situated on an oversized outdoor rug with an enormous gas fireplace in the middle. To warm the cool mountain mornings, a patio heater stood in the corner, making the space usable almost year round. Only when the snow blew did she stay indoors.

Cunningham hollered from his deck, asking what the holdup was.

Zo looked at Max. "You go ahead. I'll be right there."

Max made kissy noises in the air. "George. Here, Georgie, Georgie."

Zo bit her lip to keep from smiling. He looked sort of ridiculous calling out the name. "It's *George*," she said. "And I doubt he'll come for you."

George took that moment to prove her wrong, rolling like an orange tumbleweed onto the deck. Covered in dust, he swerved past Max's legs, leaving a faint streak of dirt behind. He meowed loudly.

"Hey buddy," said Max. "Are you hungry?"

George answered by rolling onto his back.

"Here you go, George," said Zo, filling his bowl. She hated to leave food outside because of the squirrels, but she wasn't about to wrangle him inside in front of Max. Several scratches might be involved. "Your water is over here." She pointed to the mat where she placed his food dish.

George gave her a glance and licked his paw but made no attempt to move. Zo crossed her arms. It was embarrassing that she should have to beg for his attention this way, and in front of Max. The cat had no shame.

Max squatted near the food dish. "Come on, big guy. You don't want the squirrels to get your dinner."

George followed, sniffing the air a few times before digging into his food.

Max smiled. "You know he's just showing off, right? And I'm really good with animals. He's a Maine Coon, did you know that?"

No, she didn't know that. She didn't know what a Maine Coon was or what it would be doing in South Dakota. "Interesting."

By the time they reached Cunningham's deck, she knew exactly what a Maine Coon was. Max was knowledgeable on that species and probably several others. No wonder he connected with George. He was a natural with animals, and he knew a lot about habitats.

When they reached the deck, Hattie was seated next to Cunningham under the table umbrella. Four pink cocktails sat on a plastic tray that read, "With mirth and laughter let old wrinkles come." It was Shakespeare, he'd told her once, and tried to persuade her to take his class. She had declined, saying the Zodiac Club took up any time she had for extracurricular activities. In fact, they had a meeting coming up next week, and she was looking forward to it—and summer stargazing.

"Max," greeted Cunningham, "I didn't expect to see you here. But I guess you're like that old tomcat, popping up when I least expect it."

"Max is here to talk about a magazine review. It might have something to do with Enid's death," said Zo, picking up one of the cocktails.

"Before we discuss *that* macabre subject"—Cunningham raised his glass—"a toast." He cleared his throat. "To spring, summer, and *love*. May it blossom wherever—and whenever—it grows."

Zo rolled her eyes and clinked glasses. The toast was an obvious attempt for Hattie's attention.

"Well, you're no Hemingway, Cunningham, but you make a mean drink," said Hattie.

Cunningham raised a bushy brow. "Do you know Hemingway drank thirteen of these in one afternoon in Key West? It's true. I read it in a magazine."

Hattie looked skeptical. "What magazine?"

"A men's health magazine," said Cunningham. "I like staying active," he added with a wink.

Hattie couldn't help but chuckle.

"Did you find the missing money, the twenty thousand dollars?" Zo asked Max. She took a sip of her drink, a combination of rum, grapefruit juice, and lime. It was completely plausible to her that someone could drink thirteen in an afternoon.

"No," said Max. "But Griffin confirmed that Enid told him she offered Beth twenty thousand dollars to close the lodge."

Hattie asked for an explanation, and Zo brought her up-to-date.

Max leaned forward and crossed his arms on the table. "Zo, how long has it been since you've seen Beth?"

"Almost twenty years," said Zo. "But we've stayed in touch through social media, and of course I saw her for a few hours the day of Lilly's funeral."

"I don't want to offend you, but is there any way she took the money?" asked Max. "From the looks of the lodge, she spent a lot on renovations. Maybe she's in over her head."

"Max has a point," said Cunningham before Zo could respond. "You haven't spent time with Beth for years. People change, Zo. Look at me. I'm an old man now." He gave Hattie a smile. "But 'some work of noble note, yet may be done.'"

"'Ulysses,'" said Hattie. "I love that poem."

Zo understood what they were saying. Beth had changed. She was more assertive, but so was Zo. That's what happened as people aged. They knew what they wanted and went after it. "I get what you mean, but why would Beth tell us about the money if she took it? That doesn't make sense." Zo shook her head. "Only Griffin knew about the offer."

"And Sarah," said Max. The flicker from Cunningham's tiki lamp highlighted Max's five o'clock shadow, darker than his sand-colored hair. "She said she heard Beth tell Enid it was her last night at the lodge. It sounded like a threat, and people do crazy things when they feel threatened—by animals or people. Trust me. I see a lot of it."

Zo crossed her arms. "There's a big difference between confronting Enid Barrett and a mountain lion."

"Not that big," Hattie observed wryly.

"Beth was just upset," defended Zo. It felt like they were ganging up on her. "I heard the argument. You would be mad too if someone offered to buy you out."

"Oh, I doubt that," said Cunningham. "Max would be a terrible businessman."

"What? You heard the argument?" said Max, ignoring Cunningham's remark. "Why didn't you tell me?"

"I'm telling you right now," said Zo. "I know Beth didn't kill Enid."

"That's what I'm saying," Max said. "You don't *know* that. All we know are the facts. One, Enid is dead; two, she was found dead in your friend's lodge, and three, your friend—the *new* person in this equation—allegedly threatened her the night before she died. If I were you, I wouldn't put too much faith in Beth."

She'd always trusted Beth, and she wasn't about to stop now. Sure she'd changed, but so had Zo. They weren't the same kids they used to be. But that didn't mean Beth was capable of murder, did it?

Cunningham pushed back his chair. He was determined not to let a little thing like death get in the way of his cocktail party. "Let's get another drink, Hatfield," said Cunningham, using his nickname for her. "Come on."

Hattie looked at her empty glass and stood, pushing her red spectacles to her forehead. "I could use a refresher."

Zo watched them go inside, then turned to Max. "Beth was my best friend when we were kids. She was like family to me. She wouldn't kill someone. I know it like I know…the trees will change colors in the fall."

"I understand," said Max. "But you have to be cautious."

It sounded as if he was starting to believe Brady Merrigan's accusations. If that were the case, Beth was in real trouble. Zo had a responsibility to defend her, no matter how long it had been since they'd been together. Max had been the voice of reason earlier, asking Brady to withhold judgment until they had all the facts. But Brady had a strong personality and was convinced of Beth's wrongdoing. He might have convinced Max, too.

"You're a good guy," said Zo. "I know you want to do the right thing, and I know you have a job to do. Just don't jump to conclusions. That's all I'm asking."

"Did you just say I was a good guy?" Max pretended to clean his ears. "And here I thought you didn't like me."

Zo attempted a smile. She had the feeling it looked more like a grimace.

"Look, everyone knew Enid," said Max. "That's what I'm trying to say. If someone did kill her, why do it now? And why at the lodge?"

"That's what we need to find out," said Zo. "At least three of the guests are out-of-towners. If someone killed her on purpose, it might be one of them."

He leaned back in his chair. Maybe he'd made up his mind. "But they didn't fight with Enid, not like Beth."

"You're wrong," Zo insisted. "Kaya fought with her at the chuck wagon, and Allison backed her up. And what about Robyn's review? I wasn't the only one at the library digging for it."

He shrugged. She could tell by the look in his eyes he was unconvinced. He was wondering if Beth had something to do with Enid's death, and she'd have to move mountains to persuade him otherwise. Mountains it would be then.

She slammed her glass on the table, hard. He blinked. Good. She had his attention. "Beth isn't a murderer."

"You don't know that," he said.

"Yes, I do."

"You are one stubborn woman," Max said. "You want to know how I know that?"

She didn't, but it looked as if he was going to tell her anyway.

"Because every time I try to tell you something, you don't listen. But I'm telling you this for your own stubborn good. Watch your back."

She had to restrain herself from throwing her ice cubes at him. As it was, she tightened the grip on her glass. "Stop trying to scare me, Harrington. She was my best friend. She's not a killer."

"Oh, so now I'm *Harrington*?" said Max. "What happened to being a good guy?"

She pushed back her chair and stood. Despite all appearances, maybe Max was not such a good guy.

Chapter Ten

That night, Zo didn't sleep. She lay tossing and turning about Max. She flopped her pillow over her head. Of all people who might keep her awake, Maxwell Harrington was not one of them. He was like…the wildlife whisperer of Spirit Canyon. What did he know about anything? The only problem he'd probably ever had to overcome was wet matches.

She turned to her side. *That wasn't fair.* Her temper was getting the best of her. But Max looked so dang smug sitting at Cunningham's, acting as if he knew Beth better than she did. The problem was his words had a ring of truth to them. It stung that he was half right. It'd been years since she'd spent time with Beth, who had a husband, family, and business now. She was all grown up. They both were. But they were still friends; no amount of questioning would change that.

She flipped to her stomach. Maybe Max was just a skeptical person. He was skeptical about her tours at Happy Camper. When he came to the store, he said she didn't know the canyon well enough to give tours, and for a split second, she believed him. Then she came to her senses. She'd lived in Spirit Canyon thirty-three years; of course she knew the area. Besides, it wasn't as if hers were whitewater-rafting tours. Most of them were walking tours. Sometimes she ventured into the hills, but she followed the popular paths and never trusted strangers. Just as she'd learned in school, trusting strangers was a mistake.

Like when she trusted the Merrigans. Before opening the original Happy Camper, she signed a year-long lease with Patrick Merrigan, the owner of the downtown storefront. Everything she read said to lock into a longer lease, but she believed him when he said he had nothing planned for the area. They were a well-known family in town; she had no reason to distrust them. Plus, she thought the shorter lease would give her more options if the store didn't go over as well as she anticipated. It turned out it gave her no options whatsoever when he wouldn't renew the lease. He opened a sporting goods store of his own, which was conveniently located next to his hardware store. That's when she moved here, to a house and business she loved more every day. She turned to her back. Maybe it was fate, the stars aligning for her benefit.

Fate or not, if Brady tried to put Beth in jail, she would call down the thunder of Spirit Canyon on the Merrigans. She swore to God she would. She tossed off her down comforter and got out of bed, grabbing her robe from the closet hook. A cup of nighttime tea might help get her mind off murder and the Merrigans. *Hmm, murder and the Merrigans.* It had a nice ring.

Her tiny kitchen was dark. She flipped on the light above the sink and popped a mug of water into the microwave. As the water heated, she rummaged for the new tea she'd bought at the Green Market. She found it still in a bag on the counter. It'd been a crazy couple of days. She hadn't even had time to put the tea leaves into the canister. When the microwave beeped, she placed the tea diffuser into the cup, and the air filled with smells of vanilla and caramel. Inhaling deeply, she stood at the window, waiting for the herbs to take effect.

The night sky was as clear as water, the stars like fish. Orion, her favorite constellation, had disappeared and wouldn't reappear until winter. She felt a little pang of loss. Maybe it was the arrangement of stars—a hunter and shield—that made her feel safe, or maybe it was the story. Like her, Orion was given up at birth. When he fell in love with Artemis, the moon goddess, his brother, Apollo, objected, and Zeus put Orion in the winter sky to keep the two from fighting. If Max's suspicions kept up, someone might need to put him in another sky to keep her from killing him. Otherwise, Brady might have two deaths to investigate.

A loud thump startled her, and she jostled her mug, a few hot drops of tea landing on her hand. For a second, she thought someone was on her deck steps, and she glanced at the lock to make sure it was turned. It was. The sound of her heartbeat filled her ears as she tiptoed across the linoleum and peeked out the window. From a cedar post, George's yellow eyes stared back at her. His mouth opened into a loud meow. She let out a breath.

"Dang it, George," she scolded, setting down her mug on the counter. "You scared me."

She slid open the door, and he crouched down. "Come on then."

He jumped off the post and stretched. She attempted to be casual, but a low rumble in the canyon disturbed her, and she wondered if a storm might roll in later. She looked at the clear night sky. Impossible. Yet there was the rumble again.

She reached for him, and he ducked out of her grasp. *So, it's going to be this way,* she thought. Tying her robe tighter, she stepped onto the deck, chasing him all the way to the steps before catching him. He didn't fight or scratch her this time. He hung in her arms like a giant scarf. It was an improvement.

"Just for tonight," she said as she brought him into the house. "Okay?" To reward him for not tearing her to pieces, she opened a can of soft cat food. He ate the food, and she drank the tea. Then she went to bed.

* * * *

As it happened, she hadn't needed to set her alarm, for in the early morning, George woke her up. His orange paws massaged the comforter for a full minute before he plopped down beside her, purring. Without moving, she gave him a glance. *Incredible.* Were they finally starting to bond? She avoided pondering the question. She wasn't sure she was ready for an answer.

Though it was Memorial Day, tourists expected stores to be open on holidays, and her store was no exception. Happy Camper was open from noon until five, so Harley was taking the short shift. That meant Zo could spend the day at Spirit Canyon Lodge with Beth, who'd invited her for a barbeque. Despite the untimely death of Enid Barrett, she was pressing on with the holiday event. Really, it was all she could do. Guests had paid for the add-on, and for all anyone knew, Enid had died of a heart attack. None of them would know for sure until the preliminary autopsy labs came back. Until then, Zo was going to enjoy her day off. She stretched lazily. Her single hamburger patty wouldn't be used after all.

After petting George for several minutes and feeling like a genuine cat owner, she got out of bed. She checked her email while the coffee brewed. There was a reminder from the Zodiac Club. Barring bad weather, the group would meet at the observatory at Black Mountain College tomorrow, the first meeting of the summer. Hunter, her ex-boyfriend, would be there. It had been three months since they dated, and Zo hoped it wouldn't be awkward. They'd fought during their breakup. Actually, *she'd* fought during the breakup. He had leaned back in his chair, scratching his chin. He hadn't seen why talking about himself three quarters of the time was a problem. She tried to educate him. But he was a kind man, and she doubted he held grudges. They would probably disrupt his chakra.

After pouring a cup of strong coffee, she pulled up the picture of Robyn's review of Serenity Hills on her MacBook, where she could see it better than on her phone. As she reread it, she wondered how Griffin could marry someone who said such awful things about the family business. It must have been love. She'd heard it made one do strange things. Then again, so did hate. The night Enid died, Griffin looked like he despised his mother. Zo shivered. Brady Merrigan said Griffin was a mama's boy, but even mama's boys had their limits. She couldn't imagine being told what to do at thirty-three. By the time she was his age, she'd be even less willing to take orders.

Griffin could have killed Enid that night. He knew her medications and her heart condition better than anybody else and had a strong motive. The trouble with that theory was Griffin seemed genuinely distraught when they found her the next morning. Robyn, on the other hand, was unaffected. She comforted Griffin, as any fiancée would, but she felt no personal loss from the death. She was coolheaded and smart. Zo had a feeling if anyone could pull off a murder in the middle of the night, it was Robyn. If she thought Enid would tell Griffin about her lover last fall, she might feel threatened. But threatened enough to murder Enid? Zo wasn't sure.

She finished the last drops of her coffee and placed the cup in the sink. She opened the deck door for George, who'd been pawing at the window ever since he'd finished his breakfast. She had to give him credit; he'd been as domestic as he'd ever been. But the day was a gorgeous mix of blue and yellow, and she didn't blame him for wanting out. She did, too. After a quick run through the shower, she was off to the canyon.

Even though the morning was crisp, Zo opened the windows of her Outback. Days like these, sunny and fresh, reminded her how much she loved it. Unlike Beth, she didn't have a husband, kids, or even a promising relationship, but she had Happy Camper, a place where she could share her enthusiasm for the canyon with customers.

As the days warmed and summer progressed, more tourists would arrive, and Happy Camper would be packed with moms, dads, and hipsters wanting to rent bikes or kayaks or purchase souvenirs. Zo loved their zeal. She'd seen city dwellers turn into nature lovers after a few nights in the canyon. Scouring for vacation rentals, they promised to come back year after year, and many did. If campers were anything it was loyal. They frequented the places they fell in love with again and again.

Zo closed her windows as she approached the gravel path of Spirit Canyon Lodge. It looked like the same rustic lodge it had on Saturday night. *But it didn't feel like it,* she thought as she got out of her car. The canyon was rife with questions about Enid's death, and Zo was determined to find the answers. She would know soon enough whether or not her death was natural, maybe even today.

She walked up the curvy path to the lodge, putting aside the nagging question. She was here to spend time with Beth and her family. All their interactions thus far had revolved around Enid. Zo wanted today to be about them. As Max pointed out, she and Beth had been apart for many years. They had a lot of catching up to do.

The screen door shut behind her, and Beth looked up from the front desk. "I'm so glad you came early. Isn't it a gorgeous morning?"

Every day was gorgeous to Beth. Even with Enid's death looming over the lodge, Beth still had the fervor of a tourist, probably because she was one for so many years. "I was thinking the same thing on my drive out here," said Zo.

"I mean, it's chilly," said Beth, retying her summer sweater as she came out from behind the desk. She wore jeggings and flowered flats. "But it's going to be perfect later this afternoon, for the barbeque."

Zo glanced around the empty room. "Everyone is still here?"

Beth nodded. "They booked the entire week. They don't leave until Friday. Of course Griffin and Robyn checked out yesterday, which was to be expected."

Zo remembered them leaving right after their interviews with Max and Brady. They had to get back to Spirit Canyon to make arrangements for Enid's funeral.

"I keep kicking myself," Beth continued. "I wish I would have read the signs better. They say nausea is one of the symptoms of a heart attack, and you know she didn't eat. Maybe I should have asked more questions about how she was feeling."

"It's not your fault," Zo said. "We were all there, even her son. She seemed fine to me, and she must have seemed fine to Griffin because he didn't ask if she felt sick."

"Still, I'm the hostess," said Beth. "I should have pressed her about why she wasn't eating. I thought she was just being cranky. Muffin?"

Zo nodded and followed her to the dining area, selecting a chocolate chip pastry from the breakfast bar. They sat at a round table, and Beth sipped her coffee while Zo unwrapped the muffin paper. "She *was* being cranky. She was jealous of your success. That's why she offered you money to close the lodge. She knew she would lose a lot of business to you."

Beth tapped the sides of her coffee mug with manicured fingernails; they were bright pink. Some things hadn't changed, like her choice of fingernail polish. "Twenty thousand dollars is a lot of money, but it's nothing compared to what Jack and I have invested. Do you think she really thought I would take the money and shut down the lodge?"

Zo chewed her muffin, thinking about the question for a moment. "Enid was used to getting her way, so yeah, I do. If someone had offered me twenty thousand dollars after the first Happy Camper closed, I would have been tempted to take the money and pay off my credit card."

"Tempted, but you wouldn't have taken it," said Beth. "You love your store too much."

"I do," Zo agreed. "Money couldn't replace the happiness it brings me."

"As a business owner, do you think my grand opening was successful? I mean, despite Enid's death."

"Absolutely," said Zo. "If Enid hadn't been there, it would have been the perfect evening. Even with the storm and the blackout, it was fun. I felt like a kid again, taking cover from the rain, and I bet the other guests did, too."

Beth smiled. "I feel that way all the time. This place has brought back all the good memories—and you."

Zo returned the smile, happy her friend felt the same way she did. But the feeling was short lived. The front door opened, and she knew it was Max before she even turned around. His heavy footstep gave him away. Brady Merrigan from the Spirit Canyon Police Force was there also. With an investigation underway, she guessed they didn't get the holiday off.

"Hi Zo," said Max. "Are we feeling better today?"

Nothing was more infuriating than the use of the royal *we*. Only the queen of England should be allowed to use it. "I'm fine. I was fine yesterday, too." Her reaction was not lost on Beth, who gave her a puzzled look. Zo hadn't told her of Max's suspicions last night. The last thing she needed to hear was that Max didn't trust her.

Brady also watched the exchange with interest, spinning the emerald ring on his pinky finger. Zo wouldn't be surprised if it had a Merrigan crest on it—or a shamrock.

"Can I get you anything, officers?" Beth asked, standing. "Coffee or a muffin?"

Brady motioned for her to sit back down and joined them at the table. "No thanks."

Standing rigid, like an oak tree, Max glanced at Zo. She knew right away it was bad news.

Brady opened a leather folder. The inner flap held an envelope. He unfolded a piece of paper. "These are the results of Enid's blood test, done postmortem. They show she died of digoxin intoxication. She had nearly twice the therapeutic amount in her bloodstream."

"Wait," said Zo. "Digoxin? Griffin said she took that for her heart."

"And what do you mean by *intoxication*?" added Beth. "She didn't have anything to drink Saturday night, just one glass of sherry. She wasn't drunk."

Max elaborated on the report. "What he means is that she died of a digoxin overdose, not that she was intoxicated by anything she drank."

"So, she took too much of her heart medication?" asked Beth. Her face brightened. "That actually makes sense. I was just telling Zo she didn't eat anything. Maybe her lack of appetite was a sign of a heart attack. Maybe she took a second dose…to alleviate her symptoms."

Max cleared his throat. "It's possible, Beth. It's also possible that she overdosed on purpose. A lot of elderly people choose to take their own lives when their health fails."

"And why not do it in Beth's lodge as a last-ditch effort to cause a scandal?" said Zo, thinking out loud. "When Beth refused to take the money, it could have sent her over the edge."

"Sixty-five isn't elderly, kids," said Brady. "I hate to be the one to tell you that, but somebody has to. Enid might have had a heart problem, but she wasn't suicidal. I'd bet my police pension on it."

Brady was like a dog with a bone. He thought Beth had something to do with Enid's death and was determined to prove it. Zo tried to think of a way to deter him.

"You know," said Beth, "I have to agree with Officer Merrigan. I'd only just met Enid, but she didn't come off as depressed. She seemed very sure of herself, on top of it."

Zo rubbed her forehead. Her friend wasn't doing herself any favors.

Brady looked pleased by the comment. "Enid Barrett *was* very on top of it. She was a good businesswoman and an upstanding citizen."

Beth ignored the look. "Not quite upstanding. An upstanding citizen wouldn't come into another person's business with twenty thousand dollars and the notion of shutting it down. That's not normal."

Zo agreed and was glad Beth pointed out the discrepancy. Although Enid was a savvy businesswoman, the action was over the top, even for her. "Beth is right. Why was she so intent on closing Spirit Canyon Lodge?"

The room went quiet as they considered the possibilities—at least Zo did. Brady sat with his fingers laced, waiting for a plausible answer. Zo recalled what she knew of Enid. The woman certainly wasn't afraid to speak her mind even when it might offend others. It was as if she didn't have a filter. *Like when she mentioned Beth's aunt Lilly.* Zo snapped her fingers. "Maybe she had a grudge against Lilly. The night of the chuck wagon, Enid said she knew Lilly and Pete. She seemed...I don't know... jealous of them."

"She made a similar comment to me," said Beth. "What did she say to you?"

"She said they were young fools," said Zo. "She said you were just like them."

"That's right." Beth nodded.

"Had you ever met Enid before that night?" Max walked back and forth as he asked the question. "Did she ever come to the lodge?"

Beth looked at Zo in question, but Zo didn't know the answer. If they'd met her when they were kids, she couldn't remember.

"I don't think so," said Beth. "I'll ask my mom. She might remember Lilly mentioning her."

Zo turned to Max, who was still pacing. "Why don't you sit down? You're like a black cloud hovering over me."

Max took a chair from a nearby table and positioned it close to hers. "Bad habit. Is this better?"

No, it wasn't better. It was worse. He *smelled* like the Black Hills, woodsy and crisp, if that was even possible. She swallowed hard, deciding not to let the pleasant scent distract her.

Max spoke to Beth. "If it's possible, we'd like to take another look at the room where Enid stayed. Now that we know she overdosed on digoxin, we have a better idea what we're looking for."

"Of course it's possible," said Brady. "We're investigating a homicide now."

Zo exchanged a glance with Beth. There it was—murder. The question of Enid's death had been officially answered.

"No problem," said Beth. "I've left the room just as you asked."

"Nobody's had access to it?" said Max.

"No, it's been locked," said Beth.

"Except one person," said Brady, his chair squeaking loudly as he stood.

"Who?" asked Beth, clearly puzzled.

But Zo knew who he meant before his answer left his mouth.

"You."

Chapter Eleven

For the next hour, Max and Brady scoured the lodge for evidence, and Zo helped Beth with the preparations for the barbeque. They made a potato salad large enough to feed an army, let alone the four remaining guests. While quartering potatoes, Zo decided this was what she remembered most about Spirit Canyon Lodge: the food and friendship. There was always an abundance of both, and with family gathered around, the girls vying for Beth's attention, Zo was struck with a feeling of déjà vu. Twenty years ago, it was Beth and Zo clamoring for Lilly's attention, always aimed in the direction of the kitchen. All Zo had to do was close her eyes and she could see the young versions of themselves, sneaking snacks, pulling pranks, talking incessantly. *It was nice to remember.*

Zo refocused on what Beth's youngest daughter, Molly, was saying. Her curls were bouncing up and down as she talked animatedly about the barbeque and her plans to sing afterwards. She was definitely the performer in the family.

"I think it's a fabulous idea," said Zo. "I can't wait to hear you. Your uncle Pete used to sing campfire songs. Remember that, Beth?"

Beth stopped chopping onions. The kitchen island was covered in glass bowls in various states of being filled. Vi, making a large bowl of coleslaw, was shredding cabbage. Her knife was the only sound, slicing vegetables. "He was great, wasn't he? Do you remember that old six string he used to have?" asked Beth.

Zo nodded. "I do. In fact, I bought one at an estate sale to sell in the store. At first, I priced it, but now I have it sitting in the window." She shook her head. "I just couldn't part with it."

"And that song he used to sing, 'Hello Darlin'?" Beth said. She tilted her head toward the window as if she could hear the song playing in the distance. "Lilly loved it when he sang that song."

Vi let out a small snort. "You two are too young to know who Conway Twitty was."

"Yes! It was Conway Twitty," said Beth. "Pete sang his songs all the time."

"He was a true blue cowboy," Vi said.

The way she said it made it sound like a criticism.

"Well Lilly loved him—cowboy or not," said Beth.

"Gran prefers pop music," said Megan with a smile. Her pretty brown hair was done in a French braid, pulled forward over her shoulder. It was hard not to compare her to Beth because Beth looked exactly the same way twenty years ago. They had the same mannerisms and habit of sweeping back their hair with their fingertips.

Vi shrugged. The morning was chilly, and she had on a bright athletic jacket. "Music today is more upbeat. Besides, we didn't have a lot of cowboys in Chicago. I suppose that's why Lilly was so attracted to him."

"Vi, that reminds me, did Lilly ever mention an Enid?" asked Zo. "The night she died, she told me Beth reminded her of Lilly, so they must have known each other in some capacity." For a moment Vi's knife stopped cutting, and Zo wondered if she should've brought up the touchy subject. She knew Vi begrudged Lilly for running off, but the sisters had to talk sometime, especially with Beth staying at the lodge in the summers.

"I've been thinking about that ever since she died," said Vi. "You know my sister couldn't have children. That's why she liked to take Elizabeth for the summer."

"*Mom,*" said Beth in a warning tone.

She plopped a large dollop of mayonnaise in a bowl. "I'm not saying anything that isn't true."

"But did she mention an Enid?" asked Beth.

"That's what I was getting to." Vi gave her a look. "When you told me about Enid knowing Lilly, I remembered Lilly talking about a friend named E who was going to help her adopt a baby. I wondered if it could be the same person."

"I didn't know Lilly wanted a baby," said Beth.

"Me neither," said Zo.

"You were too young," said Vi. "She wouldn't have mentioned such things to you. As she grew older, she grew more anxious to have a child."

Zo considered the information. Lilly was older than Enid. She would want a baby before she reached middle age. Still, something didn't add up.

Zo shook her head. "Enid was in the hotel business, though. How could she help Lilly adopt a baby?"

Beth gave Zo a look that said Vi might be wrong. Vi wasn't close to Lilly and might be missing critical information. Besides, Vi didn't recognize the name, and *Enid* was unique. Still, E could have been a nickname.

Vi stopped stirring. "I don't know. Maybe Enid's husband had connections."

That was true. Zo didn't know much about Enid's husband. Maybe he was E.

Vi continued tossing the coleslaw. "I don't recall exactly, but I do remember that Lilly was excited about the prospect of a baby. And I was excited, too. I thought I'd finally get to spend a summer with my youngest daughter."

Beth wiped her hands on a kitchen towel and walked over to Vi, giving her a squeeze. "You could've said no."

"You liked it here so much," said Vi. "I couldn't do that to you. Besides, we're spending the summer together now, aren't we?" She elbowed Beth.

Beth smiled.

"So, what happened to the baby?" asked Megan. She and Molly had been as quiet as mice listening to the grownups' conversation. But Meg wanted the rest of the story.

So did Zo.

"I don't know," said Vi. "Maybe Enid couldn't *deliver.*"

Zo laughed.

"Ha ha, very funny Mom," said Beth.

Vi pointed her knife at Zo. "Zo thought it was."

Zo agreed. She thought the older woman was hilarious.

"Zo, you said something about the canyon being haunted," said Vi. "And I heard some nonsense about it when I went into town. What's the official story?"

Zo glanced at Megan and Molly, who were still listening intently. Beth understood the gesture.

"Go check the front desk, would you girls?" asked Beth. "I want to make sure I haven't missed any calls."

"*Please,*" said Meg. "As if we're scared of ghosts. Come on, Mol."

"*I'm* scared of ghosts," said Molly as they left the kitchen. She quickened her pace. "I call hitting the voice-mail button!"

Zo turned to Vi. "The official story goes like this. A couple of young lovers were walking though the canyon one spring day when it began to rain. The girl ran ahead, finding a cave. The boy went to gather firewood.

When he returned, a rockslide had blocked the cave's entrance, and he could hear his lover inside, crying for help. He began to dig with his hands, then with a piece of the wood he'd brought back. But the rock was loose and began to fall. He was crushed by the rubble, and they were both found dead many days later. Locals say they haunt the canyon, still looking for one another. Their spirits won't be satisfied until they are reunited on the other side."

Beth clutched her chest. "That's tragic!"

"That's poppycock," declared Vi.

Zo chuckled at their different reactions. Vi wasn't a believer in anything she couldn't see with her own eyes—or turn on with a click of a button. She was into technology. Beth was only interested in the story because it involved a pair of star-crossed lovers.

"The Black Hills are full of tragedy, when you think about it," said Zo. "Like the ghosts of men who worked on Mount Rushmore—they still haunt Mountain View Cemetery. Then there are the miners and prospectors who came here, looking for gold but dying in the mines. Wild Bill Hickok, Calamity Jane, and Seth Bullock are all buried in Deadwood, and Bullock's hotel is famous for its hauntings. That doesn't even touch on the stories of the Lakota, who suffered plenty themselves."

"I'm so glad we moved here, dear," Vi said to Beth. "Such a *pleasant* past."

Finished with the salad, Beth unraveled the plastic wrap, preparing the dishes for storage. She pulled open the fridge door then stopped. "Mom, tell Zo about Aunt Lilly and the blue dress."

"It's nothing," said Vi.

Zo could tell by Beth's face, it was something. "What about Lilly and a blue dress?"

All business, Vi told her that she had a dream about Lilly, who was wearing a blue dress. She appeared in a powder blue gown, the kind she would have worn to a party in Chicago. In the dream, Vi tried to talk to her, but she disappeared. Vi said she must have woken up.

"Maybe Lilly's trying to tell you something," said Zo.

"That I shouldn't eat ice cream after eight?" said Vi. "It always does weird things to me at night. The whole thing was just odd."

It could have been the ice cream, or it could have been Lilly's ghost. Pete and Lilly had lived here many years, had built the lodge with their own hands. If Lilly were to return anywhere, it would be here. Of course it might have also been a dream. Being a vivid dreamer herself, Zo understood how real dreams could feel. Dream or specter, the important detail here seemed to be the blue dress.

"Did you recognize the dress?" Zo asked. "Does it mean anything to you?"

"Lilly never attended her debut." Vi rapidly peeled a cucumber, the pieces flying into the sink. "She never wore a gown like that. She left us all standing at her party like idiots. Maybe she's rubbing my face in it."

"Mom is ten years younger than Lilly," explained Beth. "She thinks Lilly's running away affected her own reputation."

"It did!" said Vi. "Our name was mud after she left."

Zo doubted that. They were a well-known family in Chicago. The elopement might have caused a passing scandal but probably didn't tarnish their name. It was obviously a touchy subject, though, so she kept her suppositions to herself. She'd think on the information later. Right now, she heard a commotion outside the kitchen door and wanted to check it out.

"That sounds like Max or Brady," said Zo. "Come on. Let's see what they found."

Vi and Beth followed her into the great room, where Max, still wearing gloves, was carrying a plastic baggie. It looked as if he'd collected an empty water bottle from Enid's room. Zo asked him if that's what it was. Brady answered.

"Yes indeed," said Brady, coming down the stairs with heavy footsteps. "We've found our murder weapon."

Murder, thought Zo. *He had to say it out loud.* She hoped the guests hadn't heard.

Max held the bag into the sunlight. "See this chalky residue? Enid's water was tampered with."

"And I'm going to take a wild guess here and say the residue is digoxin," added Brady. "This is how the extra doses were ingested Saturday night. Now we just need to find out who gave her the water. Maybe you can help me with that, Mrs. Everett?"

"I gave it to her, of course," Beth offered. "I leave bottles of water for all my guests—along with bottles of shampoo, conditioner, and body wash."

"Well that answers that," said Brady.

"You can't possibly believe I would murder an old woman." Beth was clearly aghast.

"Look at me," said Vi. "I'm still here. And I've done a lot worse things than Enid Barrett. Believe you me, my daughter has the patience of a saint."

"Besides, Beth wasn't the only person in the lodge." Zo pointed above her head. "Four perfect suspects are upstairs right now. They all fought with Enid."

"And don't forget," said Brady. "You stayed here, too."

"Well I'm not going anywhere," said Zo. "The guests won't be staying forever."

"Can you tell them not to leave town?" asked Vi. "That always works on TV."

"No." A smile touched Max's lips. "That's not a real thing. They just say it on television."

"Oh, don't worry." Beth gestured to the calendar at the front desk. "We have time. They're not leaving until Friday."

* * * *

As Zo waited for Beth on the front porch, she wondered about her friend. Either Beth didn't understand the threat was real, or she wasn't afraid of the threat. It was encouraging that she thought the truth would prevail, but Zo was less confident. At the *Star*, she'd shared stories of innocent people going to jail for crimes they didn't commit, only to be released years later. And Beth had just returned to the area. Zo didn't want her to leave again so soon.

She glanced at Brady. He might look like a gentleman, but he was as clever as any Merrigan. They could get people to do things just by flashing their smiles. Brady was out to catch a killer, and he didn't care who it was. Actually, that wasn't true. He preferred it to be someone like Beth, someone from Chicago. Then he could blame the murder on a stranger, keeping his town's reputation squeaky clean.

She noticed Max placing evidence bags in Brady's police cruiser. Whether she liked it or not, he was her only hope in this matter, and even he suspected Beth. He'd told her to watch her back last night. Why else would he say that unless he thought Beth was capable of murder?

It was impossible. A few hours in the kitchen had reminded Zo that Beth was interested in weddings, not funerals. And like Vi said, she could be patient to a fault. It was what made her a great mom and friend. Zo just hoped she wasn't *too* patient with Brady Merrigan. Patrick Merrigan had almost ruined her business; with enough talk of murder, Brady could do the same thing to Beth's.

Dressed in khaki shorts, long socks, and hiking boots, Allison appeared on the far end of the property. Zo guessed she had been trekking one of the surrounding trails this morning. Spirit Canyon Lodge had five within walking distance. From the look of her pale legs, she spent a lot of time indoors with her books. Then again, it was only Memorial Day, and she'd been teaching all year. Cunningham had said something about a lab at

Homestake Mine, but Zo couldn't remember exactly what was researched there. As Allison greeted her, Zo decided to ask.

"How was your hike?" asked Zo. "It's the perfect morning for one." Allison took off her cap. "Exhilarating. It's great to be outdoors after the long winter."

"I read the other day that just five minutes in nature can improve your mood." Zo was always looking for positive tidbits to pass on to her customers.

"I believe it," said Allison. "It always makes me feel better."

"Beth is bringing out iced tea if you'd like some." Zo motioned to the open chair next to hers. "We're taking a break from prepping for the barbeque this afternoon."

"She's a good hostess." Allison sat down. "The extras have been worth every penny."

Zo noticed Max glancing in her direction. She'd better get around to what she had to ask before he approached them. "I know one of your colleagues. Russell Cunningham?"

Allison nodded with recognition. "Yes, I know him. I think he's in the English department."

"He's my neighbor," said Zo.

"He knows a lot about literature." She squinted in Max's direction, too, seeing the police car. "I like sci-fi, myself."

"That makes sense," Zo said. "Cunningham said you work at Homestake Mine. I remember reading about it in the news when it opened, but it's been a while. What do you research there?"

"It's sad, the little coverage we get," said Allison, "despite the cutting-edge technology being used. The media are more interested in the latest summer cookout than our progress—no offense to your friend."

"None taken." Zo decided not to tell her she was writing about lodging in her Curious Camper column this week. Maybe she'd check out the mine for an upcoming article.

"But it's the truth," said Allison. "Lodges, inns, and dude ranches are cropping up everywhere. If it doesn't stop, the Black Hills will become a commercial landmine."

The young professor was passionate about the subject. Zo could tell by the way she raised her voice. But Happy Camper was successful because of tourists, and Black Hills National Forest was over one million acres. It would stay mostly undeveloped as long as the land remained protected. Zo thought academics like Cunningham and Allison worried too much for no reason.

"Anyhow, to get back to your question, scientists at Homestake research everything from dark matter to star life. I led a group of graduate students out there last semester on a grant. They studied movement of underground rock." She crossed her legs in front of her. "It was a real opportunity for a fledgling scholar."

"Did they find anything?" asked Zo.

"I'm not sure what you mean."

Zo realized she'd missed the point of Allison's work. The point was the research, not the discovery. "I just meant did they find rock movement… or whatever."

"Oh," said Allison. "Right. Well, rock is always moving. That's why people should be careful where they build." She motioned to the surrounding area. "Hills erode. Rocks shift. Mountains move."

That might be overstating it, thought Zo. She knew the wilderness could be dangerous, but Allison's stance seemed extreme. People loved vacationing in the Black Hills, and plenty of homes provided them the safe opportunity. "That reminds me. Enid had a resort out near Homestake Mine, Serenity Falls. Have you ever heard of it?"

"Yes, I've heard of it. I've been there."

The answer surprised Zo. Allison lived in the area, but to be honest, she didn't seem like a person who'd take a day off to enjoy a spa. What reason would she have for going to Serenity Falls? She was only staying at Spirit Canyon Lodge because of the college reunion. "I didn't realize. What's it like?"

"I can't speak to the resort, but the area is lovely," said Allison. "It's not far from the mine."

So, maybe that's how she knew of it; she encountered it during her work at the lab.

"Here we are," said Beth, pushing open the screen door with her backside. "Iced tea—Allison! Good morning."

"Hello," said Allison.

Beth set the tray on a table. It had four glasses, a large pitcher of tea, lemon slices, and sugar. "Where are your friends?"

"They're sleeping in," said Allison. "We were up late last night, but I can never sleep past eight."

Beth gave her a sympathetic look. "I'm always amazed at what I can accomplish before my family has rolled out of bed. Here it is only eleven o'clock, and I'm ready for a break. Would you like some iced tea?"

Allison nodded.

Beth filled two tall tumblers. "I thought the officers might need something, too."

So that's why she brought out extra glasses, thought Zo. Brady was convinced she was a murderer, and here she was serving him iced tea. Beth was too nice. Or very smart. Or both.

"What are they looking for?" asked Allison.

"Clues to Enid's death," said Zo. "They say she died of digoxin intoxication." She didn't mention the bottle of water or the word *murder*. Allison might tell her friends, and they would check out early. No one would want to risk staying in the same lodge with a murderer. A thief was troubling enough, and the money was still missing.

Allison blinked a few times before answering. "Digoxin has an incredibly narrow therapeutic range. Just a little over the prescribed amount can kill a person."

"How do you know that?" Zo didn't think Allison's research had anything to do with prescription medicine.

"I entertained the idea of becoming a pharmacist before turning to geoscience." Allison took a drink of iced tea. "They make good money, you know. Teacher pay is awful."

"The *Star* covered teacher pay a couple of years ago," said Zo, nodding. "Mostly K–12 teachers, though."

"New professors make only slightly more," said Allison.

Brady and Max approached the house. They were finished with the evidence. "If you don't mind, we'll go inside to wash our hands," said Brady.

"Of course," said Beth. "The restroom is just past the reception desk. And join us for a glass of iced tea when you're finished."

"I'm on my way in, officers." Allison put down her empty glass and stood. "Let me get the door for you."

When they were gone, Zo turned to Beth. "Don't be so nice to them. They're trying to pin Enid's death on you."

Beth smiled. "They're just doing their job, Zo. You've always been so suspicious."

"You don't know the Merrigans." Zo plopped another sugar cube in her remaining iced tea. "Brady will get what he wants, and right now, he wants you in jail for Enid's murder."

"What about Max? I met him at Honey Buns, but who is he?" Beth handed Zo a spoon. "He's so handsome."

Zo couldn't believe what she was hearing. Sure he was handsome, but Beth had to remember his opinions about her tours. Zo had emailed her about it, and she'd been sympathetic. "Max is the forest ranger who thinks I shouldn't offer tours. He wants me to stick to 'knickknacks.' Remember?"

Beth nodded. "I remember. He was worried about your safety."

"Hardly," said Zo. "He doesn't think I'm qualified. In his mind, the only person qualified to give a tour is a big hairy man."

Beth scrunched up her nose. "I wouldn't call him hairy. He's pretty clean-cut. You should give him a chance."

Leave it to Beth to take the comment literally. "To what? Shut down my new store? You heard him warn me about the decals."

"You said so yourself, the decals needed to be there," said Beth. "He was only trying to help."

"Thank you," Max said as he opened the screen door and returned to the front porch. "That's what I told her, but you can see how well she listens to me."

"Excuse us," said Zo. "We were having a private conversation."

"No, please join us," said Beth. "I made tea."

"I believe I will."

Max took the chair beside Zo's. The wood creaked as he sat down, and she hoped it broke into pieces. It would serve him right for barging in on their conversation.

"So, you guys have known each other for a long time?" Beth asked.

Zo was losing patience. Maybe the fairytale romance had turned out for Beth, but it certainly hadn't for her. Every serious relationship she had ended in a haircut or tattoo. If she had any more dating disasters, a pixie cut might be her only option.

"Yep," said Max.

"Not really," said Zo. "The first time I met him was at Happy Camper. He came in to hassle me about a decal. That was just before the first store shut down. He showed up again in time to carry my HAPPY CAMPER sign to my car."

Max smiled. "I remember. You didn't want my help."

"Zo has always been very independent," said Beth, sharing the smile.

"I really haven't had any other choice," Zo said. Max and Beth quit smiling, and Zo wished she'd kept the comment to herself. Anytime she brought up her past, the conversation could get awkward. When it came to the foster system, people only knew what they saw on TV. They didn't realize those years made her the resilient person she was today.

Zo cleared her throat and continued. "Allison and I were talking about Enid's spa in Lead, Serenity Falls?"

Max nodded. "It's a huge resort."

"She said she'd been there, but I can't imagine when," said Zo. "It doesn't seem like the kind of place she'd stay."

"Why?" said Beth. "She's staying here."

Zo shook her head. "I know but she's with her friends for a college reunion. She mentioned Serenity Falls when she talked about her work at Homestake Lab. I had a feeling she wasn't there on vacation."

Beth tapped her pretty pink nails on her iced tea glass. "She did tell me once she thought too many hotels were cropping up in the Black Hills."

"She said the same thing to me." Zo glanced at Max. "You should check it out."

"I can't," said Max. "At least not today. I don't have my car here, and Brady and I have to take the evidence back to town so it can be processed tomorrow. Lab personnel aren't in because of the holiday."

Beth snapped her fingers. "Zo has her car. She could drive you. You just have to promise to bring her back before the barbeque—and join us, of course."

Zo cringed. Spending an hour in the car with Max was the last thing she wanted to do, especially after their argument last night. Beth had no idea about the quibble because Zo hadn't wanted to worry her with Max's misgivings. Zo got the feeling that even if she knew, though, she still would have suggested the idea. Beth thought throwing two people together in a car was a surefire recipe for love. Zo thought it was a surefire recipe for a car wreck. She was curious about Allison and the mine, though. If the mine somehow connected Allison to Enid Barrett, it would be worth one awkward drive with Max.

"It's up to Zo," said Max. "I'm not her favorite person these days."

"You weren't my favorite person last month either." Zo turned to Beth. "Are you sure you don't need more help?"

"Not at all," Beth said. "We finished the salads, and I promised Molly I'd help her with her new face-painting kit. Mom said it has twenty-four-hour wear. I don't want her trying it on by herself."

Zo laughed. She imagined Vi bought only the best for her grandkids.

Brady opened the screen door and stepped onto the front porch. "Sorry to keep you, Max. I was talking to that Jennifer gal. She said there's a big drawing at noon in Deadwood for Memorial Day. The whole group is headed there."

"I hope they win," said Beth.

"I hope *Jennifer* wins," Zo said. "I heard she's lost a lot of money."

"I wish I could stay for a glass of tea, but I need to get back to the station," said Brady, descending the front steps. "We'll be in touch."

Max told him to wait up. They talked, presumably about Max's change of plans, as they walked to Brady's police cruiser. At least Zo hoped that was why Brady kept looking her way.

Beth turned to Zo. "This is perfect, right? You in the car alone with that hunk for an hour?"

"I knew that's what you were thinking," said Zo. "But Max is investigating a murder, not looking for a date."

She gathered up the glasses and pitcher. "I don't see why he can't do both."

Of course she can't, thought Zo. She had a great lodge, a great husband, and a great family. Zo hadn't really thought about family until Beth returned to Spirit Canyon. It felt good having Beth back in her life, but it was hard trusting her feelings. Circumstances could change in the blink of an eye, especially when the Merrigans were involved. She glanced at Brady, who was studying the lodge from afar. She'd just have to make sure Beth's was one circumstance he didn't change.

Chapter Twelve

Driving with Max, Zo focused on the curvy road in front of her. It gave her an excuse not to think about their argument last night. She wanted to let it go, but he was right about her being stubborn. In some ways, she had to be to live in South Dakota. So did he. Maybe she could make a joke, clear the air. She gave him a sidelong glance. It looked as if he was studying road signs. Nope, she was going to save jokes for later. Taking a deep breath, she tried a gratitude exercise. She was grateful for...the radio? At least the car wasn't completely silent.

"You're speeding," he said.

Zo took her foot off the gas petal.

Max let out a laugh. "Sorry. That was my attempt at a joke."

Maybe she wasn't the only one wanting to lighten the mood. "You need practice."

"You're right." He rolled down the window. "I'm better with animals than people."

"I wish I could say the same, but you've met my cat."

Max's chuckle faded into the background music. A few minutes passed before he spoke. "I'm sorry about last night. I didn't mean to upset you."

Zo gave him a glance. "Saying you're sorry I got upset isn't the same thing as saying you're sorry for accusing Beth of murder."

"I didn't accuse her of murder," Max denied. "I said to be careful."

"I feel like it's the same thing."

"It's not."

Zo had to hand it to him. He was good at quibbling, and it was even kind of fun, but she'd had enough of the banter. "Okay, simple question, simple answer. Do you think Beth killed Enid?"

"Do you?"

The question dragged her attention from the road. "What kind of question is that? Of course I don't."

"You're not the most trusting person I know." Max shrugged. "It had to cross your mind."

She couldn't lie. She'd considered the possibility for one split second. However, she'd never admit it to Max. "I can't believe it. Beth defended you."

He quirked an eyebrow. "I wondered about that. Why *was* she defending me?"

"Beth used to coordinate a lot of weddings for her job in Chicago," said Zo. "I think she's having a hard time adjusting to life without a bride or a groom."

"So, she's playing matchmaker—on us?" He laughed.

She threw him a look. It wasn't *that* crazy of an idea. He acted as if she was the last person in the world he'd date. Well she felt the same way.

"Not that it couldn't happen, I mean," stuttered Max. "I think you're—"

"Okay, let me save you from saying something we're both going to regret." Zo lifted one hand from the steering wheel. "Just answer the question. Do you think Beth murdered Enid?"

"Hey I was going to say something nice," said Max. "But to answer your question, no. I doubt Beth had anything to do with Enid's murder."

"Thank you."

"But people surprise me all the time," he added. "Don't let your guard down."

"You sound like my old boss," said Zo. It was a line he often repeated to reporters on assignment. It was one of the beliefs she let go when she opened Happy Camper. You had to let down your guard to make meaningful connections with people.

"Didn't you work for the *Star*?"

"Yes, almost ten years."

"I read your Curious Camper column every week," said Max.

"I—really?" She checked to see if he was kidding. "You read my column?"

"Yeah," he said. "Of course. I *am* a forest ranger, as you keep reminding me. There's some good stuff in there."

Zo relaxed. "I like writing it. My degree is in journalism."

"That makes sense," said Max. "So, what made you want to go into business?"

Zo switched lanes. "I always had the idea for the store but not the money. Every morning when I drove an hour to work, I thought about it. I saved my paychecks, hoping for *someday*. Then, a few years ago, I went to work and found out I didn't have a job anymore. People weren't reading the newspaper; they were getting their news online. I figured it was a sign, my *someday*. I opened the store, and you know the rest."

"Patrick Merrigan really wouldn't renew the lease on the first place?" Max asked. "I always thought he was a nice guy."

"Oh, he is," Zo said. "He was incredibly nice when he told me he needed the space for his sporting goods store. He even offered to help me pack my things."

"Which explains why you were trying to shove your HAPPY CAMPER sign in your Outback by yourself," said Max.

She smiled. He could be funny when he wanted to be. "Your truck came in handy that day. I guess I never got a chance to thank you." She exited toward Lead. Like the resort in Spirit Canyon, Serenity Falls was on the outskirts of town. According to her GPS, it was several miles outside of the city.

"That's okay," he said. "I understand. I would have been mad, too."

From a distance, she could see the evidence of Lead's mining history. Homestake's open cut mine was a rocky hole, plunging deep into the earth. Gold was mined here from 1876 until 2001. She'd heard once that it produced ten percent of all the gold in the United States. Officially closed, it now housed a visitor's center, where tourists could find out information about the Sanford Underground Research facility, which was dedicated to projects like dark matter. Just the words *dark matter* were enough to arouse curiosity in Zo. She needed to check it out.

If not for the blue sign that read SERENITY FALLS, she would have missed her turn. As it was, she took it sharply.

"Look at this place," said Zo. "It's enormous."

"And secluded," added Max. "Customers must really be looking to get away from it all when they come here."

While the turn had been hidden by shade, the spa was in a clearing. Surrounding the main building were several executive cabins, a pool and detached steam room, and a meditation garden—the perfect accommodations to a relaxing getaway. Only the very rich could afford these digs. *There's no way Allison could swing them on her teacher's salary,* thought Zo.

Max was the first to open the door. "What do you suppose something like this costs?"

"A lot." Zo joined him. "Look at that waterfall." Despite being manmade, the waterfall spilled gallons of water over a rocky cliff, giving the illusion that the pool was its natural run off. Pots overflowed with colorful flowers, and lush green plants decorated the muted cobblestone. The spa must have had a full-time gardener, if not many, to care for the grounds and cabins. Max opened the heavy wooden door to the spa, and Zo squinted to make out the front desk. The room was painted green and had minimal lights and a small waterfall near the reception area. It was more modern than Serenity Hills in Spirit Canyon, and from all the cars in the parking lot Zo guessed it was also busier. No wonder Enid didn't mind leaving the other resort to Henry. This was where she was making her money.

"Hello," said Zo as they approached the front desk. She'd never been to a spa in her life, and the only time she got a pedicure was when the Cut Hut in town was running a special.

A woman in a high bun and black smock looked up. *This must be what flawless looks like*, thought Zo. If she had pores, Zo couldn't see them. Her makeup was perfectly applied.

"Welcome." Her nametag read CLAIRE.

"I'm Max Harrington with the Black Hills National Forest Service, and this is Zo Jones." Max stuck out his hand, and Zo noticed it was calloused from outdoor work. He obviously wasn't there for a manicure.

Claire nodded, and he continued.

"I'm investigating an accident in Spirit Canyon, and I have a couple of questions about someone who might have stayed here recently."

Zo was impressed. He sounded very official. She decided it was nice when his officialness wasn't directed toward her or her store.

"Of course." Claire said the words as if she handled inquiries like this every day. "How can I help?"

"Her name is Allison Scott," said Max. "She's a scientist, and she might have been a guest here when she was working at the Homestake Lab."

Claire's lips turned into a straight line. "You're mistaken. Allison Scott was never a guest."

"Maybe she used the facilities?" Zo tried.

Claire blinked. "That might have helped her attitude, but no."

"How do you know her, then?" asked Max. He was losing patience. She could tell by the way he crossed his arms.

"Allison wanted to do soil tests at the spa—if you can imagine." Claire was clearly horrified by the idea. "She wouldn't leave it alone, even after Enid told her no. If you're here for the same reason, I'm going to have to ask you to leave."

"We're not," Zo said in a rush. "We're here about Enid. I'm sure you heard about her death."

The receptionist looked around to make sure no one heard the unseemly word. "Of course. I was so sorry to hear of her passing."

"You got along with her?" asked Max.

"We heard she could be tough to work for," explained Zo, covering for Max's surprise.

"It's called being a boss," said Claire. "I had no problems with her."

Zo appreciated Claire's directness. "I bet Allison encountered some problems, though, when she approached Enid about the tests."

"For all her academic mumbo jumbo, Allison was a bully." Claire pursed her red lips. "Plain and simple. Enid was right to turn her down. No one wants a spa like Serenity Falls crawling with equipment and scientists. This place is the epitome of solitude. Just the idea of a problem would keep people away."

"When was the last time you saw Allison?" asked Max.

She held up her index finger as she answered the phone. It was a request for more salt in the steam room. She paged an employee then returned to Zo and Max. "I never saw her. I only took her calls—dozens of them. She claimed Homestake could mandate the tests, but of course they couldn't. This is private property."

Zo wondered about that. Yes, it was private property but private property located in the middle of a national forest. Could what Allison said be true? If so, there would be no need to contact Enid. She must have needed permission.

"Do you know if Enid ever met Allison, in person?" asked Max.

Claire gazed over his shoulder. A guest was approaching the desk. "Not that I'm aware of. She might have tried reaching her at her other property, though. You could check with them."

"Thank you for your time," said Max. "If you think of anything else, please give me a call." He slid his business card across the front desk and turned to leave. Zo followed, almost bumping into a towel-clad man. She took a moment to sneak a peek at his backside as they walked out the door.

"I'm pretty sure that guy didn't have any underwear on," Zo whispered when they were safely outside.

"Thanks for letting me know," said Max.

Zo unlocked the car doors. "I'm just saying."

The seats were warm from the sunshine overhead, and she took off her sweater before buckling her seatbelt. Max unfastened a button of his shirt, perhaps wishing he had on something lighter. He wore a park ranger uniform and his gun belt.

"I didn't know you had business cards." Zo opened the sunroof. "Maybe I should have one of them. You know, just in case."

He placed a card into the compartment near her gearshift and patted it. "You're starting to warm up to me. Admit it."

"The car is starting to warm up, if that's what you mean."

He laughed.

Zo pulled out of the resort parking lot. "I think Enid recognized Allison at the chuck wagon. Maybe not *recognized*, recognized, but she said there was something familiar about her. I bet you it was her lisp."

Max nodded. "You're right. I noticed it, too."

"It's slight," said Zo, "but distinguishable."

"What bothers me is that she never mentioned the soil tests during our conversation," said Max. "Maybe she said something to Brady, but I doubt it."

Zo signaled to get onto the highway. "And she's a scientist—who almost became a pharmacist. She would know how to go about killing Enid."

"But why would she kill Enid?" asked Max. "What's her motive? The tests? Even with Enid gone, Griffin might not agree to the equipment."

"He's younger, though," said Zo. "He and his fiancée are much more modern in their thinking."

"True," Max agreed.

"And Griffin wasn't shy about going against his mother's wishes when he asked Robyn to marry him," she pointed out.

He stared out the window. "Still, it's a stretch."

Max believed the easiest explanation was the right one. Zo assumed pretty much the opposite. She'd done enough work at the *Star* to know the tangled webs people wove, the stories that started one place and finished another. It was shocking how one event triggered another. All Max knew was the straight-and-narrow road to justice. Zo knew other ways to get there.

A shiny billboard interrupted her thoughts. It pictured a boy with a gleaming nugget of gold in his hand. Seven days a week, tourists could pan for gold at a forgotten vein of the Homestake Mine. Although one of many similar signs in the Black Hills, it gave Zo a new idea. "What if it wasn't about the soil?" Zo mused. "What if Allison found something at Serenity Falls?"

Max turned from the window. "Like a discovery?"

"Like gold."

Chapter Thirteen

Despite the look on Max's face, it wasn't that crazy of an idea. The Homestake Mine had produced gold until the lab took over, and gold had been found near Deadwood as early as 1865. The Gold Rush was the one and only time in history people flocked to South Dakota. Shops everywhere sold Black Hills Gold, the rose-colored mineral specific to the area. Maybe Allison found a new outcrop. Studying the land from afar, however, Allison could only speculate what lay underground. She would need proof, and a test would give her that.

"You've got a good imagination, Zo," said Max. "I can almost picture the idea in my head."

"Anything is possible, even an undiscovered gold mine. People aren't as predictable as animals. They're really kind of crazy when you get to know them."

"I'm starting to realize that." Max smirked.

"I'm being serious," Zo said.

"Okay, truce." Max held up his hands. "Actually, your theory reminded me of something else. Remember the dinosaur found near Hill City years ago?"

Zo nodded as she took the turnoff for the canyon. Of course she remembered. A paleontologist with the Black Hills Institute discovered the most complete T-rex ever found, on a ranch near Hill City. Unfortunately, he didn't get to keep it. Federal agents seized the dinosaur days later. The whole region was sad and angry. The dinosaur's name was Sue.

"Maybe Allison found something like that," said Max. "A fossil or bone."

So, Max *did* have an imagination. "That's not a bad idea. Fossils would be as valuable to her as gold. And she had to have found something of value. That's why she kept calling."

"What I don't get is why Allison didn't confront Enid." Max shook his head. "Meeting at the lodge was the perfect opportunity to plead her case in person. Why didn't she?"

No wonder he's a forest ranger, thought Zo. *The word lie isn't in his vocabulary.* "Maybe she *did* confront her. Maybe it didn't go well. Do you really think she'd admit they'd had words? No way. Allison's too smart for that. She's a professor, for Pete's sake."

"It'll be easy enough to find out why she's interested in the resort," continued Max. "She teaches at Black Mountain College. If it's work related, I can start there."

"Hey, my astronomy group meets at the college tomorrow night," said Zo. "The Zodiac Club."

"What do you guys do in that group anyway? I've always wondered."

She pulled up the drive to Spirit Canyon Lodge. "We mostly talk about stars and constellations. Sometimes we have a guest speaker or book discussion. You're welcome to join us tomorrow. We're meeting at nine o'clock at the observatory."

He turned to face her. "You can't mean that. You'd hate it if I came."

She put the car in park. "Not true. Why would you even say that?"

"Because I have no imagination." He crossed his arms. "Because I'm a Boy Scout. Because I push your buttons."

Check, check, and check. That pretty much covered it.

"See?" Max pressed. "No rebuttal."

"I'm just surprised you're interested. That's all," said Zo. "Tomorrow night's meeting would be a good chance to get inside and snoop. Allison teaches in the science department, and it's summer. No one's around."

"But the college isn't open."

"Hence the term *snoop.* Besides, the buildings *are* open, until ten." She glanced out the window. The group was back from the casino. It was after four, and Allison's Durango was parked in the drive.

Max didn't answer.

"You'll be fine," prodded Zo. "Just leave your Boy Scout badges at home."

He narrowed his eyes. "Okay, it's a date."

If he was scared of the word *snoop,* she was just as scared of the word *date.* Anytime the word entered a conversation, it ended badly. She went through boyfriends like she went through tea bags, quickly and with variety. Her independent style made relationships—even with a cat—hard. Now that her business was doing well, she was even more content to bury herself in her work.

A woman walked out of the lodge in fringed boots, and it took Zo a moment to realize it was Sarah. Usually plainly dressed, Sarah looked as if she'd been out shopping with Jennifer. The mom jeans were replaced with skinny jeans, and she wore a ruffled shirt. Maybe she'd ransacked Jennifer's closet, or maybe she'd won the jackpot they'd been talking about earlier.

Zo decided to ask her and reached for the door handle. Max did the same. "Hey Sarah." She shut the car door. "You look nice."

Not used to praise, Sarah blushed. Her brown hair was curled into waves, making it appear fuller and shinier, and her hazel eyes looked blue with the new touch of eye makeup. "Jennifer talked me into a makeover."

"Let me guess. Deadwood?" said Zo.

Sarah nodded. "She didn't win the jackpot, but she did win enough to treat us to a trip to the spa in the casino." She smoothed the ruffles on her shirt. Her nails were purple. "They had a great clothing store there, too."

"Did all of you go?" asked Max. He joined Zo by the side of the car.

She wondered if he was thinking the same thing. Four trips to the spa would cost a lot of money. Nails, hair, makeup. Jennifer must have won big, or stolen big, to recoup her losses. Was it Enid's twenty thousand dollars that paid their way?

"Except Allison." Sarah scanned the area, perhaps looking for her friend. "A.J. was covering the drawing for the TV station, and they got to talking. She wants him to cover some event for her, something to do with the college." She turned back to Zo and Max, lowering her voice. "Between you and me, I think she likes him, though she'd never admit it."

Zo thought the same thing. They looked comfortable together Saturday night in front of the fireplace. A.J. was quiet, if not altogether shy, and Allison was reserved. No matter what she did, it had the smudge of *professor* on it. A.J. lived and worked in Spirit Canyon, so there was no reason Zo couldn't talk to him about Allison. Maybe she could find out what event was coming up at the university and if it had anything to do with the Homestake Mine.

"Oh, my *gawd.*" Jennifer cracked open a can of beer. She and Kaya came from the rear of the lodge. She grinned at Sarah. "Look at you, hottie. I love the boots."

"Jennifer's right. You look great." Kaya wore her same no-nonsense attire: jeans, boots, and a sleeveless t-shirt. No fringe for her, but her nails were bright red.

"After the barbeque, we are *so* going out." Jennifer handed Sarah a can of beer and gave Max a look. "Kaya's our designated driver."

"Glad to hear it." Max nodded. "The police are out in full force for the holiday weekend."

Zo supposed he got that a lot.

"We're going to get you to relax yet, girl." Jennifer clinked her beer with Sarah's, then held her phone up to take a selfie. "Damon will regret ever leaving you when he sees this."

"You're not going to post it, are you?" Sarah's hazel eyes were wide.

"Already did." Jennifer slipped her phone into her pocket.

Kaya took a drink of her water. "Enough with the selfies. Let's play beanbag toss." Two raised platforms and several beanbags were in the front lawn. "Where's Allison?"

Allison appeared from around the corner of the house. She was tucking her phone into the inside pocket of her jacket, which was too warm for the sunny day. While the other women wore t-shirts or sleeveless tops, she wore a button-down blouse that looked like something she might wear to class. Zo had a feeling no matter what Allison wore, she would always look a little uncomfortable.

"Just when you think you've solved one fashion problem, another crops up," mumbled Jennifer as she picked up a miniature beanbag. "It's like whack-a-mole." She called out to Allison. "You're not wearing that tonight, are you?"

Allison stopped and glanced down at her outfit as if she'd forgotten what she had on.

Zo and Max took the opportunity to approach Allison before she reached her friends.

"Hey, Allison," said Zo. "How was Deadwood?"

"I attended a panel on Gender and Settlement in the Northern Plains. It was really interesting. Tomorrow there's one on Notorious Horse Thieves of the Wild West."

"We've been somewhere interesting, too," said Max. "Serenity Falls."

Zo guessed Max was going with the direct approach, which wasn't a bad idea. Allison would appreciate a straightforward question. Whether or not she would answer it was to be seen.

"Claire, the receptionist, told us she knew you," Zo said. "She said you called Serenity Falls several times in the last few months."

Allison's eyebrows shot up. "That's surprising. Every time I called, she pretended I didn't exist."

"Why didn't you tell me you knew Enid?" asked Max. His voice was laden with suspicion. "You had plenty of opportunities."

"I didn't *know* her," said Allison. "I reached out to her business as an emissary from the college."

Max crossed his arms. "Okay, then. Why didn't you tell me and Brady you'd had contact with her before last weekend? We asked you, and you lied to us."

Zo studied her response. If she was upset by the question, she didn't let on. The slight wrinkle of her forehead was the only indication that she was surprised by Max's question.

"No, I didn't," Allison denied. "I've never met her before in my life. I didn't think phone calls counted."

The way she responded made Max's question sound ridiculous, but that didn't stop Max from continuing. Allison's righteousness was hard to refute, but he wasn't easily dissuaded, a quality Zo could appreciate.

"What Claire described was harassment," said Max. "She said you wouldn't stop contacting the spa about setting up scientific tests."

Allison waved away the comment. "It was hardly harassment.. I was always polite when I called, which is more than I can say for Enid."

"Why did you want on the property in the first place?" asked Zo. "What did you find?"

For the first time, Allison hesitated. "Nothing yet. That was the problem. Research at Homestake indicated a large outcrop of minerals. But without the proper soil tests, we can't be sure."

Jennifer called out to Allison. It was her turn to toss the beanbag.

"Is that all?" asked Allison. "Or do you have more questions?"

"We'll let you know," said Max.

Allison joined her friends at the beanbag toss, and Zo and Max walked to the rear of the lodge. Zo was perplexed by Allison's response. Allison didn't deny contacting Serenity Falls and said she'd done so in her official capacity as a scientist. If that were true, why not tell Brady or Max from the beginning? Maybe she was an absent minded professor, or maybe she really didn't think it was important. She was convinced she'd done nothing wrong. Zo wasn't so sure.

The sun was bright in the sky, illuminating the pasqueflowers surrounding the inn. If Zo closed her eyes, she could feel the nearness of summer—or at least smell it. Jack was smoking baby-back ribs, and barbeque tinged the calm canyon breeze. Soon the hills would be filled with campfires and cookouts like this one. The Black Hills were a popular summer destination for good reason. Besides Mount Rushmore, hundreds of attractions dotted the area: Reptile Gardens, Bear Country, Wind Cave, and Needles Highway just to name a few. With so many sights in the area, it made a perfect getaway. Beth, Jack, and the family were on the patio, just off the lodge deck. Like the chuck wagon, the patio was carefully decorated. The picnic tables were set with red, white, and blue petunias, a miniature American flag poking out of each pot. An oversized umbrella was cranked to full size, providing shade for the majority of the seating area, and two large stainless-steel coolers, one stocked with drinks and the other with salads, were stationed nearby. Red, white, and blue dinnerware completed the Memorial Day ensemble.

"You're back!" Beth's brown ponytail swung back and forth as she hurried to greet them. "I was getting worried you wouldn't make it in time."

"Everything smells delicious," said Zo. "What can I do to help?" Guests paid additional fees for the chuck wagon and barbeque. Although Beth would never take her money, she hoped she would take her up on the offer to help.

"You can take pictures," Beth said. "I don't have a single one from the chuck wagon, and Vi is fuming that she has no fodder for her new ad campaign."

Zo took her phone out of her backpack. "Consider it done."

"How about me?" Max offered. "Is there anything I can do?"

"You can tell me what you found out at Serenity Falls." Beth motioned to the umbrella shade. "Start at the beginning."

Zo could see why Beth made a great event coordinator; she was superb at multitasking. Even in the midst of a fairly substantial dinner party, she wanted to know what they'd found. When Zo cooked, it took all her concentration not to burn something, and even with her full attention, meals could go terribly wrong. Which was probably why she dined out or with Cunningham as much as she did. Despite being a mediocre gardener, he was a fantastic cook.

Max recounted the trip to Serenity Falls, not leaving out any details. Zo added a brief description of the man in the towel. Max rolled his eyes, but Beth chuckled. Beth stopped mid-laugh. She turned her head to one side, her ponytail dipping over her shoulder.

"So, Allison *knew* Enid," said Beth.

"Yes," said Max.

"And she said nothing about it," said Beth.

"Nope," said Zo. "Not until we confronted her about it a few minutes ago."

"You were right, Zo," Beth said, looking out at the surrounding hills. A cloud crossed over the faltering sun. "The canyon does have its secrets."

Zo agreed. The hills held secrets that cast long shadows. Death was as much a part of its history as life, and although spring was in the air, it couldn't disguise the deepness of the canyon or its mysteries. But if Zo knew one thing, it was Spirit Canyon. She would find out what happened to Enid even if she had to unearth the past one piece at a time.

Chapter Fourteen

After the barbeque, Zo drove Max home. For much of the drive through the canyon, she and Max were silent, watching the light change and evening fall. They were both thinking about Enid's murder—at least Zo was. After looking into Allison's connection to Serenity Falls, she had expanded her list of motives to include a discovery, something that would help the young professor advance her career. Zo knew what it was like to be the new kid, and it wasn't fun. A discovery at Serenity Falls would make Allison's colleagues take her seriously. It would also secure her future as a scientist.

Zo let up on the gas as she approached downtown Spirit Canyon, noticing the buzz of activity that accompanied warmer weather. Summer was coming; she could feel it. At Buffalo Bill's Beer Garden, a band played on the outdoor stage while onlookers ate burgers and drank frosty pints of cream ale from the well-known local brewery. Later, diners would leave and dancers would take to the space surrounding the stage. Since Buffalo Bill's was a block kitty-corner from Zo's house, she could enjoy the music—and entertainment—from the comfort of her deck. A lover of rock and folk music, Zo enjoyed the nights they didn't play country, which were usually weekdays. In the summer, tourists dictated the music the bands played, and they wanted authentic Wild West. Of course the bands agreed; they enjoyed tips as much as anybody else.

"They must be having a Memorial Day concert," said Max, indicating out the window. "Sounds like a country band."

"Probably." Zo slowed down to the speed limit. "That's what I hear most in the summer."

"I forgot. You're right across the street. Does the noise bother you?"

"Nope," she said. "It's like background music. I always know when it's nine o'clock." A few bars of guitar floated through the window. "They're not bad. I might have to check them out later."

"Call me if you go," said Max. "I wouldn't mind a beer."

She kept her eyes on the road. It took all her resolve not to gawk in his direction. A beer with Max? Didn't he remember how their last drink had ended?

"Take a right here, on Spruce."

Zo turned the corner, picking up their earlier conversation. "No matter how cooperative Allison was today, she still lied, you know. She should have told you about her history with Serenity Falls when you and Brady interviewed her."

Max nodded. "I agree. She's hiding something. I just don't know if it's the murder of Enid Barrett. I also don't know if Brady's going to let me hang around long enough to find out."

"What do you mean?" she asked. "You're a law enforcement officer. You have every right to be there."

"Oh, so *now* I'm a law enforcement officer," said Max with a laugh. "What changed your mind? The tightening grip of desperation?"

"Look, I suppose I am sort of desperate," said Zo, also laughing. "Beth was a friend to me when I didn't have many. It meant a lot."

"I don't want to see Beth arrested for a crime she didn't commit any more than you do," said Max. "I know she's your friend."

Zo believed him. Max might have been a lot of things, but he wasn't a liar.

"Take this left," said Max. "I'm halfway down the block."

Zo was surprised Max lived downtown. For some reason, she imagined him living in a cabin somewhere in the forest, chopping his own wood. She could see him with a big ax in his hand.

Max told her to stop in front of a small green bungalow. Although tiny, it had a large overhang and porch with two wooden rocking chairs. His old pickup truck was in the driveway.

"What?" said Max. "You look surprised."

"Sorry," she said. "I thought you'd live on an acreage or something."

"Because forest rangers live in the wild?" Max rolled his eyes. "I'm just a regular guy, Zo." He pointed to the front door, where a man in tight jeans and a black t-shirt appeared. "See? I even have a roommate."

Zo recognized his roommate at once. "Duncan Hall?" She couldn't keep the shock out of her voice. Good-looking and tattooed, Duncan was known in town for being a hell raiser.

"Yeah, so?"

So? Just watching him saunter, barefoot, down the steps made her heart rate increase. The guy was an instant aphrodisiac. If she were the blushing type, she would have blushed. "He's hardly your type."

Max laughed. "That's okay because we're not dating."

"You know what I mean," Zo said, turning toward him. "He's…not like you."

"I think you've clarified that already," said Max.

She didn't have time to say anymore. Duncan was approaching the driver's side of the car. He rested his folded arms on the window frame.

"Zo Jones," said Duncan. "I know you. You're the happy camper." Despite his rough shave, his voice was like honey, smooth and sweet.

Zo chided herself for feeling flattered. "Hi, Duncan."

"And you know who I am, I guess," said Duncan. "What are you doing here?"

Zo wanted to ask him the same question. "We were at Spirit Canyon Lodge. My friend owns the place where Enid Barrett died."

"That's right." Duncan tapped the windowsill. His fingers lingered inside the car. "Max was out saving the world—again."

"It needs saving from guys like you." Max smirked, but Zo could tell they were good friends. He reached for the door handle. "Do you want to come in? I promise I won't let Duncan bite."

"Unless you want me to," whispered Duncan as Max got out of the car. "Then that can be arranged."

Zo had to admire his spirit. "A tempting offer, but I have two men waiting for me at home—my cat and Professor Cunningham. I promised Cunningham I'd listen to him recite a war poem in honor of Memorial Day."

"Is he a veteran?" asked Max. Standing together, they could have been brothers. They were both tall, muscular, and in their thirties. But that's where their similarities ended. Max was the dutiful friend. Duncan was…not.

"No, but he fights with our neighbor Midge a lot," said Zo. "Does that count?"

"If you change your mind, you know where I live," said Duncan. He gave her a wink.

Max gave him a playful shove. "But seriously, if you decide to go to Buffalo Bill's, give me a call."

"Okay. Have a good night, guys." She rolled up her window. Max waved to her as she backed out of the driveway. She wondered how long Duncan had been living with him and how long Max's patience would hold out. Duncan seemed fun, in a reckless sort of way, but so different than Max. She couldn't believe they lived under the same roof.

She pulled away from the STOP sign. She'd never roomed with anyone, except in college. Even when she was little and lived with the Joneses, she spent most of her time outdoors. The house was packed and claustrophobic. Sometimes Zo wondered if, somewhere out there, she had a sister or brother. It was possible. All she knew of her birth were the few details the Jones family had shared.

According to accounts, she'd been left inside the bathroom of the police station on New Year's Eve. She was probably two weeks old, but they didn't know for sure, so she always celebrated her birthday on Christmas, when people were giving gifts anyway. Spirit Canyon was small, and even smaller and less trendy back in the 1980s. The police station was a one-room brick building then and didn't have the surveillance system it did now. She thought it was telling, though, that she was left at a police station and not a church or front door. Her parents, whoever they were, trusted her well-being to the police. It was New Year's Eve, and if the station saw any action, it would be on that holiday. They knew she would be safe, which made her feel loved.

As Zo turned the corner onto Main Street, she saw A.J. walking out of the television station. She gave him a honk. He looked up and waved. Glad he recognized her, she pulled into an empty parking spot and got out of the car. A.J. was probably around forty but had the face of a much younger man. His skin was as light as alabaster, untouched by sun or wrinkles. It would be a long time before he looked old.

"I didn't realize cameramen worked such long hours," said Zo. "Are you just getting done for the day?"

"Finally." A.J. let out a breath. "Holidays are the worst. Justin made an unscheduled stop at Sturgis. It turned out to be nothing."

Zo could tell he was tired. Who wouldn't be, chasing stories with Justin Castle? The guy got on *her* nerves. She couldn't imagine working with him. She'd worked with enough guys *like him*, always looking for the next big break at stardom. It was as if they didn't even care about what the news was as long as it meant coverage for them. "Sarah mentioned seeing you at Deadwood. I was out at Spirit Canyon Lodge for a barbeque."

He nodded. "Sarah and her friends were at the casino for a giveaway, but Allison's not into that. Do you know she's a professor at Black Mountain College?"

The way he said *professor* made Zo understand he thought Allison was someone important. Or maybe they had a little crush on each other, like Sarah said. They were pretty cozy the night of the storm. They pored over the same book, anyway. A day spent gambling might be unattractive to a bookworm.

"She seems super smart," said Zo. "She mentioned some event coming up at the college. It has to do with science."

"They're opening an exhibit on campus later this summer, and she wants me to cover it," he said. "It's about the treasures beneath the earth's surface. Cool stuff, especially to us sci-fi geeks. I'm going to ask my editor."

"Will he go for it?" She knew much of what got covered wasn't up to the writer. It was up to the editor and the day's schedule. If nothing was going on, even a small event might get coverage, but if the day was booked, a large one might escape notice.

A.J. took off his hat, smoothed his hair, then put it on backward. "I've been there ten years. I should be able to persuade him."

"Ten years, wow," Zo said. "I didn't realize."

He shrugged. "Most people only know the face in front of the camera, not the guy behind it."

That was true. Zo would recognize Justin anywhere, and he was fairly new to the station. "Did Allison mention anything specific about the exhibit? I forgot to ask her."

"She promised a few surprises. But she might be saying that to get coverage. Why?"

"No reason. Just curious." Zo wondered if the surprise included whatever she found near Serenity Falls. With Enid out of the picture, she might be able to get her hands on the discovery more easily.

A.J. glanced over at Buffalo Bill's. Maybe he was headed to the bar for a drink. She didn't want to keep him. After a long day with Justin, he deserved it. But seeing him reminded her that Beth needed pictures of the chuck wagon, and he'd taken several. Maybe Zo could ask him? It was the least she could do to help Beth generate a little positive publicity. "I wanted to ask you something quick. Beth is looking for some footage of the chuck wagon. She's starting a new ad campaign, but she didn't get any pictures. She was too busy rushing around that night."

He thought for a moment. "I'm sure I have something she could use. I don't know if I'm supposed to do that, though. I took them with the station's equipment."

"Any little snippet might help," Zo pleaded. "If you have anything, I'd be happy to pay you for it."

"I could use the money," said A.J. "I'll see what I can come up with. Will you be at Happy Camper tomorrow?"

Zo nodded. She was scheduled for most of the day.

"I'll drop something by."

"Thanks so much, A.J. See you then."

He gave her a wave and continued walking.

Zo thought about their conversation as she drove the remaining blocks to her house. He mentioned the exhibit at the college. She wondered if Allison wanted the camera crew there because she would be making an important announcement, one that involved her discovery at Serenity Falls. A discovery of that magnitude would certainly elevate her status at the university, and she took her career seriously. Maybe it would even give her tenure, something Cunningham was always yammering about. As she parked on the street, she decided to ask him, knowing full well the answer would include a much longer explanation than needed. Turning off the ignition, she wondered if a dictionary might be quicker.

Cunningham wasn't on his deck, so she didn't have to decide right away. She glanced around for George as she walked up the deck stairs. Surprisingly, he was stretched out on the cushioned lounge chair, warming himself in the last drops of sunlight. It was a good sign. He might not live with her, but he was sticking closer to the house. With time, he might even come to think of it as home.

"Hey, George." She scratched his ears. "How's it going?"

He purred in response. She decided not to press her luck and, after one more pet, went inside to change. The night was growing cool, and she threw on a sweatshirt. After pouring a glass of merlot, she padded out to the deck in her moccasins. She turned on the fireplace, and with the flick of the flame, George startled and left. She called for him to come back, but Cunningham was the only one who heard her pleas.

From his deck, he said, "It's almost nighttime, Zo. You can't expect Saint George to remain celibate."

She adjusted the flame height. "Why *Saint* George?"

"I have a story for you," he said, toddling down his stairs and into her yard. His gray hair looked like a bush on top of his head, coarse and unruly, and his round nose was pink from the sun.

"What about the poem?" she said as he approached her deck. "I thought you were reciting one for Memorial Day."

"I am."

Zo sat down. "I think I might recite something, too."

He crinkled his brow in question. He knew she wasn't patient enough for poetry.

"Ode to a sunburnt professor," she said. "I think that's what I'll call it."

He sat down next to her. "I would like to hear that. But first, Saint George. Do you know him?"

"Not personally, but I have a feeling I'm about to get better acquainted with him."

"Your instincts serve you well," said Cunningham and began his story. According to the professor, a dragon made a nest near the ancient town of Cyrene in Libya, blocking the town's water supply. The town lured the dragon away from its nest with sheep until all the sheep were gone. Then they decided to send a maiden, and the town's princess drew the unlucky straw. But before she could meet her demise, Saint George rescued her and slayed the dragon, saving her and the town like a true prince. It was the reason St. George was depicted slaying a dragon on religious memorabilia, he explained.

"But these are modern times," said Zo, sipping her wine. "There are no dragons—or princes."

"Not a dragon or a prince, but a snake and a tomcat." He pointed into the woods. "George chased it all the way up the hill. I was gobsmacked. Cats are afraid of snakes. Hence the term scaredy-cat."

"He's a good guy," said Zo. "He just doesn't know it yet."

"Like Max Harrington?"

"Hardly," said Zo. "Max definitely knows he's a good guy—too good. Squeaky good."

"He might be *that* good," said Cunningham. "You have a hard time trusting people, Zo."

She'd heard it before. People thought because she'd grown up in the foster system that she was somehow broken. What the system did was make her grateful for the life she had right now. She was a strong believer in rising above circumstances. She had done it, and so had others. It gave her hope for the future.

When she didn't respond, Cunningham glanced at her glass of wine.

"The epitome of subtle." Zo stood. "Red or white?"

"Red, if you please. It pairs well with poetry."

Zo returned with a second glass and the bottle of wine. "Does your Memorial Day poem feature our neighbor, Midge?" she asked as she poured. "I can hear it now: The Battle of Little Main Street."

Cunningham took the glass and leaned in conspiratorially. "Did I tell you? Her birdseed is what's causing all the weeds in my garden. I found her by that dang tree today with her binoculars. When I told her about the problem, she said she'd rather see me in court than take down her bird feeder." He sipped his wine. "I'm tempted, by God."

Zo took a drink to hide her smile. Cunningham disliked Midge with a passion, and after hearing all the stories of her birds, squirrels, and feeders, Zo was thankful for the one house that separated them. From the way Cunningham made it sound, she loved all living things, except human beings, and Zo wondered if it was true. Midge never talked to her when they met out front, just touched her straw cowgirl hat. Though Zo had lived in the house a couple of years now, she knew very little about her.

"So, the poem," said Zo. "Let's hear it."

Cunningham cleared his throat. "You'll like it because it's short."

But as he began reciting the poem, she decided it wasn't short, and when he forgot a line and had to pull the creased paper from his pocket, her attention turned elsewhere. From her deck, she could see a little of Main Street. She could also see the group from the lodge entering Buffalo Bill's. Jennifer had said something about going out; Zo didn't realize she meant in Spirit Canyon. But Spirit Canyon was the closest town to the lodge, and they'd already been to Deadwood.

Zo glanced back at Cunningham, who continued with page two of his poem, then back to Buffalo Bill's. A.J. had also been walking in the direction of Buffalo Bill's. Were he and Allison meeting up, or was it a coincidence?

Cunningham finished, and Zo clapped. "I didn't know your uncle was a veteran."

"He was," said Cunningham. "Korean War, fifth battalion."

"I'd still like to hear one about Midge."

"Midge is not the kind of woman who inspires poetry."

"You said once that fire and ice make the world go round," said Zo, finishing her wine. "Maybe she's the ice to your fire."

"I said the world would *end* by fire or ice," Cunningham corrected. "And here I thought you were listening to me." He pushed away from the table. "Frost was a heck of a poet, though. If anyone has the answers, he does."

"You're not staying for another glass?" Zo held up the bottle.

"I might be an old man, but I know when someone's attention is elsewhere." Cunningham lifted his chin toward Buffalo Bill's. "Is it about a prince?"

Zo shook her head. "I told you this is modern times. Princes don't exist. The group from Spirit Canyon Lodge is at the bar."

Cunningham set his empty glass on the table. "It's the perfect night for honky-tonking. I'd come with you if I weren't so tired."

She smiled. Even *honky-tonking* sounded like poetry in his mouth. "Who says I'm going anywhere?"

"That look on your face," said Cunningham.

She couldn't deny it. She needed to see why five out of the eight guests had popped up at Buffalo Bill's. But first, she had to call Max. She decided she wanted to go out after all.

Chapter Fifteen

At Buffalo Bill's, a steady country beat shook the building. The later it got, and the more beer the tourists drank, the louder the band played. Inside, people were starting to dance, two-stepping with partners or boogying with friends. Zo waited for Max outside, hoping she wouldn't regret calling him. If he showed up in his forest ranger uniform, she was going to kill him. She'd taken off her sweatshirt, put on a cute top, and traded her flip-flops for flats. She breathed a sigh of relief when she caught him walking up in jeans and a red t-shirt, looking very unlike the Boy Scout she accused him of being.

"I didn't think you'd really call." Max ran his hand through his hair. She wondered if he'd showered. It looked damp.

"I didn't think you'd really come," said Zo. What she meant was she didn't think he'd come looking like that. It was hard to remember he was there to investigate.

"I guess we're both full of surprises."

The outdoor seating area was standing room only, so she followed Max around to the far side of the bar, where they ordered beers. Sarah, Kaya, and Jennifer were dancing near the stage, but Allison and A.J. were sitting together at a table. Across from one another, they looked like a couple on a first date, timid but excited. Allison had discarded the jacket she was wearing earlier, and A.J. had dropped the baseball cap. Zo could see now that his hair was the same color as his chin whiskers, red-brown against his light complexion.

Max pointed toward the dance floor. "They've had a couple beers."

Sarah and Jennifer were twirling each other around the dance floor, laughing and singing. Kaya was dancing near a guy who was also alone, and when the lights dimmed and a slow song started, he pulled her into a two-step.

"Look who's joining them," said Zo, nodding toward A.J. and Allison. They were approaching the dance floor like two colts standing for the first time. "A.J. said she wants him to cover an event at the college. Let's go see if we can overhear anything."

"Me?" Max choked on his beer. "I don't dance."

"Everyone dances," said Zo. "Just pretend I'm a lost animal."

"You know, that's not so big a stretch."

"Ha ha, very funny. Don't make me find someone else. You know I will."

Max set down his beer next to hers, and she led him out to the dance floor. The band was playing an Alabama song, and she put her arms around his neck. Max moved his hands up and then down her waist, not completely sure where to put them. Finally he relaxed, placing his hands just above her hips. His carefulness was kind of cute.

A.J. and Allison took up a position near the edge of the dance floor. They could have been in gym class; their form was the same one students used. It was sort of endearing, really, thought Zo. She could see A.J. respected Allison a great deal, and Allison liked him, too. She smiled more in sixty seconds than Zo had seen all weekend.

Tightening his grasp on her waist, Max steered them as close as he could to the couple without being conspicuous. Even near the perimeter of the dance floor, though, the music was loud. Zo couldn't hear a thing but the words to the song. Strain as she might, she couldn't catch any of their conversation. A.J. saw her and blinked. Allison turned around and waved, lifting her fingertips off A.J.'s shoulder. Zo thought they made a cute couple. She really hoped Allison didn't turn out to be a murderer.

"So, I guess our cover is blown," said Max, but he didn't stop dancing.

"I couldn't hear anything anyway." Zo noticed a disturbance out of the corner of her eye near the stage. Max noticed it too and turned to look. Kaya's voice was raised and not in a good way. She was angry, but her dancing partner seemed unaware of her feelings. He pulled her closer. Kaya was strong and pushed back while slipping something shiny out of her vest pocket. Zo and Kaya's dance partner realized at the same time it was a knife. Kaya held it close to his face, her eyes like two blazing fires. The music slowed, like a record on the wrong speed, then stopped.

With a few quick steps, Max was next to them, quietly asking Kaya to put away the knife. The attention of the dance floor was on her, but she didn't move. It was as if she was in another time or place, stuck in a memory or dream where she was paralyzed. If Zo were in the man's place, she would have been afraid for her life.

"I have a right to defend myself," said Kaya, her eyes not leaving the man's face.

"Absolutely," Max agreed. "And I think he's taken your point. Right, guy?" The man nodded but just barely. He didn't want the knife scraping his throat.

"I don't want to charge you with assault." Max kept his tone calm but firm. "Put away the knife."

Kaya swallowed and tucked the knife into her jacket, and the man stumbled away. Drunk, he meandered through the crowd that had gathered to see the disturbance. The band began to play again, this time a fast song, and Max led Kaya back to the table where Jennifer and Sarah sat.

"What the hell happened?" asked Jennifer. "What did that guy do?"

"I was wondering the same thing," said Zo.

"Same old story." Kaya was still tense. "You meet a guy. You think he likes you. Then he spouts some racial slur or puts his hands on you." She shook her head. "I don't know why I'm surprised."

"I think he was drunk," said Sarah.

"You think that gives him the right to say whatever he wants? You think it's an excuse?" Kaya's eyes were as sharp as the blade of her knife.

"No way." Zo answered for Sarah, who was shocked at her friend's reaction. "Nothing gives him the right to disrespect you."

Kaya took a breath. She seemed more like herself. "It's been a long day. I think we should go."

"It's still early." Jennifer took a peanut out of the basket on the table and cracked it open, tossing the shell on the floor. "Don't let that loser ruin our fun."

Sarah put her hand on Kaya's. "She's right. And besides, Allison finally found a boyfriend." She pointed toward A.J. and Allison, leaving the dance floor.

"Men," said Kaya. "This is supposed to be a girls' week anyway."

Zo empathized with Kaya but also wondered at her reaction. She looked as if she could have killed the man. Could she have killed Enid? Enid had made a remark about Native Americans at the chuck wagon. She suggested their beliefs were false, myths. Had Enid offended Kaya more than Zo realized? It was another possibility she needed to sort out.

A.J. and Allison approached the table, and A.J. gave Max a quick glance. "They say it's not a party until the cops arrive. Did you arrest that guy?"

"No, I didn't call anyone. I thought we'd had enough interaction with the Spirit Canyon police since Enid's death."

A.J. nodded in agreement. Obviously, he didn't want the night to end prematurely.

"It's hot in here," said Jennifer. "I could use another beer. Anyone else?" she asked as she rose from her chair.

"I'm good," said Kaya, who was driving.

Sarah said she'd have another.

"Thanks, but we're on our way out," said Zo. Like Kaya said, it had been a long day, and Zo didn't want to keep Max. She had a feeling the group would be on their best behavior knowing he was there. They wouldn't learn anything now, but they had learned something about Kaya. Not only was she pretty, she was tough—with good reason. Could her temper have had something to do with Enid's death?

She and Max said good-bye, trading the packed bar for wide-open sky. Stars dotted the black night, like white paint splattered across a black canvas. Zo hoped tomorrow would be just as clear and lovely. The Zodiac Club was meeting at the campus observatory. She reminded Max of her invitation.

"If tomorrow is like tonight, it's going to be perfect for stargazing," said Zo. "We're meeting at the campus observatory if you want to join us."

"No one will mind?" asked Max.

"Not at all. It's open to the public. Lots of people visit without joining."

Staring into the inky darkness, he didn't respond right away. "Do you think we'll ever find the answer?"

"I think the stars hold lots of answers," she replied. "They've been here longer than we have. They have to know more than we do."

Max looked at her and smiled. "I meant the answer to Enid's death."

Of course he meant the answer to Enid's death. What did she think he was talking about? She gave herself a mental kick. She could be an idiot sometimes.

Max briefly lifted her moon necklace. "That's why you're interested in astronomy, isn't it? You think it holds the answers you haven't been able to find yourself."

His question hit close to home, and she wondered how much he knew of her past. Probably something. Spirit Canyon was small, and everyone knew something about someone. But he hadn't grown up here. He probably moved here when he became a forest ranger. She didn't meet him until opening Happy Camper.

With his eyes on her, she felt exposed, vulnerable. She longed to flee, but she forced herself to respond. "I like the stories. I like the sky. You don't have to come to the meeting if you don't want to. It's totally up to you."

"I want to come," said Max. "I'll be there."

She turned toward the crosswalk. She couldn't deny the urge to leave any longer.

"Hey, thank you," said Max, following her.

She pushed the crosswalk button. "For what?"

"For the dance."

"It was nothing," she said and crossed the street for home. They were partners for one reason and one reason only: to solve Enid's murder. Glancing back at Max standing under the streetlight, his face as honest as the night sky, she decided he made it easy to forget.

Chapter Sixteen

Traffic hadn't subsided just because Memorial Day was over, which meant a busy Tuesday at Happy Camper. People extended their stays to enjoy the warm weather and fun events that signaled summer. Horseback excursions, helicopter rides, and kayaking tours were offering discounts for the weekend, and greening trails and calm lakes provided tourists with plenty of reasons to linger. Throughout the morning, Zo had waited on ten customers, and all had made purchases. They gushed over the new Happy Camper mugs as well as the scented candles (s'more was her favorite scent this month). One shopper considered the Remington typewriter Zo had purchased from an auction, but Zo was almost glad when she decided against it. With a cute piece of Happy Camper stationery tucked inside, it made a fun display.

When Beth rushed through the front door at eleven thirty, Zo didn't notice right away. She was on the floor, unpacking a box. It wasn't until Beth touched her shoulder that she realized it wasn't another customer.

"What a surprise," said Zo, unfolding an ENJOY THE RIDE flag. "You doing a little shopping this morning?"

Beth shook her head, her hair pulled back in a messy bun, and Zo noted her outfit. Normally a careful dresser, Beth wore a baggy sweatshirt, old jeans, and slip-on tennis shoes. No flowers in sight. She must have left in a hurry.

"Is something wrong?" Zo rose, brushing packing material from her pants.

Beth's blue-gray eyes darted to the door and back at Zo. A customer was leaving, and Zo called good-bye. After the shopper was gone, Beth answered. "It's Enid's medicine. I think I've found it."

"Where?"

Beth leaned in. "In Allison's room."

Zo was surprised, sort of. She and Max knew Allison's work involved Serenity Falls. They also knew Allison was planning an event at the college. She might have discovered something at Serenity Falls. Plus she knew the medication, digoxin. She herself said it would take very little for a person to overdose.

"I wasn't snooping," continued Beth. "I was dusting. It was right there in the dresser. The drawer was ajar."

The dresser that you own, thought Zo. She hated where her mind was taking her, but this was bad news.

"I was cleaning the rooms while they were having breakfast, and that's when I found it. It had Enid's name on the bottle," said Beth.

"So, what did you do with it?" Zo asked as she hung a flag on a display rod.

"Nothing. I shut the drawer and came here. I didn't know if I should go to the police or what."

A new group of shoppers entered the store, heading for the colorful flag Zo had just hung. The display had not only flags but welcome mats and other décor that tourists liked to display outside their RVs. After showing a customer the location of the wrapped flags on the shelf below, Zo led Beth to the cash register, where they had a little more privacy. George was sprawled out on the counter.

"I thought he ran away." Beth gave George a scratch under his chin. He didn't bother opening his eyes.

"He did, he does," said Zo. "He was hungry this morning. He'll disappear by this afternoon." She put her elbows on the counter. "Beth, was anything else in the drawer? Clothes? Books?"

Beth shook her head. "No. Nothing."

"Doesn't that seem strange?' said Zo. "I mean, if Allison did poison Enid, why not put the medicine in her suitcase or hide it in a sock? There's no reason to leave it in a drawer, where you or anyone could find it."

"You don't think *I* put it there, do you?"

Beth was so taken aback that Zo felt bad for ever even considering the idea. Maybe Cunningham was right about trust issues. She reached for Beth and gave her a big hug. "Of course not. I know you had nothing to do with Enid's death."

When they separated, Beth was smiling. "Thank goodness. If you thought I killed her, I couldn't bear it. You meant someone else is setting her up."

"I think they might be," said Zo. Their conversation was interrupting George's nap, and he jumped off the counter, a fluff of fur floating behind him. He stood next to the door, waiting for the next customer to open it.

"But who would do that?" asked Beth. "One of her friends?"

"Who else?" said Zo. "No one else is staying at the lodge. They must have decided they had to unload it somewhere. Maybe Allison was the safest bet since she's smart. They figured she'd be able to defend herself against the accusation."

"You know, I really need to install cameras," Beth mused. "At least in the main areas."

The mention of cameras reminded Zo that A.J. was stopping by the store today. He said he would drop off some footage of the lodge. She told Beth.

"You are a lifesaver," said Beth. "Thank you." She redid her bun, which was coming loose. "What am I going to do about the pills? Go to the police?"

Zo reached for Max's card in her backpack beneath the cabinet. "Maybe the police can come to us." She dialed his number and waited. When Max answered, she explained Beth's discovery.

"Has she given her statement to Brady at the station?" Max asked.

"No," said Zo. "She came straight here."

"Meet me at the station," said Max. "I can be there in ten minutes."

"I'm working," said Zo. "But I'll tell Beth to meet you there. Stop by when you're finished."

He promised he would and clicked off the phone. Zo relayed his message to her friend. Beth didn't want to go by herself, but Zo reassured her that she would be just down the street. "The station is less than a mile away. It won't take long, and by that time, Harley will be here, and we can go to lunch."

Beth still looked worried, but her step was lighter when she left. At least Beth knew Max and liked him. Zo was confident he wouldn't let Brady railroad her; Max cared about doing the right thing. Brady, on the other hand, wanted this case closed and his town's reputation restored. If he had to pressure Beth, he would. Since she was the owner of the lodge, he would try to hold her responsible even though the medicine was found in Allison's drawer.

Zo was relieved when Harley punched in early. One, she wouldn't have to worry about leaving the store, and two, a customer wished to purchase the large buffalo print hanging near the door. It took both of their strength to take it down and wrap it for travel. Without the print, the wall looked bare, and Zo shot off an email to the photographer requesting another, as well as some miniature postcard prints. She was pressing the Send button when Max and Beth returned from the police station. Max wore a short-sleeved green shirt and green uniform pants. *This* was the Max she knew.

"So now I can tell my kids I've seen the inside of a police station," said Beth. "Who would've thought that it'd be in Spirit Canyon, not Chicago? Wonders."

"Sorry I couldn't go with you," Zo said. "Harley just got here."

"Max was great," said Beth.

"Brady not so much." Max glanced at Zo. "He thinks it's 'interesting' Beth found Enid's medicine in Allison's room." He air-quoted.

"*Interesting?*" said Zo. "You'd think he'd be excited to find another clue to Enid's death."

Max shook his head. "I don't think he thinks of it that way. He's convinced Beth had something to do with it."

"I'm just glad you're not convinced," said Beth. "Without you, I don't know where I'd be—probably jail."

Though Zo hated to admit it, they needed Max's help. They needed him on their team. "We're going to go to lunch. Do you want to join us?"

"I'd love to, but I told Brady I wanted to run out to the lodge with him," he said. "I don't want him gathering evidence alone. I'll see you at the Zodiac Club, though, if you're still meeting?"

"Sure. Unless it clouds over, we'll be at the observatory at Black Mountain."

"I'll see you at dusk, then," said Max.

Zo nodded, and they watched him walk out the door.

"Max is sweet." Beth smiled. "I'm glad about your date."

"It's not a date," Zo said quickly. "The astronomy club is meeting at the college. He wants to see what it's all about."

"Right." Beth gave her a conspiratorial wink. "Because he seems like the stargazing kind of guy."

"He's a forest ranger. He's into nature."

Beth chuckled. "You don't think his interest has anything to do with you?"

"Honestly," said Zo, "it probably has something to do with *you*—or Brady. I'm starting to think he wants to prove Brady wrong. Show him he's a *real* cop, you know?"

Just then, A.J. entered Happy Camper. Zo gave him a wave, and he approached the register, but not before bumping into a customer. He apologized to the woman, moving his camera strap from his arm to his neck.

"Hey A.J.," said Zo. "Thanks for coming. Beth is excited about getting some pictures."

"You're the best," said Beth. "I need all the advertising I can afford right now."

"I bet Enid's death wasn't the coverage you were looking for this weekend," A.J. said. "Is that why Max was here? Did he have new information?"

Considering A.J.'s interest in Allison, Zo didn't think it was wise to tell him that Enid's medication had been found in her room. She'd had her fair share of dating disappointments, but no one wanted to start a relationship with a murder suspect. "No, he was just in the area."

He glanced around the shop. "I've never been in here. I like it." He pointed to a shelf. "Love the books."

"I do, too." Zo had enjoyed reading since she was little, which was probably why she majored in journalism. But now she read just for pleasure, not assignment, unless she brought in a local author. She always prepared for a book event by reading the author's work.

A.J. took a jump drive out of his pocket. "Do you have somewhere we could look at this? I just made a copy of what I had, so it might not be what you want."

"Anything will be great, I promise." Beth pulled out a checkbook from her wrist wallet. "With everything else going on, I haven't had time to think about advertising. This will make it so much easier. Is a hundred dollars enough?"

"Sure," said A.J. "Thanks."

While Beth wrote the check, Zo and A.J. chitchatted. "So, what do you like to read?" asked Zo.

"Science fiction," he said. "I'm actually working on writing a novel."

"Oh, yeah?" said Zo. "What's it about?"

A.J.'s voice grew more confident as he described the plot. For the first time, he was separate from his camera equipment, not just a journalist on assignment, but a writer with his own ideas. At the television station, he got lost behind the scenes. But here, talking about his novel, he seemed more passionate. No wonder Allison found him intriguing.

"Have you told Allison about the book?" Zo asked. "It sounds like something she would be interested in."

"It's how we started talking," said A.J. "She was reading a sci-fi book at the lodge, and I mentioned I was writing one."

That made sense. Allison was interested in anything to do with science, fiction or otherwise.

"She's really smart," continued A.J. "I've been asking her a lot of questions about planets."

Beth handed A.J. the check. "Thank you so much."

A.J. folded the check and put it in his jeans. "Thank *you*. I'm going to put it toward a sci-fi conference I want to go to. It's insane how much those things cost."

Zo had an idea. "My neighbor is an English professor. Russell Cunningham? If you'd like, I'm sure he'd take a look at your book for you. I don't know if he reads science fiction, but he has to know something about novels, right?"

"When I'm finished, I'll do that." He set the jump drive on the counter. "Thanks again."

Now that A.J. was gone, she could introduce Beth to Harley. She led Beth to a store shelf where Harley was working. "Harley, this is Beth, my friend from Spirit Canyon Lodge. This is Harley, my awesome employee. She's an accounting student at Black Mountain College."

Dressed in a short skirt and army boots, Harley gave Beth a wave. It was as close as she would get to a handshake. Though Harley wasn't as good with people as she was with numbers, she was a hard worker and a whiz at math. With her eclectic style and impressive accounting skills, she was the perfect employee for Zo.

"I've heard a lot about you," said Harley. "It's nice to finally meet."

Beth couldn't help herself. She leaned over the shelf and squeezed her hand. "I love your hair."

Harley smoothed her black and purple pixie cut and went back to unpacking a box. "Thanks."

"Beth and I are going to lunch, but I wanted you to look over the draft of the schedule," said Zo. "I left it by the counter."

"No problem," said Harley. "I'll take a look when I finish with these bird houses." Shaped like little campers, they were a perfect complement to the store.

"If you need any days off, just leave a note," said Zo.

"I don't," Harley replied. "I need as many hours as I can get before school starts. I plan on staying here from now until September. You might as well throw a cot in the back room."

"That can be arranged," Zo said with a laugh. She knew Black Mountain College was spendy, and Harley's parents weren't paying her way. She'd moved from California—and free tuition—to be close to the Black Hills. Her mom and dad thought she was crazy. Zo thought she was a perfect fit for Happy Camper. She hoped she stayed long after she graduated from college.

Chapter Seventeen

For lunch, Zo led Beth down the street to Lotsa Pasta, an Italian restaurant. Jack had insisted he could handle Brady Merrigan collecting evidence. He said Beth had already done the hard work by giving the statement, and their lawyer had just arrived. Jack wanted her to spend a few hours away from the lodge, which would be easy to do at Lotsa Pasta. Cozy and comforting, the restaurant had an authentic menu with reasonable prices. It also had an Italian wine list and outdoor seating area that Zo enjoyed at least one night a week. The smells of garlic and bread greeted her this afternoon as she opened the door. She inhaled deeply. Fresh bread was the best thing on earth.

"This place is adorable," Beth said. "How is it that I haven't been here?"

Decorated in colors of red, green, and white, the eatery had wooden tables and stucco walls that gave it a rustic and informal feeling. Waitresses handed out hunks of dough to kids, who needed a way to pass the time waiting for their pizzas, and traditional Italian music tinkled over the speakers. Today a mandolin filled the air.

Before Zo responded, the hostess led them to a two-person table by the window. "You've been a little busy opening a new lodge and dealing with Enid's murder."

Beth leaned forward, crossing her arms on the table. "It feels like I never left Spirit Canyon. Isn't that weird?"

"It is," said Zo. "But I feel the same way. It's like we've picked up right where we left off. I wondered if it would be different after all this time. I can't believe it's not."

"It's like time stood still." Beth looked out the window. "It still feels like home, which is crazy but true. It couldn't be more different from Chicago. I hope the girls feel the same way someday."

The waiter appeared with water glasses and told them he'd be back in a few minutes to take their orders. Zo sipped her water. "How are they doing? Do they like Spirit Canyon?"

"Oh, they love it." Beth flipped through the menu. "I just hope that doesn't change when school starts and they have to make new friends. Meg is at a hard age. Middle school—ugh."

Zo sympathized. Navigating the teen years was hard without a mother, but the girls had Beth, and she was a great mom. "Meg seems like she has a good head on her shoulders. I think she'll do all right. Plus she has you. What about Vi? How is she doing?"

Beth put down her menu with a slap. "With everything going on, I almost forgot. Mom had another dream last night, about Aunt Lilly. It really bothered her. I'm starting to wonder if Lilly *is* sending a message."

Vi might be unconvinced of the spirit world, but it looked as if Beth was turning into a believer. "The canyon is named *Spirit Canyon* for a reason," said Zo. "What was this dream about?"

"It was about the blue dress. Well...no, not actually the dress. This time it was a blue outfit, a baby's."

Zo was puzzled. "A baby's outfit?"

"Like a onesie," Beth explained. "The thing babies sleep in?"

Zo smirked. "I may not have kids, but I know what a onesie is."

"Anyway"—Beth shook her head—"she dreamed Lilly brought her a blue onesie, as a gift or something."

"That doesn't make sense," said Zo. "Why?"

Beth placed her napkin on her lap. "Mom tried to make a joke, saying maybe I could expect a brother soon, but I know it bothered her. When I pressed her, she brushed me off, saying Lilly was always jealous. She couldn't have kids, and my mom had three."

"But girls, right?"

Beth nodded. "I have two sisters."

"So why a *blue* onesie?" asked Zo.

"That's what I want you to find out."

* * * *

Zo had a dream dictionary in the store, as well as several other books she'd bought since joining the Zodiac Club. She first became a member to learn about the stars. A South Dakota native, she wanted to know more about what she was looking at, and the Badlands—only an hour away—provided some of the best stargazing in the nation. After hearing a talk about the constellations, she became interested in signs, dreams, and horoscopes. It was a fun hobby, and Max was right, she did wonder about her past. But she also considered herself a lifetime learner. She liked acquiring new knowledge about topics that interested her.

Zo scanned her small shelf of books on alternative health and healing. She had a few books on sleep and dreams and selected a thick book that organized dreams alphabetically. She turned to the letter B for blue, but the book said to turn to C for colors. In her mind, the thing that connected the two dreams was the color blue. The outfits didn't match. One was for a woman, and one was for a baby. One Lilly was wearing, and the other was a gift. The color had to be the connecting detail.

She scanned the text. It discussed bright colors as well as individual colors and their meanings. Blue indicated relief from worry and/or help from an outside source. Zo scratched her head. Was Lilly the outside source of help? If so, what message was she trying to relay with the blue baby outfit? The only worry surrounding the lodge was the murder of Enid Barrett. Lilly had to be giving them a clue.

She reached for her cell phone to call Max. Who was she kidding? She couldn't tell Max about a dream and expect him to take it seriously. She didn't even know if *she* took it seriously, but it was the only new piece of information she had. She decided to talk to her good friend Julia Parker instead.

Jules was the owner of Spirits & Spirits, a liquor store that doubled as a psychic shop. Jules wouldn't have agreed with the description, but that's what it was. When she wasn't selling booze, she read palms and tarot cards. She also sold spirit beads, mala beads, and dream catchers. Zo had bought her gorgeous mood ring there just last year. If Jules couldn't help, Zo would be forced to ask her ex-boyfriend, Hunter, at the Zodiac meeting tonight. Jules would normally be there, too, as she was a founding member, but she'd emailed the group, explaining that she would be absent. She had a séance. Hunter had studied philosophy in college, though, so his knowledge would be useful. He considered himself an expert on dreams, especially his.

"Would you be okay closing the store today, Harley?" Zo asked. Harley was refilling the postcard display. "I want to run to Spirits & Spirits."

"Not a problem," said Harley. "It's been slow since three."

"Great," said Zo, grabbing her helmet underneath the register. "I'm taking the bike."

Zo used the red Kawasaki motorcycle more than she rented it, but it was available in case a tourist wanted to see the Black Hills via open road. She could have walked to the store, it was so close, but she loved riding the bike in the summer months.

Main Street was less busy than it was earlier in the day, but tourists carrying packages still dotted the sidewalks. They hauled colorful bags of saltwater taffy from the candy store and sacks of kettle corn from Pop and Shop's, a neat place where customers could make their own gourmet popcorn. Zo smiled as she noticed a girl walk out with a bag of rainbow popcorn almost as big as she was, her accommodating parents holding the door.

The stoplight turned green, and Zo zipped down Main Street, still smiling. She loved the busyness of summer: the tourists, the bands, the bustle. She didn't have to travel the whole world over to meet new people. Spirit Canyon was unique that way. But the nice weather and the motorcycle ride made her long for a road trip. Though she rarely had time off, a short getaway wasn't out of the question. She might leave for a weekend after Enid's murder was solved.

As she pulled into Spirits & Spirits' parking lot, she repeated the word to herself: *murder*. As an ex-journalist, she was used to hearing the word. She just wasn't used to hearing it in Spirit Canyon. But that's exactly what had happened at the lodge. Someone killed Enid and stole her money. Or was it the other way around? She wasn't convinced they were connected. Two separate crimes had been committed that night. She was almost certain of it.

Zo took off her helmet and shook out her hair. Entering the store, she noticed the swing of the curtain of ruby red beads. Jules had just finished with a client and was leading her to the cash register. Jules had blond hair, like Zo's, but it was much longer, and the bottom layers were pink. Today she had it piled into a bun. It looked as if the pink bun came from a different head of hair.

"How about a nice merlot to take with you?" said Jules, pulling a bottle of wine from a circular rack of reds. It housed international varieties.

"Merlot is my favorite," said the customer. "How'd you know?"

Jules tapped her forehead. "I have my ways."

Zo tried not to laugh. Jules had a way, all right—with money. She'd been a rock-star entrepreneur since they were kids. She'd been capitalizing on the town's name since their teenage years. First it was Spirit Snacks, akin to a lemonade stand with goodies. Then it was Spirit Pet Sitting, which lasted two years and would have lasted longer if Jules's mother hadn't tired of pet hair. The last idea, Spirits & Spirits, was Jules's most successful venture yet. Hers wasn't the only liquor store in town, but it was definitely the busiest. Filled with a good selection of wines, whiskeys, and local beers, it was a popular spot with young people and tourists staying near Main Street.

Zo glanced at a display of growlers with the Spirits & Spirits logo on them while Jules rang up the customer. A skull tipped back a bottle of wine above a quirky font. Zo checked the price on the bottom: twenty-five dollars. Yep, Jules knew a good idea when she saw one. Zo just hoped she knew as much about dreams as business.

After the customer left, Zo approached her friend.

"You like the new growlers?" asked Jules. "They've got a Day-of-the-Dead look, huh?"

"I love them," said Zo. "I might take one to go."

Jules came out from behind the counter. Like milk chocolate, her eyes were light but warm, an unusual color. "But that's not why you're here."

"Try to remember we went to high school together."

Jules crossed her arms. "You don't believe in my abilities?"

"I believe you have the ability to make money wherever you go," Zo teased.

"You want me to prove it to you?" Jules grabbed Zo's hand. "I took an online class on palm reading. Paid a hundred bucks for it." She squinted at Zo's palm. "Oh, heck yes. This is bad."

"What? Am I going to die?"

"Not your life line, your love line," said Jules. "It's not good."

"I could have told you that—without the hundred bucks," said Zo.

"Your heart line has all these branches." She flicked her finger in different directions. Her fingernails were long and painted blue. "Here, here, and here. Either you've dated a lot or you've made great demands on your partners." She glanced up. "I'd say both."

"I'm not demanding, but I *have* dated a lot," said Zo. "Which you already knew."

Jules ignored her, bringing Zo's hand closer to her face. "But you have strong intuition lines. I guess they don't apply to boyfriends."

Zo jerked back her hand. "Okay, Nostradamus. That's enough for one day. I'm here about something else. Dreams. Do you know anything about them?"

"*Everything*," said Jules. "I did a camp with a bona fide dharma. What do you want to know?"

Zo had to admire her confidence. "A friend of mine keeps having the same color pop up in her dreams. Do you think it's important?"

She shrugged her shoulders, which were large like her personality. She was six feet tall. "Sure. Colors have meanings just like images. Snakes, bears, birds—they all signify something. What color is it?"

"Blue."

"Blue is a spiritual color." Jules walked toward the growlers and selected one for Zo. "It could represent spirits or heaven or the dreamer herself. By the way, I'm giving you a discount on this."

Zo rubbed her brow. "You think a spirit could be sending a message?"

Jules tipped her head toward her spirit beads, dolls, and other paraphernalia before placing the growler under the tap. "You know what *I* think. What do you think?"

"I think you need to come over to my house and share a beer with me."

Jules twisted the cap on as a customer entered the store. "Call me."

Zoe promised she would as she walked out, glad to have another opportunity to talk to Jules. Zo agreed with her theory and liked the idea of Lilly sending a message. Spirit Canyon Lodge had been Lilly's home for over forty years. If anyone knew what happened the night of Enid's death, it was Lilly.

Chapter Eighteen

Later that night, Zo took the Kawasaki to Black Mountain College. The weather was perfect for a short drive, and the campus was beautiful this time of year—and nearly deserted. Nestled in the heart of the hills, Black Mountain College was small but sought after because of its location. Plus it was cheaper than most of Colorado's universities, providing a nice alternative to those students looking to supplement their college experience with outdoor recreation. Zo hadn't gone to Black Mountain; she'd gone to a less expensive state school. Even then, money was tight, but she knew she'd need an education if she wanted to stay in the area. Everyone wanted to live in Spirit Canyon, including her. Without a college degree, she would have never found a job.

She inhaled the scent of pine as she curved around the mountain. It was a lovely night for stargazing, and the college's observatory was located high on a hill. One of the oldest buildings on campus, the observatory was built in the late nineteenth century out of red sandstone. It had a twenty-inch telescope that the university made available to the club once a month and more during the summer. Though students and professors still used the facility, the astronomy and physics department had newer equipment that they utilized more frequently. But Zo liked that it was old. She felt like a real astronomer as she approached the building.

Someone pulled in behind her, and in an instant, she knew it was Max. There was no mistaking his Ford pickup truck, a green-and-white classic from the 1960s. She paused while she waited for him to park, glad he'd shown up. If he hadn't, she would've tracked him down and grilled him about what happened when he and Brady collected Enid's prescription vial at the lodge. They might have discovered something else about her death.

Wearing dark jeans and a dark shirt, he blended in with the night. He pointed at the helmet hooked to the back of the Kawasaki. "I'm glad to see you wear a helmet."

She nodded. "Safety first."

"Somehow I see safety about halfway down on your list of priorities."

"Not true," she said. "It always makes the top five."

Crickets chirped in the distance as they walked up the path. It was no wonder students paid hefty tuition prices to attend Black Mountain. It was serene, picturesque, and secluded. Encircled by towering spruce trees and native wildlife, the college was a sanctuary for nature lovers. The grounds blended in with their natural surroundings, and cobblestone pathways guided visitors to the observatory and the rest of the campus.

"Tell me what happened at Spirit Canyon Lodge," said Zo. "I haven't talked to Beth since we went to lunch, but she was pretty shaken up. She couldn't believe Enid's medicine was in Allison's room."

"Brady confiscated the evidence," said Max. "He also questioned Allison. She denied taking the medication, but Brady will have it tested for prints. She claims someone planted the bottle in her room, and you can guess who she thinks that someone is."

Zo stopped on the path. "Beth?"

Max nodded. "She's the only one who has access to all the rooms."

"Any one of them could have been in Allison's room," Zo said. "They all hang out together. And the rooms are locked with an old-fashioned key, nothing fancy."

Max stuck a hand in his pocket. "I said the same thing, but Allison was pretty convincing. She lives here, and Brady trusts her."

"In my mind, it was a local who did it," said Zo. "Everyone who knew Enid hated her."

Max raised his eyebrows.

"Disliked for sure," Zo continued. "Beth would have needed more time to get to know her before she wanted to kill her."

Max chuckled. "Speak your mind, why don't you. Alison said Beth offered everyone a discount on their stay."

"Beth is so nice—too nice, maybe." Zo sighed. "This investigation is costing her, and she's too polite to say so."

"Brady thinks she has another reason for cooperating," Max said. "The longer they stay, the longer she can plant evidence on them."

"Beth isn't a thief, and she's certainly not a murderer." She started walking toward the observatory again.

"I'm telling you what Brady said. I'm not saying I believe it."

The front door swung open, and Hunter stood at the top of the stairs. Dressed in a leather jacket and jeans, he was as gorgeous as ever. His beach-blond hair gave him a punkish look that Zo used to think was sexy. Okay, she still thought it was sexy. It was his personality that was the problem. He was an egomaniac. At least that's why she guessed he talked about himself so much. He wanted her to nod and smile. But she wasn't the nodding and smiling type.

"Hey," said Hunter, shaking Max's hand. "You're new. But you"— he turned to Zo—"look familiar." He leaned in and kissed her cheek. "How *are* you?"

As if you really care, Zo thought. Still the kiss was nice. "Good. I'm looking forward to tonight. I have a question for you about dreams. I'll catch you later, after the talk."

"Your dreams have always fascinated me, Zo," Hunter said softly. "I see so many similarities to my own."

Zo almost laughed. He'd already found the perfect segue to talk about himself. "Not my dreams, someone else's." Max was five steps ahead of her. "I'll talk to you later."

Max was signing the guest book. Zo didn't even know there *was* a guest book until she saw him scrawling his name across the page.

"I didn't know you had a boyfriend," Max said as he added his email address. "You could have told me."

"I don't." Zo didn't owe him an explanation.

"Oh, I'm sorry." Max tossed the pen and stood straighter. "I thought I saw that guy's lips on your face just now."

The way he said it made it sound so much less appealing than it was. Was he irritated by Hunter, or nervous to be there? The kiss was just Hunter's way of saying hello. "Hunter and I used to date."

"Used to?" said Max. "You still look close to me."

"We're not," Zo replied flatly. "The only person Hunter is interested in is Hunter." She motioned ahead. "Let's go. The dome is open."

Above, stars beckoned like fireflies. They seemed close enough to touch but were millions of miles away and just as old. Zo liked to think of them as storybooks, the history spanning the sky, and wondered what story they would tell about her. She'd grown up like a weed, fast and unguided, clinging to the land out of sheer preservation. She smiled. Even weeds could grow and bloom, though.

Professor Linwood, the chair of the astronomy department, asked for the group's attention. Linwood was a tall man with a beard that made his face look like an oval. He spoke in a hushed voice, as if he didn't want the stars to know he was watching them. The constellation they would be viewing tonight, he explained, was Leo. Leo was associated with the Nemean Lion, and its brightest star, Regulus, was easily spotted overhead. Hercules, the Greek hero, was said to have battled the lion in his first of twelve labors. Because the beast's coat was so rugged, it couldn't be pierced with a sword, so Hercules had to strangle the lion with his own hands. He's often depicted wearing the pelt of the Nemean Lion, which functions as his armor, Linwood said.

When he was finished talking, members approached the telescope, careful not to touch it. Linwood had taken great care to find the constellation, and no one wanted to repeat the lengthy process.

"It *does* look like a lion," said Max, peering through the telescope. "I can see how someone could get into this. I mean, I've always liked looking at the stars. I just didn't know what I was looking at. It's nice to know." He glanced at Zo. "Thanks for inviting me."

"Sure." She was glad he was enjoying himself.

After she had her turn at the telescope, Hunter approached and asked her about the dream. Though he worked at the bike shop, Spokes and Stuff, he had a degree in psychology and had written his master's thesis on Carl Jung. Unfortunately, Spirit Canyon didn't have a lot of opportunities for psychologists, and he loved biking too much to relocate. She understood the dilemma; she just didn't understand why he chose the major in the first place. She suspected it had to do with the exploration of his own id.

"So, the color blue," said Hunter when she'd finished relaying the two dreams. "It connects them, and of course, so does the woman."

"Lilly," said Zo.

Hunter nodded. "Nobel laureate Francis Crick said 'We dream to forget,' but in this case, I think Violet is trying to remember something important."

"Like what?" asked Zo. She wanted something specific. He probably wanted to quote another obscure scholar.

Max crossed his arms, waiting for Hunter's response.

Hunter put a hand on her shoulder. "Patience, love. That's always been your problem. The subconscious will reveal all if you just give it time."

Max let out a small laugh.

Hunter tilted his head to one side. "We haven't had a chance to meet. I'm Hunter Michaels."

"Max Harrington," he said, sticking out his hand.

"Max might join the club," said Zo.

Hunter shook Max's hand. "I think I've seen you at Spokes and Stuff. Maybe I helped you with a supplement?"

Max shook his head. "I don't think so."

"A probiotic?" Hunter questioned.

"Do I look like I know what a probiotic is?" said Max.

Hunter blinked an answer. Zo thought it was Morse code for "Please don't make me answer that question." Hattie Fines entered the observatory and gave her a wave. Zo took the opportunity to sidestep the awkward moment. "Excuse us," she said, grabbing Max's arm.

When they were a few steps away, Max said, "I don't know what he was driving at. Do I look unhealthy?"

Zo gave him a once over. Light hair, tan skin, strong muscles. He looked like the essence of health to her. "You look fine. That's just Hunter's way of engaging."

"In a topic I know nothing about?" said Max.

"Pretty much," said Zo. "As long as he knows what he's talking about, he's happy. Conversations with him were usually one-sided."

"You dated him for the hair. Is that it?"

"And the leather jacket," said Zo with a smirk. "I've got a thing for guys in leather jackets."

Max sighed. "That settles it. I don't have a leather jacket."

"Somehow that doesn't surprise me." Zo chuckled.

"Sorry I'm late," said Hattie. "Are you leaving already?"

Zo wanted to check out the science building before it closed at ten. "I think so."

Hattie took off her red beret, which had a large gold buckle that matched the glint in her eyes. She shoved it in her windbreaker pocket. "Guess who kept me?" She didn't wait for Zo to answer. "Allison Scott."

"Really? Why?" asked Zo.

"She called the library and asked me to add an event to the community calendar," said Hattie. "She just got the date for some announcement at the college—in July." She moved closer, lowering her voice. "Cunningham said you've been asking questions about her. Putting your old journalism skills to good use."

"I am," said Zo. "That's funny. A.J. mentioned something about an announcement, too. Did she say what it was?"

Hattie shook her head. "She was tight-lipped. Even though I said I needed her to fill out an event questionnaire, she wouldn't tell me a thing."

Zo puzzled over her statement. "I didn't know the library had an event questionnaire."

"We do now." Hattie grinned and skipped off toward the rest of the amateur astronomers.

Chapter Nineteen

As they left the observatory, Zo glanced toward the main campus. Allison taught in the science department, so they might find out more about the announcement if she and Max did a little research of their own. They'd talked about the idea earlier, but it looked as if he would need some convincing. Taking a late-night tour of the campus wasn't illegal, and the Zodiac Club met here enough for her to know that the buildings were still open. There was no reason they couldn't take a little detour through the science building.

The idea was exciting. To be chasing a lead again felt good. Although she loved Happy Camper, her work at the store was relaxing. The only thing she had to track down was a model number or auction address. Now she was tracking Enid's killer and was more convinced than ever that she was zeroing in on the murderer.

Zo told Max of her plan as they approached the parking lot.

"You mean, you want to break into Allison's office?" Max asked.

Zo couldn't read his face because they were surrounded by darkness. Not until they reached the main campus would the area lighten. But he sounded hesitant. He was probably envisioning them climbing over a hedge, sneaking into an open window, and stealing Allison's papers. She set him straight. "Of course not. I'm not going to do anything illegal. I just want to check out the science building, and campus is open until ten." When he didn't answer right away, she added, "It's no big deal if you don't want to go. I can go by myself."

That got his attention.

Max started toward the main campus. "I want to go. I just don't want to go to jail. That wouldn't help anyone, especially Beth."

"We're not going to break any laws," Zo insisted. "Besides, you're a cop. How can you get arrested?"

"Brady would like nothing better than to put me in a cell for the night. Can't you tell?"

"What does he have against you, anyway?" asked Zo, walking quickly to keep pace. "I get the feeling he doesn't want you involved."

"He doesn't," said Max. "You heard him. He thinks I'm better off catching poachers and underage drinkers. He doesn't want me involved with police business in Spirit Canyon. He sees the town as his turf, the forest as mine."

"The guy's a jerk," said Zo. "Don't listen to him. He thinks he runs this town. Patrick Merrigan was the same way."

"He really forced you out of your first store?" They were under the lamplights of the campus now, and he gave her a sidelong glance. He must have wanted to see her reaction.

"You were there," she said. "You carried the sign."

"True," Max agreed.

"Part of it was my own fault. I should have signed a longer lease."

"*He* should have told you he planned to expand the hardware store," he said. "He probably got the idea when Happy Camper took off."

"Everything turned out all right, I guess." Zo glanced at him. "As long as you don't cancel my tours, I think I'll be okay."

He stopped walking. "I can't cancel them. You know that. But I can advise caution, and that's all I'm doing. It's not safe for you to be out in the woods on your own." He held up his hand. "This has nothing to do with your skills. I know you know how to handle yourself. It's about taking the forest for granted. I see locals do it all the time. They become numb to its danger."

She didn't want to argue with him, not tonight. She wanted to get to the science building before it closed, which meant no more unscheduled stops. But just because she kept walking didn't mean she agreed. Her tours were limited to Spirit Canyon, the nearby waterfall, and a couple of popular trails. She hoped one day they would take off and she could hire a designated tour guide. But for now, it was a good side source of revenue, especially when large groups came in.

The pathway split in two different directions. One led to the older part of campus and the other to the newer part. The trouble was deciding which path was the right one to the science building.

"This way." Max gestured toward a brick three-story. "The science department is in Randolph Meyers. At least it was."

They started toward the building, a large rectangle against a dark backdrop of trees. "You went to school here?"

"After I got my bachelor's degree in Montana," said Max. "I attended the National Park Service Seasonal Law Enforcement Training Program here. It's one of the few in the area."

"What's your degree in?"

"Environmental Science." He gave her a smile. "Brady was right about one thing. I am a little bit of a tree hugger. But I also studied environmental literature, so I took a lot of English classes—like you."

A chuckle escaped her lips as she envisioned him pondering Thoreau's *Walden Pond* by the edge of Pactola Lake.

"Oh, sure, laugh it up." He pulled open the door. "But I've got a brain—unlike mister surfer dude back there."

"Hey, Hunter is actually really smart." Zo rarely defended her ex, but in this case, it was valid. "He might be conceited, but he's a bright guy."

"I'll take your word for it." Max looked around the dimly lit doorway. "I think the offices are on the second floor." He pointed to the stairway at the end of the hall. "Maybe they'll have something posted on the department bulletin board."

Zo followed him down the cement-block hallway. To the right were labs with push-button-code-style locks and to the left, a small science library, standing open. They walked up the stairs. No lights were on. Lurking around in the dark, she had to admit Max was right; she was starting to feel a little bit like a criminal. She certainly wouldn't want to meet up with one of her customers, anyway, or Brady Merrigan.

She took out her phone and pressed the flashlight button. Max did the same. As she shone the light in the office windows, she noticed a theme emerging: skeletons, skulls, and charts. One skull wore a pair of 3-D glasses, which made her smile.

Allison's office was near the end of the hallway, and Zo tried the door, but it was locked. Through the door window, she noticed a large map hanging over Allison's desk. It wasn't a traditional map; it was a geologic map of the Black Hills with exposed rock layers. She took a picture so she could zoom in on it later.

"Did you find something?" Max asked, joining her.

"Just a map," said Zo. "I took a picture. There's an open door around the corner, though. Let's check it out."

Zo flipped on the light switch; the office was the faculty break room. It had a coffee pot, a half podium, and four tables. On the whiteboard was a meeting agenda dated MAY 15, probably the last one of the semester. The first item listed was HOMESTAKE MINE: ALLISON SCOTT.

"It looks like Allison had news to report at the last meeting," said Zo. "Maybe it had something to do with what she found at Serenity Falls."

"The white board doubles as a screen. Try the computer."

Zo ducked behind the podium. The computer was connected to the monitor on the desk. She pushed the button, and the computer began to boot. Max looked on over her shoulder. She could smell his woodsy cologne, or maybe that's how all forest rangers smelled: like poplars, pines, evergreens. She shivered.

"Are you cold?" Max asked.

Before she could answer, he was unzipping his sweatshirt and putting it around her shoulders. She focused on the screen, trying to ignore the chivalrous act. She could be a pushover for kindness, which seemed like a forgotten virtue these days. It always tugged at her heart when someone went out of their way to be nice.

The operating system was protected and required a username and password. She stared at the blinking cursor for a full minute before throwing up her hands and turning around. "So what do we do about the password? Any ideas?"

"Maybe my old student ID will work," Max suggested. "They never had the best security."

They switched places, and Max punched in the information on the keyboard. The ID was no longer valid.

"It was worth a try," said Zo.

"Let me try something else." Instead of entering a password, Max clicked on Cancel. The screen changed to solid blue, then populated with icons.

"That worked?" exclaimed Zo. "I can't believe it."

"I can," he said, waiting for the pointer. "It's an old campus. There isn't a huge focus on technology. The professors are worse than the students, and this is a faculty machine."

"Check out the date on that PowerPoint file." Zo pointed to the icon on the desktop. "May fifteenth."

The file must have been copied to the computer's hard drive because when Max double-clicked, the file opened. It was the department chair's agenda for the faculty meeting, and the first slide was identical to the outline on the whiteboard. The second slide was dedicated to Allison's presentation. Although no text existed in the slide, it contained a map of the convergent tectonic plate boundaries near Lead, South Dakota. At least that's what Max said they were. She had no idea what she was looking at. Max claimed only a vague understanding, but it was apparent he understood the map better than she did.

"When plates collide," he said, "they don't always create mountain ranges. They create the right conditions for minerals, too. Rocks from the earth's mantle can find their way to the surface."

"Minerals like gold?" asked Zo.

Max nodded. "Gold, silver, ore."

"How would somebody know which mineral they're dealing with?"

"They'd have to do a magnetic survey or a soil test to be sure."

"But gold isn't magnetic," said Zo. "Is it?"

"No, but it doesn't matter." He shrugged. "The un-magnetized areas can tell you just as much as the magnetized."

"Which probably explains why Allison wanted access to the land." She considered the problem. "She needed to do more tests. Go to the next slide."

Unfortunately, the slide moved to the following item on the agenda: professors' final dates to enter grades. Max clicked on the other slides, but there was nothing else related to Allison's research, so he closed the file.

"Maybe Allison found gold—or silver," she said. "Something worth killing for."

Max snapped his fingers. "Without testing Enid's land, she couldn't know for sure. The map isn't conclusive, and she'd need proof before going public with her discovery. Evidence is mandatory—just like in police work. If I learned anything hanging around the science department, it was that."

"And Homestake Mine is just a few miles away. Don't they say if you find gold, it's probably going to be around another vein?"

He smiled. "They do say that."

"See?" said Zo. "Living here has taught me a thing or two about science—and gold."

Max logged off and shut down the computer. "People think it's everywhere. All they need is a pan and a crevassing tool, and they can strike it rich."

"I don't care about striking it rich, but I do care about catching Enid's killer," said Zo. "The sooner we do, the sooner Beth can get back to business at the lodge." She started to shrug off his sweatshirt, but he stopped her.

"Keep it," he said. "I'll get it next time."

Next time. It wasn't such a bad prospect after all.

Chapter Twenty

Zo parked the bike at the store and skipped up the back steps. She and Max were one step closer to finding a motive, and what better motives than fortune and fame? Even if Allison didn't get the gold, she would get the find. She would be credited with the discovery, and for a young scientist, there could be no better recognition. It would propel her career into new directions and maybe even secure her a position at the Homestake Lab or another distinguished research facility.

Everyone cared about making a name for themselves in some way. Like her, they wanted their work to matter. Zo was just glad her work wasn't as competitive as Allison's. She enjoyed contributing in a small way to the community, selling antiques, books, and memorabilia. She liked being the store that people came to when they needed a pick-me-up. Putting smiles on peoples' faces was a great way to earn a living.

From the deck, Zo gave her backyard a quick scan. George was nowhere to be seen. *So much for sainthood*, she thought as she opened the deck door. She stopped short when she saw him lying inside on the kitchen counter, licking a large orange paw. He paused, paw in the air, and meowed.

She jumped at the sound, closing the door a second later. George was outside when she left; she would have never put him inside on a clear night like this. So, who'd let him in? She glanced out the window at Cunningham's house. The lights were off, but it was the only explanation that made sense. None of the other neighbors would have been so bold as to open her door for the cat, and although George was smart, he couldn't let himself in—unless he was performing miracles now, too.

She gave George a scratch under his chin, but he wasn't interested. It was bath time, and the counter was his bathing area. She picked him up and put him on the couch, much to his dismay. Then she put a mug of water in the microwave. George returned to the kitchen, swishing his orange-and-white tail by the deck door as she made a cup of tea.

"You're going to have to wait a minute," she said. She took the mug out of the microwave and filled a tea infuser with chamomile and lemon balm tea. Dropping it in the mug, she turned toward George. "Who let you in, anyway?"

His answer was a meow.

She slid open the door and watched him creep across the deck. A bird was perched on a post, and George was doing his best to go undetected. She went back to her tea, absently dunking the infuser into the hot water. George never wanted in. She had to lure him with treats or canned food if she wanted to capture him for the night. So, how did Cunningham get him to come inside tonight? She'd have to get the story from him tomorrow. It was nearly eleven o'clock; she couldn't disturb him at this hour.

Thumbing through the mail, she saw it out of the corner of her eye—a muddy footprint on the hardwood floor. She dropped an envelope, her heartbeat increasing as she studied it from afar. Someone had been in her house. Is that how George had gotten inside? She walked to the hall and turned on the light. Her legs began to quake as she bent down to inspect the mark. It wasn't a footprint but half of a footprint, the ball of a shoe. It was too large to be hers. It came from a loafer or boot, and this time of year, she usually wore flip-flops. She glanced around her house with new eyes. Cunningham wouldn't have come inside her house. They'd been neighbors for two years and knew each other's boundaries. Sure, he might let in the cat if he thought it was warranted, but he would never enter her house unannounced. Someone else had been in her home, someone who accidently let in the cat.

She tiptoed to the stairs that led to the store. Her hand on the door handle, she turned gently. Her stomach dropped when it opened. She never left it unlocked. Someone might be in the store—a robber or vandal. Fear turned to anger as she returned for the mace in her backpack. She also grabbed a kitchen knife, though she had no idea what she'd do with it. Adrenaline was doing the thinking. Her heart and soul were in her store, and she wasn't going to let someone ransack it without a fight.

She flung open the door and flipped on the light. She wanted the robber to know she was there, though he probably already did. He had to have heard her when she drove up on the motorcycle. She stomped down the wooden stairs, each footstep noisier than the last. When she got to the dark store, she stood for a moment, listening. All was silent.

She turned on the store lights. They buzzed with their usual industrial sound. The front door was locked, no windows were broken, and the HAPPY CAMPER sign was turned to CLOSED. Zo checked the till. It was empty, which was normal. Harley would have taken out the cash when she closed the store.

Zo put the knife and mace down on the counter. If someone had been in the store, they were long gone. They were also very tidy. Nothing was out of place.

She took her cell phone out of her back pocket. Max's phone number was in her contact list. She'd put him under Favorites in case something else went wrong at the lodge. She pressed his number now. "Hey Max. It's Zo. I hope it's not too late."

"Not at all," he said. "I just got home. What's up?"

"I think someone was in my house." Her voice trembled slightly. "I found a footprint on the floor, and the interior door to Happy Camper was open. I thought I should call someone."

"Yeah," said Max. "Of course. I'll be right there."

"You don't have to come," she said quickly. "I just wanted your opinion."

"Is anything missing?"

That was a good question. Zo hadn't checked her house before coming down to the store. "I'm not sure."

"Just wait for me," he said. "We'll look together."

She thanked him, ended the call, and went back upstairs, locking the door behind her. She wondered if she should call Cunningham and decided against it. He was probably sleeping, and she knew he wasn't the one in the house or store.

Max had asked if anything was missing. She checked the canister in the kitchen where she kept some cash. The money was still in inside. The living room looked fine, except for the rug. She thought it was slightly askew. So was the old wooden trunk that functioned as a coffee table.

She scanned the bookshelf. It held nothing of real value, just books and vinyl records. Her TV, a 42-inch flat screen, had cost some money, and one of the doors on its stand was open. Still, she could have left it open. She crouched down, letting her finger slide over the movie titles. Most of them were chick flicks; some were old black-and-whites that she found at auctions or rummage sales. When she went shopping for Happy Camper, she often came home with something for her house, which explained the eclectic décor. She loved the mix of old and new, the shabby chic look.

Even though she was expecting it, Max's knock on the deck door made her jump. She walked into the kitchen and opened the door, glad for the company. This was one time she could appreciate the presence of a big, solid forest ranger. She was pretty sure he had a gun and knew how to use it.

"You all right?" he asked.

She appreciated his quickness—and his concern. Maybe it was just a cop reflex, but he looked genuinely worried for her safety. She could tell by his eyes. "I'm fine. It's just kind of creepy thinking someone could have been in my house." She told him about George, the footprint, and the door.

"Show me," he said.

She led him to the hallway. With all the lights on and him there, she barely noticed it. It was a smudge on the hardwood floor, an outline. He bent down to inspect it.

"I took a picture," she said. "I thought we could blow it up or something."

"I don't think there's enough here to blow up," said Max. "I'm not even sure it's a shoe."

Of course it was a shoe. The outline was shaped like the ridge of a man's boot. She bent down next to him. "What else could it be?"

He shook his head. "I don't know. Let's look around."

She pointed to the living room. "The TV cabinet door was open."

He walked over to it. "Makes sense. Electronics are expensive and can be resold." He looked inside the cabinet then glanced back at her, smiling. "Fan of old movies?"

"Old everything, really."

"Your headphones are still here," said Max. "What about other electronics? iPad, computer, stuff like that?"

"In my office." She led the way. She had two dormer rooms in her house. The area was more spacious than a traditional story-and-a-half, or at least taller, and the bedrooms had large windows that faced a side street. She loved her spot above the store. It was just the right size.

She flipped on the light to her study. Her laptop was still on her desk, a good sign. So was her Curious Camper column, *which needed to be turned in by Friday*, she needled herself. She would get to it tomorrow for sure. "My computer's still here."

"This is a pretty cool house," said Max. "Is that your column?"

She nodded. "Five hundred words of it, anyway."

"What are you writing about?" He moved closer to the column, propped up on a stand.

"Mostly Spirit Canyon Lodge's reopening." She shrugged. "I decided on the topic before Enid's death. It hasn't been as easy to write as I thought it would be."

"You'll finish it," he assured her. "Anything else?"

"The bedroom is this way." Zo pointed. "My iPad is in there."

She didn't see the iPad on her nightstand, so she checked the sling chair in the corner. She found it on top of a stack of books next to the ottoman. She held it up.

"What about jewelry?" he said, pointing to her armoire.

She opened the drawers, which were filled with lots of hoop earrings and bracelets but nothing of real value. The scarves were still folded nicely. If someone had rummaged through them, she would've been able to tell. "All okay."

They returned to the living room. "You want a beer?" Zo didn't want to be alone right now, though she would have never admitted it to Max or anyone else. Being alone was sort of her thing. She wasn't easily scared, but Enid's death had gotten under her skin. She couldn't help but think the break-in was somehow related.

Max sat down on the couch. "Sure."

She poured two glasses of beer from Jules's Spirts & Spirits growler and brought them into the living room. She couldn't wait to tell Jules she'd drunk her beer with a police officer.

Selecting the chair across from Max, she held up her glass. "Cheers."

"Thanks." Max took a swig. "First Enid's prescription popping up at the lodge, now this? I wonder if they're connected." He took another drink.

"That's exactly what I was thinking," said Zo. "I've never had this kind of trouble. Why now?"

"Was anything missing from the store?" asked Max.

"Not that I could tell, but to be honest, I didn't look very hard. I wanted to get back upstairs." Zo couldn't imagine anyone who would wish her or her business harm. Everyone in town had supported the store from the get-go. Even Patrick Merrigan had come to her second grand opening and made an extravagant purchase, as if money could make up for the extra work and worry she'd gone through. Still it was a nice gesture.

Max interrupted her thoughts. "It was strange walking around campus tonight. All those old buildings. They looked spooky in the dark."

Some of them *did* look haunted. But the dark didn't scare her. She loved the night sky. "I wasn't creeped out. That's not why I called."

"And here I thought it was because you were beginning to like me," said Max with a small grin.

"You know what I mean."

"I know what you mean." He set his glass on the trunk, on top of the Pacific Railroad logo. "We're going to find out who was in here."

She was relieved he believed her. If he had thought she was being paranoid, she wouldn't have been able to continue the conversation, no matter how much she wanted someone's company. "Do you think Brady could find out anything by looking at the footprint? Maybe he could dust for fingerprints or something."

"If something was taken, I would say yes, but without a theft, I don't know what he could do." He scratched his head. "It might draw more attention to you, and Beth."

She understood his logic. Besides, she didn't really want Brady snooping around her house and business if he couldn't help her anyway. "So, what now?"

"We figure out who was in your house," said Max. "What do you have that someone wants?"

It wasn't money, and it wasn't electronics. Maybe it was about the store. Several valuable items were downstairs, including antiques, typewriters, and art. She told Max the idea.

"It's a possibility," said Max, finishing his beer. "Since your house is connected to the store, we can't rule it out, but you didn't notice anything missing. Do you have a security camera we could review?"

Zo shook her head. "No. I've looked at a few systems. I just haven't had the time or the money to install one yet. This is only my second year here."

"But you usually lock your door, right?"

Of course she locked her door—usually. "I was in a hurry tonight. I was running late."

He stood. "I know Spirit Canyon is small, but you have to lock your door. Every time."

She walked him to the door. "I will. Scout's honor." She crossed her heart.

"You know I wasn't actually a Boy Scout, right?"

She laughed. "Yeah, I know. You told me once before."

"Lock this," he said, then he was gone.

Chapter Twenty-One

The next morning, Zo went downstairs to Happy Camper early. She perused the walls for missing memorabilia in the light of day. She started with the most expensive items: the prints, the antiques, the collectibles. All were accounted for. She walked the aisles, slowly scanning the merchandise. Every shelf was in order, every display untouched. No muddy footprints marked the floor. With the birds chirping their morning melody, Happy Camper was as peaceful as ever. No one would have guessed that someone had broken into the store last night.

Zo flipped the sign to OPEN, grabbed the newspaper outside the front door, and returned to the counter with her coffee. Harley appeared a few minutes later, and Zo was glad they could discuss last night's break-in alone. Mornings were one of the few times they could talk without customer interruptions.

As Zo recounted the story, Harley scanned the store. "You mean someone was here, in the store?" she whispered. In her black shirtdress with lace sleeves, Harley looked a little more goth than usual. It could have been the outfit, or it could have been the extra coat of black eye liner.

Zo tried to assure her they were safe. "Whoever was here is gone now. But we need to be extra vigilant for the next couple of days. You didn't see anything unusual last night when you were locking up? A suspicious customer hanging around?"

"Nothing," Harley said. "I had two women come in late. One bought a birdhouse. I locked the door when I left. Promise."

"I believe you," said Zo. "It's my fault. I left my deck door unlocked. Just be careful."

Harley agreed and began updating the website with an upcoming event. Zo pored over the newspaper while she drank her coffee. She was tired and needed a few extra minutes because of the late night and her lousy sleep. Also, the paper contained a piece about Enid. Spread out next to the cash register, the story filled the entire page. It said visitation would begin tonight at five o'clock at Tall Pines. The funeral would be held Thursday. The holiday must have delayed everything by a day.

"You know they charge per word for those things?" said Harley, who was typing in the date for a book signing. A local author was coming to the store to talk about birding in the canyon. "They must have paid some money for that."

Harley was right, but the piece wasn't an ordinary obituary. Scanning the text, Zo realized it was a feature article with a byline. Enid was an important business owner in the community. It made sense that the newspaper covered her death. "It says that Griffin will take over operations at Serenity Falls. No surprise there," Zo muttered, taking another sip of her coffee.

"What about the resort in Spirit Canyon?" asked Harley. Her purple-streaked hair was a nice contrast to her dark outfit.

"Henry told me she left it to him, and he wasn't lying," said Zo. "It says 'In a show of philanthropic goodwill, Enid Barrett willed Serenity Hills to her longtime manager, Henry Miller.'" She glanced up.

Harley rolled her eyes. "Enid didn't have a philanthropic bone in her body. It's probably back pay of wages."

What Harley said was true. Enid Barrett didn't do anything without getting something in return. What she got out of leaving the resort to Henry, Zo couldn't guess. She might have felt sorry for him; maybe she didn't pay him well, as Harley suggested. Enid's husband had been gone several years. Despite her independent personality, she had to get lonely. Henry said she called every night to discuss business. Maybe she appreciated his loyalty and rewarded it by leaving him Serenity Hills, which he obviously cared about. After visiting Serenity Falls, Zo realized *that* resort was the real moneymaker.

A customer entered, and Harley greeted her. Zo decided this was her cue to get busy. The newspaper had mentioned several upcoming estate sales, including Enid Barrett's. She marked the ones that contained old signs, books, or memorabilia and shut the newspaper. Her cell phone rang as she was updating her calendar.

It took a few moments to recognize the voice. Clearly frantic for help, Vi said Beth was being arrested. She needed Zo to come to the lodge.

"I'll be right there," said Zo. "Give me twenty minutes."

She shoved her phone into her jean jacket, grabbed the motorcycle keys, and told Harley she'd check in later. Beth was in trouble. Melissa from the visitor's center could watch the store when Harley needed to break for lunch.

Minutes later, Zo was cruising through the canyon, curving around the twisty road as fast as she dared. The cool blast awoke her senses, and the sleepless night was forgotten by the time she arrived at the lodge. Two police cars were parked in the lot. Thankfully they were empty. *Beth must still be inside*, thought Zo as she booted the kickstand into place and ran up to the door.

The great room was a mess of people: Beth, Vi, Sarah, Kaya, Allison, and Jennifer stood in various states of distress. Jack must've been with the girls, which made Zo feel a little better. At least the kids wouldn't see their mother hauled off to jail in a police car.

"Zo, thanks for coming." Vi met her at the door. "These oafs are about to arrest Beth. Jack called the lawyer, but I told him to take the kids and wait at the cottage. He's a nervous wreck."

Vi was a wreck, too. Instead of trendy clothes, she wore a baseball cap, striped lounge pants, and no makeup. Her lax attire made her no less fierce, however. She spat out each word of her explanation. The twenty thousand dollars had been found in the closet beneath the stairs by one of the guests, who alerted the police.

"Since Beth is the owner of the lodge, they're charging her with possession of stolen property. My daughter! Can you believe it? I told her we shouldn't have moved here. I said, there's a reason they call it the Wild West." She pointed toward Brady Merrigan. "People like him."

Zo took Vi's outstretched hand. She spoke quietly. "Don't worry, Vi. I'll talk to them. Just try to stay calm. Getting upset will only make things worse."

Vi took a shaky breath. "Can you talk some sense into them?"

Zo squeezed her hand. "I'll try."

She approached Beth and the officers. Beth wasn't half as upset as her mother. She greeted Zo with steadfast calm. Her resolve was commendable, really. Zo hadn't realized how strong a woman she'd become until this moment, and she felt a new kinship with her. Despite the hardships she'd endured opening weekend, she was determined to keep the lodge.

"How are you doing?" asked Zo.

"I understand the officers have a job to perform," said Beth, "and I don't have a record. I'm sure I'll be released right away. At least Mom's here to run things until I get back."

Beth made it sound like a mini-vacation. But Zo wasn't having it. They'd played nice long enough. Beth was about to go to jail, and Zo needed to stop it. Like Beth, she was determined—to keep her friend right where she was. She turned to Brady. "This is a setup, and I'm going to find out who's behind it. Why would Beth take the money only to hide it where anybody could find it?" She shook her head. "It doesn't make sense."

Brady's eyes were as smooth as glass. "It was in the supply closet, not exactly guest quarters."

That's right. The supply closet wasn't a place where guests should be poking around, so why were they? "Who found it?"

Brady crossed his arms, refusing to say.

"I did," said Sarah. She had been sitting on the staircase with the rest of the group but walked over now. "I needed more shampoo, and I didn't want to bother Beth. I'm sorry."

Beth smiled patiently. "It's not your fault, Sarah. Don't worry about it. Anyone might have found it."

But Zo wasn't so sure. Sarah's eyes were wet with tears, and her hair was pulled away from her round face in a mini ponytail. It was too short for an up-do. Actually, thought Zo, it was too short for an extra bottle of shampoo.

"I thought you refilled supplies every day?" Zo said to Beth.

"I did. I do." Beth shrugged. "Some people use more supplies than others."

"I stayed here, Officer Merrigan." Zo returned to Brady. Vi was right; he did look like a cowboy from a bad western. "Only Rapunzel would need two bottles of Beth's generous samples. Look at Sarah's short hair. She's lying."

"Good point, Zo," Vi piped up from behind the desk. "Sarah would need half a bottle on a good day."

Sarah made a noise, and Kaya stood and joined her, putting a protective arm around her.

"Sarah's not the one under arrest," Brady said. "I don't care if she pilfered the entire closet for free samples. Everyone does that on vacation. Beth was found in possession of the stolen property—twenty thousand dollars—and there's nothing you can do about it."

Zo was desperate to help Beth but knew Brady was half right. Beth was the one under arrest, and the only way to help her was to discover who placed the money in the closet. Giving Sarah a glance, she had a good idea where to start. There was no way she stumbled upon the money by accident. She either put it there for herself or a friend.

Brady led Beth to the squad car as the rest of them watched in disbelief. Vi was the most upset, heading to the restroom as soon as they left, probably to grab a tissue. But Sarah was upset, too, and Zo decided to ask her questions while the image of Beth getting hauled off in a police car was still fresh in her head. Maybe she could appeal to her as a mother.

"Beth is a mom, too, you know." Zo nodded toward the front door. "She has two little girls who depend on her."

"I know," said Sarah.

"How are they going to feel when they realize their mother's in jail?"

Sarah swallowed hard. "You heard her. She doesn't have a record. She's going to get out."

"For how long?" asked Zo. "It won't take much investigating for Brady to decide the money was a motive for Enid's death. It's the only way he can link the two crimes together."

"Beth is no murderer," said Jennifer. She was texting on her phone and didn't look up. "She might have taken the old lady's cash, but she didn't kill her."

"That's easy for us to say. We know Beth well enough to know she couldn't have done it," said Zo. "But look at it from the police's perspective. The medicine was found in the lodge, and now so was the money."

"Don't look at me," said Allison, though nobody was. "I don't know how Enid's prescription got into my dresser. If I killed her, which I didn't, I wouldn't have placed the evidence in my own room. Obviously."

Vi returned from the bathroom, blowing her nose. She looked pallid and small. Zo had to get Beth back as soon as possible for the sake of Vi's health. There was no way Vi could handle seeing Beth in a courtroom.

"Look, Sarah," said Zo, "if you know something about the money, you have to tell me. That's all I'm saying."

"I don't know why you're accusing me!" Sarah held up one hand. "I'm sorry about Beth, but I don't know anything about the money."

"Why don't you lay off her?" Kaya's voice was icy. "She has her own problems, and you're making them worse."

Zo wanted to ask if those problems involved money for her daughter's leukemia treatment but stopped herself. No matter the motive, the money had been returned, and while Sarah didn't have a threatening bone in her body, Kaya was strong. After the incident in the bar, Zo knew she wasn't afraid to act. The last thing Zo needed was a fistfight with Kaya. She would be the next one hauled off to jail, put into a cell next to Beth. Like Max had said at Black Mountain College, that would do no one any good.

"What about *my* daughter's problems?" asked Vi. "She's on her way to jail right now because of one of you yahoos."

Vi wasn't afraid of agitating Kaya or anyone else, but Zo knew Beth wouldn't want Vi accusing the guests. One bad review could ruin a potential customer's impression, and Memorial Day weekend was her grand opening. She would depend on initial reviews to get the word out.

"My daughter has leukemia," Sarah said quietly.

For a moment, the room was silent. Jennifer looked up from her phone, and Allison opened her mouth, then decided against speaking. Kaya glared.

"Then you know what it feels like to have your daughter in danger," said Vi.

"I do," Sarah acknowledged.

"And you know you'd do or say anything to fix it," Vi pushed.

Slowly, Sarah nodded, a motion that felt like an understood agreement, and the tension in the room evaporated. Jennifer went back to her phone, and Allison approached the coffeemaker. Kaya remained by Sarah's side.

Zo followed Vi to the reception desk for a private conversation. "I'm going to follow Beth to the police station and bring Max with me. Maybe he can talk some sense into Brady."

"I wish I could go with you, but I have to stay here." Vi flipped on the computer screen. "Beth needs me to hold down the fort."

Zo leaned over the desk. "Keep an eye on them, will you? I get the feeling they know something about the money, something they're not saying."

"I will," Vi said softly. "You just help Beth. I'm counting on you."

Chapter Twenty-Two

Vi's words stayed in her head on the drive through the canyon. With each curve, Zo recalled Vi's blue-gray eyes as she pleaded for help. Vi was a strong woman, but seeing her daughter taken away was too much. She was upset about the accusations facing Beth, and who wouldn't be? Zo still couldn't believe Brady was charging her. Allison hadn't been charged with stealing Enid's medication. Wasn't that the same thing? It didn't make sense, yet here was Zo, driving to the police station.

As she approached the scattered buildings on the edge of town, leaving the rocky canyon walls behind, she reproached herself for not calling the police about the break-in last night. It could've had something to do with the money being found, but what? Nothing was taken from her house or store. Zo thought Enid's murder and the theft were unrelated. Maybe the break-in and money turning up were unrelated, too.

Zo pulled into an empty spot in front of the new two-story police building, an outcast among older structures. It had a sign shaped like a half moon with a picture of a pine tree that read POLICE. For a police station, it looked welcoming.

She took off her helmet, shook out her hair, and called Max.

"Hey, I was going to call you this morning, to see how the rest of the night went," Max said. "How are you doing?"

"The night was fine, but this morning is a mess," said Zo. "Sarah found the twenty thousand dollars in Beth's storage closet, and Brady brought Beth to the station. He's charging her with possession of stolen property. I'm here now."

"You're kidding," said Max.

"Afraid not. I think we should have told him about the break-in. Maybe they're related. Do you want to meet me? It might be helpful if you corroborate my story."

"Already have my coat on," said Max. "I'll be there in two minutes."

She ended the call, shoving her cell phone in her backpack. She tucked her helmet under her arm and opened the door. The inside had modern gray tile around a sign that read MAIN DESK and back-to-back cherry wood benches in the reception area. She approached the employee under the sign—an older woman, who wore her hair pulled back and sported a pair of large black glasses. She was writing something on a piece of paper. Zo didn't recognize her, but her nametag read CAROL.

"Hi, I'm Zo Jones. My friend Elizabeth Everett was just brought in. She's being charged with a crime, and I want to see her."

"Take a seat," said Carol, her pen pausing as she spoke. "I'll be with you in a minute."

Zo looked around. She was the only person in the waiting area. What was the holdup? "I *will* be able to see her, right?"

Carol repositioned her glasses and motioned to the benches with her index finger.

Zo walked to a bench and sat down. A moment later, Max burst through the door. He walked to the front desk without noticing her.

"Hey Carol," said Max. "Is Brady here?"

"In back, dear," said Carol, buzzing open the door.

"Max!" Zo said.

Max spun around at the sound of her voice. He was red-cheeked and out of breath. It was nice of him to hurry.

"I thought you were already back there. Sorry," said Max.

"Where do you think you're going?" Carol said to Zo. "I told you to sit down."

"We both need to talk to Brady," said Max. "It involves the case he's working on. It'll only take a second." Max flashed her a smile.

"Oh, you're too cute for your own good, Max." Carol buzzed the door a second time. "By the way, my granddaughter says thank you for rescuing Mittens. My daughter thought she'd never get that cat down from the tree."

"Tell her she's very welcome," said Max. "Call any time."

Zo smiled. So he was good with cats. No wonder George liked him.

Max led her to a large room divided into several cubicles. Each cubby had a gray wall, computer, and file holder, and some had officers completing paperwork. In the back of the room was a regular office with windows.

Brady was standing near it, talking to an officer. They met him in the middle of the room.

"Where's Beth?" asked Zo.

Brady didn't answer. He narrowed his eyes at Max. "What is *she* doing back here?"

"Listen, can we go to your office and talk?" asked Max.

An officer glanced up from his computer screen, waiting to see what Brady would do.

"Your friend's arraignment is set for Monday," Brady said to Zo. "I've released her on personal recognizance, so you can quit throwing daggers my way."

"Great, but we still need to talk," said Max.

"Come on," said Brady.

Relieved by the news that Beth was free, Zo followed Max into Brady's office. If the police didn't set bail, it meant they believed Beth would show up for arraignment, which of course she would. But Beth didn't have many ties to the area, only the lodge. For all they knew, she would split town the moment she was released. Zo was glad for the small show of trust. It was a giant leap on Brady's part.

His office was decorated with old cowboy memorabilia: a rope, a hat, a buffalo head. Zo checked her reaction. Brady must have thought of himself as an Irish John Wayne. She plopped into a cushioned chair across from Brady's oversized desk, waiting for him to shut the door.

"So, what's this about, Max?" asked Brady as he positioned himself in his leather chair. "And please remember there's a civilian in the room."

The way he said *civilian* made her fists clench. She felt unwelcome at best, second-class at worst. She wondered if the lasso on the wall would fit around his large neck. She'd been to her fair share of rodeos.

"Someone broke into Zo's house last night," said Max. "We think it had something to do with what's going on at the lodge."

Brady's brow furrowed. "I didn't see a report filed. Did you call the police, Ms. Jones?"

"No, I didn't," Zo replied. "Nothing was taken, at least that I could find, so I decided not to call."

Brady leaned back in his chair, folding his hands across his stomach. "If nothing was taken, how do you know someone broke in?"

Zo had a feeling he wouldn't believe her, no matter what she said, but she had to try. "First, my cat was in the house, and I'd left him outside. Second, there was a big muddy footprint in my hallway."

"That was nice of the burglar, to let the cat in," said Brady with a guffaw.

"She's telling the truth. I was there. I saw the footprint." Max asked Zo to show Brady the photo. Zo took out her cell phone and found the picture. She handed him the phone.

Brady squinted at the picture.

"The person was looking for something," Max continued. "We don't know what."

Brady handed the phone back to Zo. "I didn't realize you and Miss Happy Camper were so close, Max. Were you on a date?"

Zo stood. He didn't believe someone had broken into her house, or if he did, he didn't care. She didn't have to listen to him scrutinize her whereabouts. Beth was being released. She had found out what she needed to know. If she stayed any longer, she would say something she would regret.

"Zo, wait." Max reached for her arm.

"Sorry, Max. You might work with him, but I don't. I don't have to listen to this." She walked out the door without a backward glance. When she reached the reception area, she was surprised to see Beth sitting on a bench. Zo rushed up to her, giving her a hug.

"I was so worried about you," said Zo. "Are you okay?"

Beth nodded. "I'm fine." Her face began to crumble, and she covered her eyes with her hands. "No, I'm not fine." She sniffed. "They fingerprinted me!"

"Come on," Zo offered. "Let's go to my house for a cup of tea."

"Just let me call Jack and tell him I'm all right."

Zo led her outside for privacy. "Vi said he was pretty upset."

She gave Zo a look and pulled out her cell phone. "That's the understatement of the century. He was a maniac. I had to make him take the kids away so he wouldn't get into an argument with the police."

Zo had a hard time imagining Jack arguing with anybody. He was an accountant, not a lawyer. He must have been really angry.

Beth dialed the number and told Jack where she was. She explained Zo would bring her home after a cup of tea to settle her nerves. She clicked off the phone. "Jack said to take my time. The lawyer won't be there for a while."

"So, he's doing better?" Zo said as they got onto her motorcycle.

"I think so," said Beth, grabbing the bar on the back of the bike. "The lawyer assured him everything would be fine."

Zo started the bike, and they were at her house in less than five minutes. At least one thing was going her way. The parking lot of Happy Camper was full. Tourist season had officially begun, and she would be busy from now until late fall. Business was one less problem on her mind.

She parked the bike, and Beth followed her up the deck stairs. George was curled up like a Russian hat on the deck railing. He was watching

Cunningham, working in his garden below. Now Zo could ask Cunningham about last night. Even though she knew he hadn't been the one in her house, it didn't hurt to make sure. Maybe he'd seen someone poking around the area.

"Hey, Cunningham," she called out.

He squinted at her from beneath his straw hat. "Hi Zo...and friend."

"This is Beth, the one I've been telling you about," Zo said.

"Hello." Beth waved.

Zo moved closer to the steps. "I have to ask you a weird question."

"I'm used to your weird questions." Cunningham smiled. "No need to warn me."

Zo took a deep breath. "Were you in my house last night, by any chance? Did you let George inside?"

He stood to stretch and pull his hat off. "Of course not. I wouldn't darken your doorway without permission."

She and Beth shared a small smile and headed for the door.

"Why do you ask?" Cunningham wiped his forehead with a handkerchief. The midday sun was raining down like bullets with no clouds to provide protection.

"Someone was in my house last night." Zo inserted her key in the door as she called back to Cunningham. "They let George in. I thought maybe it was you."

"This is concerning, Zo," said Cunningham, replacing his hat. Even from a distance, Zo could see he was worried.

"It is," she agreed. "Keep your doors locked until we figure out what's going on."

"You didn't tell me someone broke into your house." Beth shut the door behind them. "What happened?"

Zo filled the teakettle with water. "I came home last night, and George was inside, which was odd. He stays outdoors—obviously." She nodded toward the deck, where the fat cat perched. "There was also a muddy footprint. It was too big to be mine."

Beth sat down on one of the stools at the kitchen island. "Did they steal anything?"

Zo took out her bluebird teapot and filled the infuser with loose-leaf tea. "Not that I can tell. I wasn't in the store long when Vi called, but nothing looked out of place." She joined Beth at the island as she waited for the kettle to whistle. "I just have this feeling it has something to do with the money, or the murder. Someone thinks I have something, but what?"

"Not the twenty thousand dollars," said Beth, rolling her eyes. "That was neatly tucked under my staircase all along."

Zo shook her head. "No, it wasn't. Think about it. You would have seen it when you restocked supplies."

"You're right," said Beth. "I restock every day. So, who put it there?"

"That's the question. My bet is Sarah. She acted so weird after you left. And she's the one who *found* the money."

Beth wrinkled her forehead. "But she's so nice."

"Thieves can be nice."

"I know," Beth said. "I've worked in the hospitality business for years, but it doesn't make it any easier to believe. Sarah's a mom."

"Of a very sick child," added Zo. The kettle whistled, and she filled the teapot with water. "Life is hard for her. But maybe she couldn't go through with it. Maybe that's why she returned the money."

"To my supply closet, thank you very much. But why, and what does it have to do with your break-in?"

Zo took out two colorful Happy Camper mugs. "That's what we need to figure out."

"And before my arraignment on Monday," said Beth. "Otherwise Enid might get her wish after all, and I'll have to close Spirit Canyon Lodge."

Chapter Twenty-Three

After taking Beth home, Zo went back to the store. She needed to get some work done before going to Enid's visitation at Tall Pines Funeral Home. Now that summer was in full swing, the front window needed a new display, and she had the perfect idea. Recently, she'd ordered a hammock chair and aqua pillow. She would hang the chair from the ceiling and add a side table stacked with the books she'd purchased at a going-out-of-business sale at the used bookstore. Some were hardcover and would complete the book nook. Maybe she would add the plastic iced tea set, too, which included a pitcher and glasses. It was an adorable set, yellow and aqua, and travelers appreciated its durability. She'd sold several sets last year.

After helping her hang the hammock chair, Harley returned to the computer, crunching sales numbers while Zo set up the display. It looked so inviting that Zo wanted to curl up in the seat and flip through the pages of one of the books. But now wasn't the time for reading, stargazing, or any of the other hobbies that usually occupied her summers. Beth was counting on her to figure out who set her up, and she hoped Enid's visitation would reveal more information. Family members would be there, and Zo hadn't had time to talk to Griffin or Robyn. Tonight would give her the opportunity. They might divulge a detail about Enid or themselves that would give her another direction to explore.

She stood back and admired her work. It was lovely and so summery. She noticed the bar at the top of the hammock chair was tilting to the right. *Dang.* It would have to be fixed. She climbed up the ladder, still near the display, realizing too late she should have repositioned it closer to the chair. Thinking it was close enough, she reached for the bar and almost fell off the ladder. She let out a small yelp just as someone entered Happy Camper.

"Whoa, let me help you," said a male voice.

Zo knew it was Max without turning around. "I got it."

He put his hand on the ladder anyway. "I wanted to stop and say I'm sorry for the way Brady acted this morning."

She straightened the hammock chair and stepped down the ladder. "I didn't expect anything different."

"Still, he didn't have to be a jerk."

There was that concern again. She could tell he felt bad about the encounter and appreciated his thoughtfulness. She returned to the display. One of the books had fallen off the side table. "It's not your fault. He wasn't exactly nice to you either."

"I told you he doesn't like me," said Max. "It doesn't matter that I'm a law enforcement officer. I'm a wannabe as far as he's concerned."

"What about the break-in?" Zo asked. "Does he really think we made it up?"

"I don't know. He said he's going to check with the businesses on Main Street." Max shrugged. "He thought one of them might have a surveillance system."

"That's something at least."

Max nodded. "True. What about Beth? How's she doing? I suppose you took her home after you left."

"I did," said Zo. "She was pretty shaken up about the arraignment, and I don't blame her. If she's charged with a crime, it could mean the end of her business."

"So, what's your next move?" Max asked.

She gave him a smile, the first one all day. "How do you know I have a next move?"

"I just know." Max returned the smile. "I can tell by your face."

She didn't deny it. She'd been planning her strategy ever since reading the morning's newspaper. "I'm going to Enid's visitation tonight. It was mentioned in the paper. Griffin will be there and probably Robyn. I'd like another chance to talk to both of them."

"Good idea," he said. "Brady hasn't done enough investigating in that direction. He thinks Griffin's a harmless mama's boy."

Zo straightened the stack of books and stood back from the display, admiring her work. "Mama's boy, yes. Harmless, I'm not so sure."

"Mind if I join you?" asked Max.

"Not at all," she said. "Far be it from me to prevent you from paying your last respects.

* * * *

At five o'clock, Zo left the store in Harley's capable hands and went upstairs to change. Most of her clothes were casual, but like most women, she had a nice black dress that suited every occasion. It was dressy but not too dressy and looked good paired with sandals. *Now if I could just do something with my hair*, she thought as she looked in the mirror. The motorcycle ride through the canyon hadn't done her any favors. Her blond hair was all over the place. Normally she didn't mind the messy look, but tonight required something dressier. She grabbed a black barrette and clipped her long bangs to the side. That was better. The backpack couldn't be helped. It was the only purse that held her notebook, and she didn't want to be without paper tonight. Something might need to be jotted down. She tossed the bag over her shoulder and walked out the door.

Tall Pines was a funeral home on the east side of town, and Zo drove her Outback so as not to cause any more hair problems. From a block away, she could see the place was packed. It didn't surprise her. Enid was an important person in town, and now, so was her son. She'd lived here her entire life and made lots of friends, or if not friends, acquaintances. People in Spirit Canyon were accustomed to doing the right thing, especially when it came to weddings or funerals. They wouldn't miss the visitation just because Enid could be hard to get along with.

Zo signed a sympathy card on the wheel of her car and headed inside. The reception area was full of people waiting to extend their condolences to Griffin, who was standing near the casket with Robyn. *Enid would have been horrified at that arrangement*, thought Zo. Enid didn't like Robyn, and Robyn didn't like her. But as Griffin's fiancée, she had every right to be there, despite the damning review she had written on Serenity Hills.

As long as the line was, Zo wouldn't be entering the room anytime soon, so she meandered toward a table filled with cookies. Since she hadn't eaten before she left, she grabbed two treats to tide her over. She was thankful to see A.J. pouring a glass of water. At least she knew one person and could talk to him while she waited.

"Hey, A.J. How's it going?"

A.J. was dressed up. A clean-shaven face and a button-down shirt replaced his usual stubble and t-shirt. "Hi, Zo. I didn't expect to see you here."

"I wanted to pay my respects," said Zo. Even to her ears, the words sounded false. She turned the attention to him. "How about you? Are you here for KRSO?" He didn't have his camera, but then again, Zo didn't think this was the type of story that required pictures.

He shook his head. "My dad worked for Enid. I'm here because of him."

She puzzled over his answer. "Your dad?"

"Henry Miller," said A.J. "He's my dad."

"I had no idea," said Zo. She knew they had the same last name, Miller, but Miller was so common she didn't consider they might be related. Now that she knew, though, she could see a resemblance. They both had the same hair color, red-brown, but Henry's was mostly gray. And A.J. was quiet, like Henry. He had the same unobtrusive manner and easy ways.

"I talked to your dad a few days ago," Zo continued. "He seemed pretty upset by Enid's death. I suppose they were close after working together all those years."

"Everyone else thought she was cruel." He looked in his dad's direction. Henry was talking to a townsperson. "But he didn't. He was loyal to her until the end." A.J. shrugged. "She left him Serenity Hills, so maybe he was right. Maybe there was more to her than people knew."

"I read about that in the paper," said Zo. "I was surprised, to say the least. Do you know why she left him the resort?"

"My dad's taken care of the property for years. I'm sure it seemed natural for him to have it. I don't think Griffin had anything to do with the place, or if he did, I didn't see him around."

His comment reminded Zo of a question. "Do you think Enid knew about Griffin's engagement to Robyn? Before the chuck wagon?"

A.J. shook his head. "No way. She was blindsided by his announcement that night at the lodge. Don't you think?"

Zo tossed her napkin in the trash. She was finished with her cookies. "It seemed that way to me."

"Who knows?" A.J. said. "Maybe it was the news that gave her the heart attack."

"Maybe." She kept her answer noncommittal. Obviously, he didn't know about the digoxin found in Enid's water bottle. The longer the news was kept out of the press, the better.

Zo heard a noise at the door and turned to see Justin Castle. She knew reporters like him, making an entrance wherever they went. It made her glad to be out of media. He gave A.J. a vague wave before turning to a woman in a short brown dress.

"I thought KRSO wasn't here for a story?" said Zo. With Justin tracking Enid's memorial, word was certain to get out about Beth's arraignment.

"We're not," said A.J. "Not officially, anyway. Justin likes to keep tabs on what's going on in the community."

Is that what you call it? Justin's tabs were more like talons. "Will the station do another story on Spirit Canyon Lodge?"

He shook his head. "Probably not. Justin has his other pet projects to cover."

Zo heard the disgust in his voice loud and clear. She decided it was safe to be candid with him. "Like Jennifer Greene?"

He smiled. "You don't know the half of it. He leaves behind a lot of loose ends. I'm just glad Jennifer wasn't the clingy type."

The comment gave Zo pause. "I don't think you have to worry about that. Jennifer seems anything but clingy."

A.J. looked in Justin's direction. "I'd better check if he needs anything."

"I'll see you later." Zo turned toward the casket room. Fewer people were in line now, and while waiting, she glanced at a large poster board surrounded by a heart bouquet. Zo didn't know Enid when she was young: tall, slender, her curly hair untouched by the flat iron. She looked innocent, nice even. Then she met her husband, who was older than she was. It looked as if Enid's transformation took place the moment she married him. She went from girl to woman to mother in the series of a dozen pictures. Zo glanced at Griffin. He had his dad's good looks, sleek and sophisticated. No wonder Robyn was willing to put up with Enid. But now she didn't have to, and Zo wondered if that could have been the plan all along.

Approaching the casket, Zo shook Robyn's hand while Griffin finished speaking to a relative. "How are you doing?"

"I'll be better when this is over," said Robyn. Dressed in a simple black dress, she was plain but confident. Her straight shoulders were thrust back, ready to face whatever came her way. "Who knew Enid Barrett had so many friends?"

"A lot of business people from Spirit Canyon are here," said Zo.

"I guess that's why you're here," said Robyn.

Zo nodded. It was as good of an excuse as any other. An older man joined the men talking to Griffin, and Zo took the opportunity to mention the money. "They found Enid's money at the lodge. They're trying to stick the theft on Beth."

Robyn's brow wrinkled. "Was any of the cash missing?"

"No, it was all accounted for."

Robyn looked confused. "So, how is that theft?"

Zo thought it was a good question, one that she was going to bring up to Brady. Could Beth eventually be charged with theft if all the money had been returned to its rightful owner? "A guest found the money in the supply closet and called the police. Since Beth owns the property, she was charged with possession."

"What's this about the money?" Griffin asked. He'd overheard the last bit of the conversation. Robyn repeated the rest.

"Why haven't the police returned it, then?" asked Griffin. "It belongs to me. Us," he added, glancing at Robyn.

"I'm sure they will," said Zo. The woman behind her cleared her throat. She wanted to keep the line moving, and the previous gentlemen had already caused a delay. "It probably has to go through the proper channels first."

"I guess one thing turned out the way Mom wanted," said Griffin with a shrug. "If Beth is arrested, Spirit Canyon Lodge will be forced to close after all."

"I wouldn't be so sure of that," said Zo, but as she passed the closed casket, she realized it was true. Despite her death, Enid had gotten her way—like she always did. If Beth was charged, she would be forced to shut down the lodge.

She looked back at Griffin and Robyn, the new power couple in Spirit Canyon. Could they have gotten rid of Enid for love, money, or both? They were the first ones in the room when Zo awoke Saturday morning. They'd had words the night before, and as her son, Griffin would know all her medications. He had to be embarrassed to find her checking up on him, and Robyn was furious he hadn't told his mom about their upcoming nuptials. It all added up.

Still, it was hard to believe Griffin could murder his own mother. *But she wasn't Robyn's mother*, Zo thought. And Robyn had guts. She wasn't afraid to speak her mind; maybe she wasn't afraid to commit murder either.

Chapter Twenty-Four

Leaving Tall Pines, Zo ran into Max in the parking lot. She remembered he said he'd see her there but had forgotten he was coming until just now. He was dressed in a black suit jacket and hiking boots. No matter what he wore, though, he always looked ready to do battle with a rogue tent pole or stray animal. As he got closer, she noticed he was frowning. She doubted it was out of sadness for Enid's passing. Something was wrong.

She didn't bother with a greeting. "What's up?"

"I'm glad I caught you," he said. "You've been inside?"

She nodded.

"Enid's bottle of water tested positive for digoxin," said Max. "No surprise there. We sort of guessed it when we found the bottle. Still, it's another strike against Beth."

"Great." Zo leaned against a car.

"First Enid's prescription, then the money, now this?" said Max. "It doesn't look good."

Zo could feel her shoulders tense. "What are you saying? You think she's guilty?"

"No," said Max.

A couple got out of a nearby car, and Zo waited for them to pass before she continued. "Good, because the more I think about it, the more I realize any one of the guests might have killed Enid. Justin Castle, for instance. He keeps hanging around. Why? He's inside right now. He seems to have taken a personal interest in this story."

"You don't have to convince me," said Max. "I'm on your side."

"Sometimes I wonder about that," Zo shot back. It was a stupid retort, and she regretted it the moment it flew out of her mouth. The hurt look on his face reminded her of Beth's.

Max shoved his hands into his jacket pockets. "I didn't have to tell you, you know. I didn't have to come here at all. I thought you'd want to know."

"Look, I'm sorry. I appreciate you telling me. This thing with Beth is driving me crazy. She moved her entire family here, even her mom, and she doesn't know a soul in town. I feel responsible for what happens to her."

They stood in silence as the wind crept up a nearby maple tree, rustling its leaves. On a top branch, a cardinal tweeted, the voice loud and certain. Zo wished she was as certain about the future. Beth was one step closer to going to jail, and Zo had taken one step back from the only man who could help her. She needed to get a grip and fast.

"You want to grab dinner?" she asked. "I haven't eaten yet, and I'm starving."

Max glanced at the funeral home. "What about the visitation?"

"I've been there. I can tell you what I found."

Max hesitated, and Zo worried he'd say no. She hadn't asked anyone to dinner in a long time. The moment felt like a lifetime.

"Okay," said Max. "How about the Presidents' Club?"

"We've got the right clothes for it, and they have great food."

"Good. Let's take your car. My truck is a mess."

The Presidents' Club was a tall building shaped like the White House. The drive was curved, and a valet waited to park her car. As she turned over her keys to him, she remembered the last time she was here it was with Hattie, who was a huge history buff. Hattie enjoyed the presidential memorabilia. Zo enjoyed it, too. The Black Hills were known for Mount Rushmore, so of course Presidents Washington, Lincoln, Jefferson, and Roosevelt were represented. They were the first portraits to greet diners when they entered the reception area.

But all the past presidents had space on the walls, and the dining areas were named for presidents' wives. Replications of their china patterns graced the tables, and Zo was glad to be led to the Eleanor Roosevelt room, one of her favorites. Mrs. Roosevelt had overcome a difficult childhood and the loss of both of her parents to become one of the most influential women in history. She was an advocate for human and civil rights, and Zo admired her work a great deal. It gave her hope. If Roosevelt could overcome so much, surely Zo could overcome her trust issues.

After she sat down, Zo placed her napkin on her lap. "I'm surprised it isn't busier."

Max scanned the room. "True, but it's a weeknight, and half the town is at Enid's visitation."

The waiter, dressed in formalwear, shared the evening's specials with them, then asked what they'd like to drink.

"You like wine, right?" asked Max. She nodded, and he ordered a bottle of Cabernet Sauvignon from Napa Valley.

"I didn't know you were a wine drinker," said Zo, looking at the menu.

"There's a lot you don't know about me. Next I'm going to order escargot and really surprise you."

She glanced up.

"Just kidding," he said with a grin. "I'm having steak. Are you?"

"I think so." She shut the menu, deciding on the Filet Oscar. The Presidents' Club was known for its tender cuts of meat.

The waiter returned with the wine, pouring Max a small sample before filling both glasses half full. He took their order, then scooted away.

Max held up his glass. "Here's to not having dinner with Duncan tonight."

Zo smiled and clinked his glass. "Is he really that bad?"

"Worse," Max answered, straight-faced.

She let out a laugh. "So, why is he living with you?"

Max took a long sip of his wine and set down his glass. "Believe it or not, I'm a sucker for hard luck stories. He lost his job as a guitar instructor when the music store shut down, and his landlord wouldn't let him give private lessons in his apartment. I said he could stay at my house until he found something of his own."

"That was really sweet of you." It was endearing to think Max saved not only animals but humans as well.

"To be honest, I'm starting to regret it," said Max.

Zo took a roll out of the newly placed breadbasket. "Why?"

Max gave her a look as he passed the butter. "Twelve-year-olds are really bad at guitar."

She chuckled. "I never played an instrument, but I always wanted to."

The salads arrived, and after he poured on his dressing, he gave her a glance. "Can I ask what happened to your parents? Do you mind?"

"No," she said. "I don't mind. I was left at the Spirit Canyon police station as a baby. I was under a month old."

"Were you put with a family?"

"Right away," said Zo. "Everybody wants a newborn. I was taken in by the Jones family, but it didn't last. They were charged with neglect—there were ten of us—and I was put into the foster care system. Unfortunately getting placed as a kid wasn't as easy as getting placed as a baby. Spirit Canyon Lodge was the only house that really felt like a home."

The steaks arrived, and she was glad for the break in conversation. Although she didn't mind talking about her past, it could be challenging for others, and they'd had enough challenging topics to discuss lately. She could never explain those years. Parents, kids, teachers—people passed in and out of her life like scenes from a movie. She could hardly remember them. Despite a difficult start, she'd been able to go to college, land a good job, and open a business. Her success made her optimistic that any story could end happily.

After a few bites of food, Max asked about the break-in. He wanted to know if she'd found anything missing at Happy Camper.

"Nothing," she said. "I checked again. I have no idea what the person was looking for—maybe an antique. I attend a lot of auctions. Who knows? Maybe I picked up something priceless, and I'll be on *Antiques Roadshow*." She took a bite of her steak, imagining she might dine like this every night if she had stumbled upon something of value. It would be delicious, but hardly her style.

"Did you call about a security system?" asked Max.

"Not yet," said Zo. "Do you really think I found something valuable?"

"Maybe," said Max. "But nothing is missing. Either the thief didn't find what he was looking for, or he did, and you don't miss it yet."

There was a third alternative, but she didn't say it aloud. The person might not have been looking for a thing but a person—her. When he didn't find her, he disappeared, leaving only the trace of his boot. Would he return? That was the question she pondered the rest of the night.

Chapter Twenty-Five

After opening Happy Camper on Thursday, Zo drove to Spirit Canyon Lodge. The guests would be checking out tomorrow, and she was running out of time. She wondered how Beth's family was faring after Beth's trip to the police station. Beth would probably be okay. She didn't have time to worry about herself. But Zo wasn't as sure about Vi, who was concerned for her daughter. Zo was concerned, too. After her conversation with Max last night, she was afraid Beth would be charged with not only theft but murder. The police had everything: the motive—money, means—digoxin, and method—water bottle. All they needed now was an arrest warrant.

When Zo arrived at the lodge, she noticed Vi and Molly on the front lawn. Curls springing up and down, Molly ran to greet her as she shut off the ignition. That was the great thing about kids. They kept life moving even when disaster struck.

"Gran and I are having a picnic!" exclaimed Molly. "Come see, come see."

"I'd love to," said Zo, but Molly wasn't waiting around for her answer. She ran ahead to the blanket where Vi sat with a visor pulled low over her forehead. Even with the hat, Zo could see the worry etched on her face. Vi was doing a good job pretending, for Molly's sake, but nothing could disguise the hurt she must be feeling over Beth's arrest.

"Zo, I'm glad you're here," said Vi. "Sit down." Sandwiches, chips, and juice boxes were scattered on the oversized blanket. Zo glanced at the house and decided to sit. She would check on Beth after talking with Vi. She needed the company more than anyone right now.

"Grape juice?" asked Molly.

"Why not," said Zo, taking the box and inserting the straw.

"Molly, be a good girl, and go get Gran a couple of those leftover brownies, will you? I've got a hankering for something sweet."

"Sure." Molly skipped toward the cottage.

"We can't let this thing go to trial," said Vi as soon as the girl was out of earshot. "It'll ruin the business whether Beth is found guilty or not. Nobody wants to stay at a thief's place."

"Or a murderer's." Zo told Vi about the digoxin and water bottle.

"Good lord. What are we going to do?"

"I'm going to talk to Sarah and her friends," said Zo. "I have a feeling they know something about the money. That's why I'm here."

Vi wiped a few stray crumbs off the blanket. "I don't know how much you'll find out. I followed Sarah everywhere yesterday, and she didn't say a word about the money."

"What about the others?" asked Zo.

"Nada."

The conversation dwindled into silence. Zo watched a hawk on a post that marked a nearby hiking trail. From the dream book, Zo had learned the hawk was a symbol of bright prospects. *I could use a prospect right now.* Recalling the past few days, she remembered her conversation with Jules about dreams, and asked Vi if she'd had any more encounters with Lilly's ghost. After their discussion, that's what she was calling them. Maybe it was a desperate attempt for another direction, but it was all she had.

"It wasn't an encounter," said Vi. "It was heartburn."

Zo restated the question. "Have you had more dreams about Lilly, or anything at all?"

"Just the new one about the baby's outfit," said Vi. "Beth said she told you."

"She did," said Zo. "But Lilly couldn't have children, and you had girls. The outfit was blue. Do you think Lilly's trying to tell you about a different baby? Maybe the one she wanted to adopt?"

"I don't know." Vi considered the question. "With her early diagnosis of heart disease, Lilly didn't look into adoption later in life. Things were different then. They didn't have as many pills to keep people alive as they do now. But she loved kids. She really did."

What Vi said was true. Lilly once said children's footsteps on the stairs was music to her ears. She never minded that Zo stayed for most of the summer. She'd told her she would have adopted Zo herself if she had a stronger heart. The last thing Zo needed was to lose another family, she'd said.

Zo thought a minute. "Lilly knew Enid, and Enid had a boy, Griffin. Could that be it? Could Lilly be telling us that Griffin is the murderer?"

"If I believed in ghosts—which I don't—that might make sense," said Vi. "Lilly would know that if we can't figure out who killed Enid, then Beth will be charged, and the lodge will close." Vi took in the canyon. "She gave up everything to come here. I don't see her letting it go now."

Zo didn't see Lilly letting it go either—or allowing Beth to hang for Griffin's crime. There had to be a connection between Enid, Griffin, and Lilly that they hadn't discovered. "Maybe we could find something in her personal effects? Beth said you guys are going through her things."

"We are," said Vi. "But we haven't been up in the attic yet, and that's where her hope chest is. We'll go through it and let you know what we find."

From the back of the lodge, Molly appeared with two sticky brownies in hand. Zo finished her juice and stood, dusting off her jean capris. "I'm going to go in and talk to Beth—and Sarah. We're getting close, Vi. I promise."

Vi nodded but didn't respond. Molly had rejoined them.

"Thank you for the juice, Molly," said Zo.

"You're welcome," Molly replied. "You aren't staying?"

"I need to talk to your mom," Zo said. "Is she inside?"

Molly nodded. "Gran says she looks *haggard*."

Zo smiled and told her good-bye. Molly had already stuffed a brownie into her mouth, so she simply waved.

When Zo entered the lodge, she noticed Beth's look. It *was* haggard. Her brown hair was twisted into a messy bun with stray pieces sticking out, and her blue-gray eyes had dark shadows beneath them. Zo wondered if she was sleeping at all. When the screen door slapped shut, Beth startled and looked up from the reception desk, giving Zo her usual warm smile. She was trying her best to be strong, but Zo knew the investigation was taking a toll on her.

"Zo," she said. "I'm glad to see you."

"I can be here night or day. I'm just a phone call away." Zo meant it, too. It felt good to have someone rely on her. George and Cunningham were pretty independent. So was Harley. It was probably why they all got along as well as they did.

Beth took a sip of coffee from the mug on the desk. "I don't know what we'd do without you right now. I'm afraid Mom has all her hopes pinned on you. Did you see her outside?"

Zo nodded. "She's with Molly."

Beth sighed. "It's crazy how fast kids grow up. I mean, I know everybody tells you that, but until Meg turned twelve, I didn't realize how true it was. Now most of my conversations with Meg involve hair care products or shopping trips."

"I wouldn't mind having a built-in shopping partner," Zo said. "She'll have to come with me to an auction some time."

"She would love that," said Beth. "So would I—if this mess ever gets fixed. Do you have news? Is that why you're here?"

Zo didn't want to tell her about Enid's water bottle, but she had to, and it was better she heard it from Zo than someone else, someone like Brady Merrigan. As she relayed the information, Beth nodded, but she was blinking back tears.

When Beth swiped her eyes, a little of her eyeliner smeared. "The police are certain the overdose wasn't an accident?"

Zo handed her one of the tissues on the desk. "Enid would have no reason to dissolve her medication in water."

Beth dabbed her eyes, threw away the tissue, and shook her head. "I delivered the water, but the digoxin was in Allison's room. Allison has to be the one who snuck into the room and poisoned Enid."

"It's possible," Zo admitted. "Any one of them, really, could have tampered with it. They all slept upstairs. But you're right. Allison knows the most about medicine, and the digoxin was found in her room."

"She's a much better suspect than I am," said Beth. "If only the police would see it that way…"

Sarah and Jennifer walked down the stairs. It looked as if Jennifer was still picking out Sarah's clothes, because instead of mom jeans, Sarah wore leggings and a clingy top. Zo lowered her voice. "I want to talk to Sarah again," she whispered. "She knows more than she's telling."

"You'd better be quick. They're on their way to Keystone. They want to pick up some souvenirs before they leave Friday. I don't know why. Who'd want to remember this trip?" She flung up her hands.

"That's not true, Beth. I promise." Zo took in the great room. The crackling fire was the same, the winding staircase was the same, the warm friendship was the same. "Some of my best memories come from this place. I'll never forget them."

Beth smiled. "Thanks, Zo. I needed to hear that."

Zo followed Sarah to the dining area, where she was visiting what was left of the continental breakfast buffet. She was selecting a muffin to go. Jennifer declared she didn't eat carbs—or breakfast. She would have a Bloody Mary when they got to Keystone.

Zo saw an opportunity to enter the conversation. "They have awesome saltwater taffy there. It's made in the store. It's stretched out on this machine, and they have all sorts of flavors. Your daughter will love it."

"Lexy loves anything sweet," Sarah said. A devoted mom, she got excited any time she could talk about her daughter. "And cookies! That girl is crazy about cookies." She wrapped a napkin around her blueberry muffin. "Are you ready?" she said to Jennifer.

"*Darn*," Jennifer said. "I forgot my sunglasses in my room. I'll meet you outside."

Zo was happy to be alone with Sarah. She could press her about the money without one of Sarah's friends saving her from answering, and frankly, she was running out of time. The only way to get the information was to ask.

When Jennifer was gone, Zo turned to face her. "I don't blame you for taking the money." She held up her hand to quiet Sarah's objection. "I would have done the same thing if I had a sick kid."

Sarah glanced up the stairs, maybe looking for one of her friends. Seeing no one, she responded reluctantly. "I don't know what you're talking about. I found the money in the storage closet, just like I said."

Zo wondered how far she could press her before she would dart. Sarah was used to having her friends around and seemed uncomfortable by the turn of events. Zo focused on the positive. "You returned the money. You're obviously a good person. I know that you don't want Beth to go to jail for a crime she didn't commit."

"Beth has been very kind to me," said Sarah. "Of course I don't want her to go to jail. But I didn't take the money, so stop harassing me."

It was the first Zo had heard Sarah assert herself, and she questioned who else could have taken it if not her. As Jennifer appeared from the staircase, Zo wondered if Sarah was protecting a friend—or friends.

"You ready?" Jennifer breezed past them, sunglasses in hand.

Zo followed them to the door, wishing them a good time. They hopped into Allison's Durango without giving Zo a second glance. She didn't see Allison or Kaya. They must have had other plans.

Zo turned around to see Beth's hopeful face staring back at her.

"Any luck?" she asked.

Zo hated disappointing her friend. "Sorry, Beth. I got nothing."

Beth shook off the bad news. "That's okay because I have something for you—lunch."

Chapter Twenty-Six

Over lunch, Zo told Beth about her conversation with Sarah. They were sitting on Beth's cottage deck, munching cucumber sandwiches. The cottage was a gray ranch with white shutters, just a short walk from the lodge. With its cobblestone path and window flower boxes, it looked more whimsical than the rustic inn. But it suited Beth and the family perfectly. It had three bedrooms on the main floor and a mother-in-law apartment in the walkout basement. Vi had her own space and a great view of the canyon. The deck had a great view, too. Beth said now that the lodge had been remodeled, she was going to tackle the house, which needed new carpet and fixtures. Zo could imagine how cute it would be after Beth was finished redecorating.

Jack joined them late, taking in the table with a smile. It was dressed with a white linen tablecloth and matching napkins. A pansy-colored cozy hugged the teapot, keeping the orange-spiced liquid warm, while a little vase of matching flowers provided a centerpiece.

"Every time I sit down to eat, I feel like I'm at a wedding." Jack unfolded his napkin and placed it on his lap. "Aren't I lucky?"

"You're incredibly lucky," agreed Zo. She'd just finished the last morsel of a cinnamon coffee cake fresh from Vi's oven. She'd run to a hundred specialty stores for spices if it meant eating tasty desserts like this every day.

"Decorating is the only thing keeping my mind off jail these days," said Beth. "When I focus on details, I don't think about anything else. It's like when I was planning weddings. I get into the zone and everything else disappears."

"Do you ever miss your job in Chicago?" Zo asked. She thought she knew the answer.

"A little," Beth admitted. "The romance, the love—the fights. Oh, do people fight while planning a wedding! Some of the mothers-in-law I've met would make you run the other direction." Beth smiled and shook her head, perhaps remembering a recent argument.

"What about you?" asked Jack. "Beth said you used to be a journalist. Do you ever miss that work?" He stacked the remaining tea sandwiches into one big double-decker sandwich. Beth looked on with a frown, but he didn't notice.

Zo thought before answering. She didn't miss the commute or the office politics, but she did miss the stories. She liked searching for answers and eventually finding them. She liked owning the store more, though. Finally, she had something to call her own. "I miss the action. Tracking a story is kind of addicting. But my Curious Camper column keeps me writing."

"She's writing about lodging this week," Beth explained to Jack. "She's including the lodge in her column."

"Which is due tomorrow." Zo groaned. Her editor, Harriet Hobbs, hated it when things came in last minute. But this week it would have to be last minute. Zo hadn't had time to finish. Harriet was a pro, though. She would understand the predicament. Zo was counting on it.

"I don't envy you." Jack slurped his tea. Dressed in a paint speckled t-shirt, he looked comical drinking from the delicate teacup. "Murderers and thieves aren't my definition of curious campers."

"Jack!" said Beth. "She's not going to mention them." She turned to Zo. "Are you?"

"Of course not," said Zo. "I'll put in a little plug for the lodge. You'll see."

"Feel free to put in a big one," said Jack. "We'll need it if word of Beth's arraignment gets out. An arraignment!" He set down his cup with a clink on the saucer. "Can you believe it?"

"Sarah had to have taken the money," Zo mused. "I'm positive of it. She was the only one who overheard Enid offer Beth twenty thousand dollars. My guess is Sarah went back into the room when Enid was sleeping and swapped the cash with the stationery from the lodge. The next morning, when Enid was found dead, she realized what a terrible mistake she'd made. She hadn't just stolen money from a wicked old lady; she'd stolen it from a dead woman. Big difference."

"I can't imagine Sarah poisoning Enid, though," said Jack. "She's too... *nice* to be a murderer."

"Zo doesn't think the thief and the murderer are the same person." Beth refilled her teacup. "More?"

Zo nodded.

"Then who?" Jack wondered. He munched his stacked sandwich as they considered the question. After a moment, he answered. "I overheard Kaya tell Molly she got that scar above her eye at a protest."

Zo put down her teacup, remembering the knife in the bar. "What was she protesting?"

"I don't think she said, but she carries a gun," said Jack. "I saw it."

"Carrying a gun doesn't make someone a murderer," Beth argued.

"Lots of people carry around here," said Zo. "Nobody wants to be caught without protection in the forest. But I'd like to find out what she was protesting."

"I hope you find *something*," said Jack. "I don't care who did it as long as Beth isn't charged. This has gone way too far. The lawyer we hired agrees."

Zo agreed, too. If Beth went to trial, it would tarnish her reputation, no matter the outcome. The news station would get ahold of it, if they hadn't already, and it would be the biggest story of the summer. She needed to find something and quick. "Jennifer and Sarah went to Keystone. Where are Kaya and Allison?"

"They're hiking out to Iron Creek Lake," said Beth. "They left this morning with a sack lunch."

Iron Creek was a twelve-mile hike west of the canyon. They wouldn't be back for a while. Zo pushed back her chair. "Let's go back to the lodge. I have an idea."

Beth looked at Jack and then Zo.

"Don't let me stop you," said Jack, popping the last bit of sandwich in his mouth.

Beth's eyes narrowed. "I've seen that look in your eye before, when you were twelve years old and convinced me to sneak out of the lodge. You wanted to see if the blue moon was really blue."

Zo grinned. "I remember. It wasn't. I was so disappointed." She also remembered that Beth took some convincing. With the trial pending, she hoped she would need less persuading.

"I think I like this idea, Beth." Jack pointed toward the lodge. "Go."

Beth stood. "Okay, okay. You don't need to gang up on me."

Zo was glad for Jack's nudge. Beth wouldn't like the idea of snooping through her guests' rooms, but they had to look for some clue to the stolen money while the group was away. Griffin and Robyn had left right after Enid's death. It had to be one of the women who returned the money. She was sure of it.

Zo explained her plan as they entered the lodge through the rear entrance.

"You mean go through their *personal* belongings?" whispered Beth.

Zo could tell by the tone of her voice she was bothered by the idea. She tried another idea. "The envelope was filled with stationery from the lodge, right?"

"Right," said Beth.

"So, somebody's stationery must be missing," said Zo. "All we need to do is find the missing stationery, and we'll have our thief."

Beth bit her lip. "And we wouldn't be going through anybody's stuff. We'd be restocking supplies."

"Exactly," said Zo. She started toward the staircase before Beth could change her mind. "Where do you put the stationery? On the desks?"

"Most rooms have a desk or table," said Beth. "I usually set it in one place or the other, along with a pen."

"Let's start with Sarah's room," said Zo as they approached the upstairs hallway. With all the doors shut, it was dark, and Zo felt a little like a kid again. The big old lodge, she and Beth exploring places they weren't supposed to. It was thrilling. Beth hesitated outside Sarah's door. Obviously, she didn't feel the same way.

"It's okay for you to restock supplies," said Zo. "You're fine."

Beth took a breath and opened the door with the key.

It was much brighter in Sarah's room. The large window facing the canyon was open. Sunshine covered the room like a warm blanket, and Zo went to the small writing desk. Postcards, gum, and an e-reader were scattered atop. She opened the drawer. No paper. She smiled.

"Zo," said Beth.

Zo turned. Beth was holding the notepad in her hand.

"It was on her nightstand," Beth said. "It hasn't been used."

Zo was stunned. She had been certain Sarah was the thief. "Let's check Jennifer's room. She won a lot of cash at the casino. Maybe that's why she returned Enid's money."

Beth locked the door behind them. The locks were originals and used keys, but a good shove could have opened any of the doors. They were part of the lodge's rustic charm but not very safe. Zo would have to talk to Beth about installing keycards when this was over.

Though Jennifer's bed was made, the rest of the room was a mess. Clothes, makeup, and shoes lay all over. She didn't have a desk but a table, and Zo started there. After pushing aside necklaces and bracelets, Zo found the lodge notepad—untouched. She looked at Beth, who was standing next to her. Beth shrugged.

"You haven't replaced any of these?"

"None," said Beth. "I never thought to check."

"Come on," said Zo. "Whose room is next?"

"Kaya's," said Beth.

Kaya's room was neat. She had her suitcase propped up on the luggage holder, and her leather jacket hung on the back of the desk chair. On the desk were several brochures on area attractions, tidily arranged. Zo was careful not to mess them up, for she had a feeling Kaya would notice if something was out of place.

Zo lifted the desk phone. No paper there. She checked under the binder of local attractions. Nothing. She opened the tiny desk drawer, and there was the used notepad. Only one piece of lodge stationery was left! Kaya was the one who'd stolen the money, but why?

A noise happened downstairs, and Beth, who'd been staring at the empty notepad with her, gasped. Now wasn't the time for asking questions. They needed to get out of there, or at least Zo did. Beth had an excuse to be in the room. It was her lodge. Zo couldn't think of a reason for being upstairs.

"What are we going to do?" whispered Beth.

Zo shut the desk drawer. "If it's Kaya and Allison, get them into the kitchen. Tell them you have something you want them to taste. I'll leave when they're gone."

"What about the stationery?"

"Leave it," said Zo. "I'll see what I can find on Kaya at the library."

They ducked out of the room. Zo noticed Beth was shaking as she turned the key to the lock. Poor Beth. She'd been through so much. Theft, murder, arrest. Opening weekend was not the reunion they'd planned.

From the dim hallway, Zo could hear Beth downstairs talking about a new breakfast muffin. It was loaded with egg, cheese, and bacon. She wanted someone to taste-test it. Zo recognized Kaya's voice. It sounded as if Kaya wanted to take a shower, but when Beth insisted, they must have agreed. The great room was quiet again.

Zo tiptoed down the stairs, glancing at the fireplace and bookshelves. No one was there. She scooted through the front door, closing the screen silently behind her. Then she darted toward the parking lot, jumping into her Subaru, her heart pounding all the way back to Spirit Canyon.

Chapter Twenty-Seven

Kaya had stolen the money, or at least filled the envelope with paper, but why—and when? Unlike Sarah, Kaya had been downstairs when Enid offered Beth the cash. Zo was the only other person in the hallway, except Griffin and Robyn, who were fighting in their room. It didn't make sense.

Zo rolled down the window, allowing the late afternoon sun in. Beth had seen the money that afternoon, when she brought the bottle of water to Enid's room. She told Zo she wanted to ask Enid to put it in a safe but decided against it. But had Beth seen the money that night, when the offer was made? Zo pushed the phone button on her steering wheel. She could easily find out with a call.

Beth answered right away. "I didn't even hear you leave, you sneaky thing," she whispered.

"I'm pretty good at getting myself out of a jam," said Zo.

"Can you believe it was Kaya?" said Beth. "I wouldn't have guessed."

"Me neither." Zo paused for a moment. "Beth, did you see the money that night? When Enid offered it to you in exchange for closing the lodge?"

"Yes," Beth said. "It was in the envelope on the table. She pointed to it."

Zo slowed down as she approached the outskirts of town. "But did you actually *see* the bills?"

The line was quiet for a moment. "I knew it was there because I'd seen it that afternoon. But no, now that I think about it, she didn't physically show me the cash. Why? Is it important?"

Zo wasn't sure. The information only changed the timeline in her head. "I assumed the money was taken Saturday night, after your argument with Enid, but it might have been switched earlier. Enid didn't open the envelope, and you didn't see the money that night."

"You're right," said Beth. "Kaya could have swapped it out any time. Enid started snooping around the grounds the moment she checked in."

Zo stopped at the light. "I'm almost to the library. I'll see what I can find and let you know." She ended the call.

Tourists were on their late afternoon hiatus, and Main Street looked neat and pretty. Giant baskets of purple and pink impatiens hung from timeworn lampposts, and the scrolled metal benches were empty. People would return tonight for dinner, for drinks, for a show at the historic opera house. *Brigadoon* was playing this month and next month *A Midsummer Night's Dream*. But for now, Main Street was clear, waiting patiently for nightfall.

The library wasn't as quiet. Hattie always had something going on, and today she'd invited a local brewing expert to speak—and pour. The talk was over, and participants were huddled around the table, tasting a pale ale. After all, it was five o'clock somewhere.

Zo spotted Jules in the crowd. Six feet tall with a curvy figure, Jules was hard to miss even with her hair down. It hung past her shoulders, the pink streaks buried beneath a mass of yellow. Zo took a quick detour in her direction.

"Thinking about adding another brew at Spirits & Spirits?" Zo asked, touching Jules's arm.

"Taste this," said Jules, handing her a tiny plastic glass. "It's perfect for summer."

Zo took a sip. "I like it. It has a twist of lemon."

Jules took another glass for herself. "Me, too. What are you doing here?"

"Trying to help my friend Beth," said Zo. "The one I told you about who moved back to the area."

"Ah." Jules nodded. "The one who's being haunted."

"You're thinking of her mother, but yes, same family."

"Has the mom had any other *visitors*?"

"Only the cops. That's why I'm here, exploring new leads."

"That's not a good sign." Jules squinted. "Maybe it's time for a spirit intervention."

"Is that a real thing?"

"Would I suggest it if wasn't?" asked Jules.

"Depends on your fee." Zo gave Jules a playful nudge. "I'm just kidding. I might take you up on it, but I'm going to try the newspaper database first. It's free and doesn't require candles."

"We both have our ways of finding information." Jules held up her plastic cup. "But my store has beer, so you tell me whose way is superior."

"Yours is definitely more exciting. I'll give you that."

"I have to get back," said Jules. "When are you going to stop by again?"

"Very soon," said Zo. "I need a refill on my growler. Max Harrington and I had a few glasses the other night."

Jules's brown eyes opened wide. "Ranger Max?"

"Yep." Zo wished she could take a snapshot of Jules's face. It was a mixture of excitement and annoyance.

"You just don't drop a bomb on me like that before I have to leave," said Jules.

Zo chuckled. "It's not a bomb. It was a few beers."

"I expect you in for a tarot card reading—ASAP." Jules tossed her cup in the garbage. "We need to see where this is headed."

Zo promised she would check her schedule before saying good-bye, smiling at Jules as she walked away.

Zo scanned the library. Hattie was at the reference desk. The area, shaped like a triangle, was Hattie's cockpit. Zo imagined her running the entire library from here, pushing keys, scanning cards, answering phones. She was scribbling something on one of those tiny slips of paper only found in a library. Looking up, she stuck her pencil behind one ear. "Are you here for the beer?"

"No—but it was good," said Zo. "I had a taste. I came to find information on a person who lives in Gillette, Wyoming. Do you have the newspaper for that city?"

"Sure, *The Gillette News Record*," said Hattie. She stood and led Zo to the computers. "Is this about the lodge?"

Zo nodded. "One of Beth's guests lives there. I want to see if I can find anything on her. She and Enid had words Saturday night."

Hattie punched a few keys on the keyboard and opened the library portal. "I imagine Enid had words with lots of people. She had the tendency to rub people the wrong way." She found *The Gillette News Record* database. "The nice thing about using this is you won't have to pay for the articles. Otherwise, try LexisNexis."

Zo knew from her work as a journalist that LexisNexis contained all the newspapers in the US. If she struck out in *The Gillette News Record*, she could try a national search. "Thanks, Hattie."

"I'll be right over there if you need me."

Zo sat down at the computer, deciding she'd search for the protest first and money second. She typed in Kaya's name and the word *protest*, and the cursor began to spin. Zo opened the articles, scanning the highlighted text for Kaya's name. After ten minutes of scrolling, she found a mention.

The article reported that one protester, Kaya Cantrell, had been taken to the hospital after she clashed with an opposing demonstrator and had her own knife used against her. Zo kept reading. The protest had to do with a mosque that had recently opened in Wyoming. Though Kaya wasn't Islamic, she was a strong supporter of religious freedom. She was quoted in the article saying that Native American practices had been forbidden; she didn't want to see another group's religious freedom limited.

Zo closed the article. Kaya was passionate enough to fight for someone else's religious freedom. She was likely to fight twice as hard for her own. Enid's comment the night of the chuck wagon was a direct affront to her beliefs, but would Kaya have killed Enid over it? She wasn't afraid to use her knife that night in the bar...

Zo tried a second search using Kaya's name and various combinations of the word *money* but no results returned. LexisNexis might yield something, so she tried that. The database was larger and harder to navigate, and it took a few tries to limit the search to a manageable list. An article appeared from the newspaper in Rapid City; it was a feature story on Kaya and her sorority sisters—Allison, Sarah, and Jennifer—ten years ago. They were promoting their fund-raising event for Parkinson's disease.

Zo remembered they'd all gone to the same college; that's why they'd come to Spirit Canyon Lodge in the first place. She zoomed in on the picture of the girls and their house mom, Sandy Faucher, who suffered from the disease. Arms linked, they looked like a real family. No wonder they'd come back for a reunion. They'd lived together in the same house and were like sisters. The house mom had been with the Greek sorority for twenty-five years.

Zo let out a groan of frustration. She knew Kaya took the money but didn't know why. She knew Enid was murdered but didn't know who was responsible. What was she missing?

She clicked the internet icon. It opened to the library homepage, and she switched to Google and typed *Enid Barrett*. She'd checked out all of the guests. The one person she hadn't looked into, however, was the dead woman herself.

From her backpack, Zo pulled out the visitation program while the search results appeared. The obituary didn't tell her anything she didn't already know. Enid was from Wales—a fact Enid made well known—sixty-five years old, married for forty years, and had one son, Griffin. She'd met her husband, John Barrett, in Denver, Colorado. When they returned to Spirit Canyon, they purchased one hotel, then the second near Lead, and lived happily ever after—or as happily as Enid could manage.

Actually, it did tell her something new. Zo didn't know Enid met her husband in Denver. Why was she in Colorado? The obituary didn't mention college or a degree. Maybe Enid was visiting family when she met her husband. But Zo thought all of Enid's family had returned to Wales when Enid was young. She bragged about her distinguished lineage and going overseas once a year, returning with china, art, and glassware. If family hadn't brought her to Denver, what had?

The internet results didn't say. There were facts on Serenity Hills and Serenity Falls, but nothing personal on Enid Barrett. Zo thought she might find a past grievance, but everything was related to the resort, and the bad reviews didn't mention Enid by name. She was left with one new piece of information: Enid's trip to Denver and her courtship with John Barrett.

Zo could ask Griffin. He might know the story, but he'd been aloof at the visitation. There had to be someone else she could ask. She tapped her stubby pencil on the edge of the keyboard. Two people came to mind: Beth's deceased aunt Lilly and Henry Miller. Lilly knew Enid. Maybe Beth would find something in Lilly's belongings. She and Vi had started to go through them, and Vi promised to check the attic. But in Spirit Canyon, Henry was closer to Enid than anyone else, perhaps even Griffin. It was time to see what else he knew about his boss. She glanced at her watch. It was after five, and she hadn't finished her Curious Camper column. The visit would have to wait until tomorrow.

Driving home, Zo saw the KRSO van in the Happy Camper parking lot and took a sharp turn. What were they doing at the store? The workday was over. Was something wrong? Harley would have called her. Zo checked her phone as she got out of the car. No missed calls. She hurried inside.

"Zo Jones," said Justin. "Just the person we wanted to see."

A.J. was unfolding a camera tripod and lifted his eyes. He mouthed the word, "Sorry."

Zo ignored Justin and went right to Harley, who explained they'd arrived a few minutes ago. She was just dialing Zo's number. Clearly flustered, Harley dropped her phone, and Zo picked it up, telling her not to worry and that she'd done the right thing. Then she turned to Justin. "What's this about?"

Justin smiled his million-dollar smile. Zo was unaffected. He adjusted his approach, taking a miniature recording device out of his designer shirt pocket and smoothing the puckered fabric. Zo supposed this was his professional tactic. "KRSO has recently learned Elizabeth Everett has been charged with possession of stolen property at Spirit Canyon Lodge. As her closest friend in the area—her only friend—did the theft come as a surprise to you? Did you know she was having financial difficulties? And could those difficulties have anything to do with Enid Barrett's death?"

The questions came lightning quick, and Zo found herself wondering what it would feel like to punch out his white teeth one at a time.

He stuck out the recording device. "Ms. Jones?"

"I'm pretty sure this is the place where I say 'No comment,' but you were there that night. You know as well as I do that Beth had nothing to do with Enid's death. And she didn't steal her stupid money."

"Can I quote you on that?" said Justin.

"You want an official quote?" Zo pretended to consider the question. "Okay. Justin Castle spent a lot of time covering one of the guests instead of the grand opening at Spirit Canyon Lodge. How does that work for you? Will *that* make the ten o'clock news?"

Out of the corner of her eye, Zo saw A.J. smirk.

Justin slipped his recorder into his suit jacket. "Pack up, A.J. This is a lost cause." He held out his hand. Zo crossed her arms, so he laughed and turned toward the door. "I'll get the story with or without your help. You can count on it."

George was waiting on the other side of the door and hissed.

"Good boy, George." Zo turned to Harley after Justin and A.J. got into their van. "Can you believe that jerk?"

Harley joined her at the door. "He thinks a lot of himself. He tried his smooth talk on me, and I said I was calling you. His camera guy seemed embarrassed."

"A.J.'s a nice person." She checked her watch. "I need to finish my column for tomorrow. Do you mind closing up? I know you're scheduled to open tomorrow."

"You know I don't," said Harley. She put her hands in the pockets of her overalls. "What's the column about?"

"Nothing yet," muttered Zo. She sighed. "It's on lodging. Spirit Canyon Lodge."

Harley lifted her dark eyebrows. "Unlucky topic."

"I know," said Zo. "This is why I went into business."

Zo left via the front entrance, looking for George, but his miracles must have been limited to one a day. He wasn't anywhere to be seen. Cunningham wasn't outside either. His garden was a quiet patch of tangle.

Once inside her house, she made a chicken salad croissant and a cup of tea and took them with her to her office. She switched on her desk light, remembering the days when the lamp signaled work. Now it signaled hobby. It was amazing how priorities could change with the flick of a light. But she still got a buzz from writing, researching stories, and punching keys. The thrill was irreplaceable.

She munched on her sandwich as she turned on her computer. Then she opened the file and stared at the blinking cursor as she sipped her tea. In a week, everything had changed. Beth was back in her life, her cat was living with her part-time, and business was booming. She highlighted the two paragraphs she had previously written and deleted them. The story needed a new beginning. It also needed a happy ending.

She began to type. *In the heart of Spirit Canyon stands a lodge made of cedar wood...*

Chapter Twenty-Eight

Friday morning set Zo's brain racing. The moment she opened her eyes she was keenly aware today was the last day to *do* something. Kaya, Sarah, Allison, and Jennifer would be checking out of the lodge, and while Allison would remain in the area, the rest of them would disappear.

Zo devised a plan as she showered. She had to get Kaya to admit to stealing the money before she left. Kaya was protective of all of her friends, but especially Sarah because she'd been through so much. If Zo confronted Kaya with the missing stationery, she would say she wrote a lot of letters. Her resolve was steely. But if Zo questioned Sarah, Kaya might admit to her wrongdoing to prevent her friend from enduring any more hardships. Plus, Sarah had found the money and called the police. It would sound natural for Zo to ask her a few more questions.

She glanced at her bicycle wall clock as she stepped out of the shower and towel dried her hair. It was only seven o'clock. She would stop at Serenity Hills before she drove to the lodge. Henry lived at the resort; he was always available. She could ask him about Enid's trip to Denver, which had been bothering her since her stop at the library. Henry wouldn't think twice about her showing up again. She would tell him she was writing about lodges in the area and mentioning Serenity Hills in her column.

After throwing on a sweatshirt and jean shorts, she ate a quick bowl of granola and took her coffee to-go. She hardly noticed the dark clouds when she shoved her Subaru into reverse and started toward Serenity Hills. It took a flash of lightning for her to realize a storm was on its way. Leaving the downtown area, she saw another flash: police lights. She pulled over to allow the trooper to pass and realized the lights were for her. Dang. It was Brady Merrigan. She could tell by the way he sidled up to her window. They were on opposite sides of most everything, which now included her window.

"Ms. Jones, I always knew I'd catch you speeding, but I thought it would be on that red motorcycle of yours." He rocked back on his boot heels. "Some things never change."

"How fast was I going?" Zo kept her hands on the wheel. It prevented her from forming a fist.

"Thirty-eight in a thirty—that's eight miles per hour over the speed limit."

"I can do basic math, thanks." She handed him her license and registration. "Just give me the ticket, and I'll be on my way."

"Where are you going in such a hurry?" asked Brady.

Zo guessed he wasn't anxious to let her leave. "Serenity Hills. My column this week is about places to stay in the area."

"It's too bad about Spirit Canyon Lodge." Brady typed up her information on his tablet. "I've always liked that hotel. Maybe someone will buy it out. My brother's always on the lookout for new properties." He glanced up from the e-ticket. "I don't have to tell you that."

Don't take the bait, thought Zo. "I'm well aware of the Merrigans' business pursuits, but I wouldn't discount Beth just yet. She's a savvy businesswoman herself. She'll figure out a way to keep the lodge. It's a piece of her history."

He tore the paper from the machine. "For her sake, I hope she does." He touched his hat. "Watch your speeding, young lady."

She bit her lip until he returned to his car, glancing down at the ticket after he was gone. A hundred dollars! She crumpled the paper and shoved it into the cup holder. It took all her restraint not to speed away. That didn't mean she couldn't curse Brady Merrigan as loud as she wanted to for the next ten minutes, and she did just that. When she was done and had arrived at Serenity Hills, she took out the ticket and smoothed it over her knee. Excessive or not, the stupid fine would have to be paid.

The tinkling spa music wasn't as soothing as it had been days ago, and unthinkingly, Zo let the door slam behind her. Two guests in the lobby looked up from their morning tea, startled. It was still early. She smoothed her hair and took a breath. "Oops," she said, smiling at the guests. "Sorry about that."

Henry was at the front desk on a phone call. He held up a finger, indicating it would be a minute. She nodded, pausing at the tea display, noting all the varieties of black, green, and herbal teas. She was always on the lookout for new flavors.

"Hey Zo."

Zo was surprised to see A.J. at her elbow. His camera work must've made him good at blending into his surroundings. "Hi. I didn't know you stayed here."

He adjusted his baseball cap, the same gray one she'd seen him wear many times. It made a shadow on his fair skin. "Sometimes. I was outside, replacing a propane tank."

"It's a big place." Zo glanced around the room. Another guest came downstairs for coffee. "Your dad must appreciate the help."

A pitcher filled with ice, water, and lemons sat next to the tea for those guests who wanted a cold refreshment. A.J. poured himself a glass. "He's a much better handyman than I am, but he's getting older. It's getting harder for him to do heavy lifting—just don't tell him that."

Zo smiled. A.J. was a good son.

"I try to drop in once a week," he continued.

"It's not a bad place to spend time."

"The rooms are posh, for sure." He downed the water in one long swallow.

"I'm surprised Enid went for that, you spending the night at the resort. She wasn't the most hospitable person I'd ever met."

"She didn't even know," said A.J. "It's not like she lived here. She had her own castle up on snob hill."

That was true. Henry managed the resort. Enid's only reason for coming would be to check up on the property. And A.J. wasn't the kind of guy to make waves. Like he said, she probably didn't notice.

A.J. glanced at his dad, who was motioning her over. He was off the phone. "Are you here to talk to Dad?"

"My column this week is on lodging," said Zo. "I'm turning it in today."

"Put in a good word for him, will you?" whispered A.J. "He needs all the good press he can get. Bird's Eye Reviews flayed the resort last fall."

"I heard," Zo said. "Were you here for that?"

He nodded. "Looking back, it makes sense. Robyn's so...haughty. Nothing or no one could be good enough for her—except Griffin Barrett. They're a perfect match."

It was an interesting comment, one Zo didn't disagree with. "Do you know her?"

He nodded again. "She was at the chuck wagon. Remember? I talked to her that night."

Henry called out, and she stepped toward the reception desk. "Right. I'd better go. Your dad is waiting, and I need to get my column in."

"I need to leave for the station." He took a step and stopped. "By the way, I'm sorry about Justin barging into Happy Camper last night. It was a ridiculous attempt to rattle you."

She shrugged. "It's not your fault."

"It's like he's obsessed with this story," said A.J. "He's thinking about running another feature on the lodge—this one not so favorable. He wants to go over what we have from the night of Enid's death."

"*Great*," Zo muttered. "Just what Beth needs."

The smattering of freckles on his cheeks darkened as his cheeks flushed. "I I…" he stuttered. "I'm worried he's going to find out I gave Beth a copy of the video," he continued in a rush. "I know I'm being a chicken, but I checked, and it's against station policy. I need my job. Do you still have the jump drive? I haven't cashed the check."

Zo felt bad for him. It was a difficult question to ask. She also felt bad for Beth because she wouldn't be able to use the material. Zo had watched the footage, and it was gorgeous. But she hurried to reassure A.J. it was fine. "I understand completely, and so will Beth. I'll update her on the situation and stop by with it later—right after I get my column turned in."

A.J. looked relieved. "Thanks a lot." He waved to his dad. "I'll see you then."

"Good-bye, son," said Henry as Zo approached the front desk. "That is a hard worker, right there."

"He must take after his dad," said Zo.

Henry smiled. To be a hard worker in this part of the world was the greatest compliment of all.

"I didn't expect to see you again," said Henry. "Everything okay?"

"Yes, fine," said Zo. "My Curious Camper column is on lodging this week. I was wondering if I could ask a few questions about the resort and Enid."

Henry smiled, and Zo noticed the gray hair at his temples. It seemed as if he'd like nothing better than to spend time recalling memories of his former boss. He was the perfect gentleman. If he had objections, he wouldn't voice them.

"Not at all." He motioned to the alcove by the window, and she followed him, taking a seat on the flowered settee. Henry had a way of making her feel at ease. She bet he made guests feel the same way. She liked the way he didn't rush.

"I know Enid's family lives in Wales, but the program at the visitation said she met her husband in Denver," said Zo. "Why was she in Colorado? Did it have anything to do with buying the resort?"

Henry looked thoughtful. "Her family moved back to Wales when Enid was seventeen, but I believe she had a relative in Denver. Yes, an aunt."

"So, she must have met her husband, John, while visiting her aunt," said Zo. "Was she close to her?"

"I don't believe so."

Zo's face must have given away her confusion because Henry quickly added, "What I meant to say is they must not have stayed close because I never heard Enid talk about her."

"John was older than Enid?"

He folded his hands across his lap. "Quite a bit older and very wealthy. Her family approved of the match, of course, so they married."

"What about the sixties and women's rights?" said Zo. "Didn't she have a say?"

"I like your spirit, Zo," said Henry, a smile crossing his face. "But things were different for Enid. She had to protect her family name."

"What do you mean 'protect'? Was she in trouble?"

He crossed his arms. "Are you sure you're not still writing for the *Star*?"

Zo leaned back in her chair and smiled. She was coming on too strong. "I guess I still have the bad habit of getting caught up in a story."

"It's not a bad habit as far as I'm concerned," he said. "Did A.J. tell you he's writing a novel? My son is so talented."

"He did." Zo stood and so did Henry. "A science fiction book. I bet it'll be great."

"Do you have any other questions for the column?"

Zo shook her head. She didn't want to admit she had the article written already. "I've taken up enough of your time, and I need to get out to Spirit Canyon Lodge."

"If you need anything else, you might ask Griffin. I'm sure he'd be a better resource for you. I'm just a forgetful old man."

"No way," Zo said. "You've been a great help. Thank you."

As she walked to her car, though, she decided Henry had a point. Griffin would know how his parents met, wouldn't he? She jumped into her Subaru and started the engine. *Shoot.* A.J.'s jump drive was in her cup holder. She'd forgotten she'd put it in her car to take to Beth. She could have given it to A.J. then and there. She shoved it into her backpack. It was yet another thing on her to-do list, and she was running out of time. Beth's guests were checking out today.

She'd never been to Griffin's house but guessed it was up on "snob hill," as A.J. had called it. She verified the address with a quick internet search, but no phone number was listed. Few people had landlines these days. The house was five miles away.

Her car zigzagged deeper and deeper into the forest until she reached Eagle's Nest, a development that afforded residents several acres of prime location. Griffin's house wasn't as large as some of the others. One of the first homes on the hill, it was a small A-frame with green shingles and shutters. She was relieved to see a black Jeep in the drive. Of course it was still early. Why wouldn't he be home?

Up close, the house needed more work than she suspected. It needed to be restained, and the landscaping needed weeding. *Crazy*, she thought as she approached the front. *Having a house like this and not bothering to pull the weeds.* Maybe Enid had been right; maybe Griffin was a bum who took her money for granted.

"What a surprise," said Griffin after he opened the door. He stood in the entrance in lounge pants, holding a cup of coffee. He didn't bother to move or ask her if she'd like to come in.

"Hey Griffin," said Zo. "I hate to bother you, but I couldn't find your phone number and was wondering if I could get a quote for my Curious Camper column." She smiled. "Would you mind?"

"No, of course." He hesitated then moved aside. "Come in. Robyn and I were just having coffee. Do you want a cup?"

"No." Zo took out her notebook. "I'll just be a minute, but thank you. Hi Robyn."

"Hey Zo." Robyn sat on an expensive leather couch that went well with the masculine décor.

Zo avoided looking at the taxidermy on the walls. Though it was popular in the West, she hated seeing animals used for decoration. The glass eyes always gave her the creeps.

"Dead animals are so homey, right?" said Robyn with a laugh. "Believe me, this is all going to change when we get married."

Zo smiled. "I don't blame you."

Griffin sat down on the couch next to Robyn. He motioned for Zo to join them, so she took the nearby chair. "Zo needs a quote for her column... What do you call it?"

She could tell by the tone of his voice that he thought it was silly. What she thought was silly was she'd *just* told him the name. "Curious Camper."

"I didn't know you were a writer," said Robyn.

"Oh, I'm not." Zo held up one hand. "I own the Happy Camper store, so I was a natural fit for writing the column. Plus, I used to work at the *Star*."

Robyn tilted her head. "Is it a weekly column?"

Zo nodded.

"That takes work—and talent," said Robyn. "I'm going to have to check it out."

Griffin squeezed her knee. "It's not like *your* column."

"It's a great idea," said Robyn, ignoring Griffin. "I bet locals love it. So, you're writing an article about Serenity Falls?"

Zo didn't want to admit that the column was mainly about Spirit Canyon Lodge, so she avoided answering the question. She opened her notebook instead. "I started writing my column before Enid's death, and now that she's gone, I need something different. Maybe we could focus on the future. You could tell me about your plans for the resorts."

"One word: expansion," said Griffin. "We're dropping the old B&B model and focusing on the spa experience at Serenity Falls, out near Lead." Griffin nodded to Robyn. "She's an expert on what's in vogue in the tourism industry. There's a whole new generation to appeal to."

"I get it." Zo scribbled in her notebook. "You're leaving the past behind and focusing on younger clientele."

"Mom would have agreed, you know," said Griffin. He was a bit defensive. "That's why she gave Serenity Hills to the old innkeeper. It was worthless. Her main focus was Serenity Falls after the—"

Bad review came out. Zo finished the sentence in her head, but Griffin tried to dodge the awkward moment.

"More coffee, hon?" He stood and picked up Robyn's cup. He scooted into the kitchen.

Robyn nodded in his direction and murmured, "Not the smoothest operator, but I love him anyway." She shrugged. "Maybe that's *why* I love him. He's so...vulnerable. I think it's sexy."

"You know who he reminds me of?" said Zo. "A.J. Miller. He can be shy like that."

"You're right," said Robyn. "He can."

A new thought occurred to Zo. "You probably met A.J. during your stay at Serenity Hills."

"I did," said Robyn. "He was the only good experience I had. Too bad I couldn't put *that* in the review."

Zo forced herself to blink. She never expected Robyn to come out with the information so directly. Then again, she was outspoken—and incredibly blunt.

"I'm only telling you because you're not a prude and you're pretty smart." She crossed her legs. "You had to have seen my reaction when I saw him at the lodge."

"I thought there was something…besides being on TV."

"*Was* something," said Robyn. "Not anymore. I'm engaged now. At the time, Griffin and I'd just started dating. It wasn't serious. And A.J. was so persuasive." Robyn seemed to be remembering the encounter. "It's always the quiet ones that surprise you."

"Did Enid know—"

"Heck no," Robyn replied. "Can you imagine? She was ancient, just like her resort. Having that old innkeeper catch me leaving A.J.'s room was horrifying enough. He blushed and everything." She leaned in closer. "Then again, I *was* in my undies."

Griffin returned with her coffee, and Robyn took a dainty sip.

Zo glanced at her notes. She needed to get to the question she came here to ask. "Your name, Griffin. That's Welsh. Do you have any family in the US? The program at the visitation said your parents met in Denver."

"No," said Griffin. "I had an aunt who lived in Denver. Mom talked about her sometimes. She didn't care for her much, though. We never met."

"They weren't close?"

Griffin looked at her as if she were deaf. "Not at all."

But Zo knew she wasn't deaf, dumb, or crazy. She also knew Enid wouldn't go all the way to Denver to visit an aunt she disliked for no reason. But what that reason was, she couldn't say. Neither could Griffin. She stood. "Thanks again for your time. I know it's been a difficult week, and I hated to drop by unannounced. Let me know if you need anything at all."

They stood and walked to the door.

"We will," said Robyn. "Thanks for coming."

As Zo drove back down the curvy hill, she realized two things: one, Enid knew about Robyn and A.J.'s one-nighter. She and Henry were close, and he would have told her. Two, Robyn hadn't made the connection between the encounter and Enid's comments at the lodge, which meant Robyn didn't poison Enid to keep her quiet about the affair. Besides, she wasn't that quiet about it herself. Maybe her relationship with Griffin had been as new as she claimed. Maybe they weren't seeing each other on a regular basis. What still puzzled Zo was A.J.'s involvement in the affair. He didn't seem like the type to have a one-night-stand, and he hadn't mentioned their relationship. Quiet, shy, and bookish, he seemed the consummate introvert. It was probably just like Robyn said: it was always the quiet ones that surprised you.

Chapter Twenty-Nine

As Zo drove away from Eagle's Nest, her phone rang over her car speakers, and she pressed the Accept button on her dash. It was Beth, and she was giddy. She needed to show Zo something right away. Zo said she was already on her way and stepped on the gas, hoping Brady Merrigan wasn't hiding somewhere, clocking her speed.

Driving through the canyon was as close as she felt to Spirit Canyon. Not particularly kind or even hospitable, the land had spirit and that spirit was in Zo. It gave her a sense of confidence. She knew she would discover the secret behind Enid's death one way or the other, maybe even today.

Beth had a funny look on her face when Zo walked into the lodge. Holding a piece of paper, Beth no longer looked like an organized event planner. In fact, she reminded Zo of the young girl she knew as a kid— flushed, giddy, and a bit of a schemer. It was great having her back.

"You've found something," said Zo.

"After you left, Mom and I went through Lilly's hope chest," Beth said. "Lilly was an avid letter writer, so we started with her papers."

They walked over to the couch near the fireplace, where a log was just beginning to crackle. After they sat down, Beth handed Zo the piece of paper. "I think it's something important."

Zo scanned it quickly. "It's a letter from Enid to Lilly."

"Read it."

The type was cursive and had a heavy slant. Pretentious, just like Enid. It took a few minutes to decipher. When Zo got to the end, she read the last words out loud: "*I know you want to help, but I need to deal with this in my own way. I wish you understood.*" She looked up at Beth. "This is signed *E. Williams*—the nickname your mom mentioned. It was written before she was married because of the maiden name."

"It sounds like they were friends back then," added Beth. "Whatever happened changed their relationship for good. The night of the chuck wagon, Enid definitely didn't act like a friend."

Zo leaned back into the soft cushion. "The letter is vague. It doesn't say what she needed to deal with."

"*Too vague*," said Beth. "As if she doesn't want to put the secret down on paper."

"True." Zo considered why. When Enid came back from Denver, she was married and had a child shortly thereafter. Maybe she was already pregnant? Maybe it was a shotgun wedding? She told Beth her theory.

"It could be," said Beth. "Griffin is around forty, right?"

Zo turned over the letter. "Right, but there's no date on this. Was it in an envelope?"

"It's in the hope chest in the attic," said Beth. "Come on."

Zo stood. She wasn't sure what this had to do with Enid's death, but some connection had to exist; she just had to figure out what it was. Secrets had a way of finding their way to the surface sooner or later. The problem Enid had to deal with in the past might have become a problem in the future, a problem that incited her murder.

"Good morning, Vi," said Zo as they passed the reception desk.

Vi forewent a greeting. "We're down two reservations. Word's getting out about that old devil's death on social media. Thirty-five comments about it on Facebook alone!"

"*Mom*," said Beth.

Vi lifted her reading glasses, placing them on her forehead. "She's driving away business, and I can't call her an old devil? Humph."

Beth kept walking to the stairs, and Zo followed. When Beth got to the end of the hallway on the second floor, she quietly pulled down the ladder that led to the attic. The guests were still getting ready, and Zo wanted to keep it that way. She needed to confront them about the theft before they checked out, but she was too excited about the new information to wait around.

As she climbed the rickety ladder, memories washed over her in miniature waves: the dormer windows, the old wooden rocking chair, the faint smell of lilacs. "Lilacs," Zo said out loud.

Beth turned back and smiled. "Lilly's sachets." She motioned to the trunk in the corner. "It's over here."

Beth slipped in a key and opened the lid. A waft of cedar greeted Zo. All of Lilly's most personal possessions were in here: her marriage license, the blueprint for the lodge, a photo album filled with pictures of Beth.

Beth opened the album. "She even kept a lock of my hair."

"It's like you were her own child," said Zo.

"You don't even want to know what my mom said when we found it."

Beth took a stack of papers, looking for the envelope, and Zo glanced through the chest. They were personal mementos, so she was very careful about what she picked up or took out. Underneath a family bible she found a pair of baby booties—blue and beautifully crocheted. She held them up for Beth to see. "Look at these. Why would Lilly have baby booties?"

Beth shook her head. "I don't know. She did crochet, though."

Zo sat back on her legs, turning them over in her hands.

"Here it is!" said Beth. She squinted at the postmark on the envelope then counted the years on her fingers. "Forty-five years. The letter was sent forty-five years ago."

Zo thought through the timeline out loud. "So, if we're assuming the problem she mentioned in the letter was an unexpected pregnancy, this would make sense. The obituary said Enid was married for forty years. This was written forty-five years ago. That would mean Enid wasn't married when she got pregnant. The trip to Denver might have been a way to hide the pregnancy."

Beth scrunched up her nose. "Griffin doesn't seem that old."

"Maybe it's his mod clothes..." But that didn't exactly explain it. Something niggled at the back of Zo's mind, a memory. She shrugged it off and focused on what they did know. They were running out of time. "So, what about these?" She held up the booties. "Do you think Lilly thought Enid might give her the baby, Griffin? Maybe that's what the letter meant by *help*."

"And they are blue," said Beth.

A bell went off. "Blue, like Vi's dreams."

Beth hastily shut the lid, and they hurried downstairs. Zo wanted to explain the connection to Vi. It was just as Zo thought: Lilly *was* trying to help them solve the murder and keep Beth out of jail. The color blue symbolized Enid's baby boy.

Vi was on her cell phone, posting a picture to social media when they joined her at the front desk. Complete with a cool filter, it showcased the Memorial Day barbeque.

"Instagram, too, Mom? Do you really think that's necessary?" Beth asked, peering over her shoulder.

"Absolutely," said Vi. "It's the only way young people communicate."

Beth squinted. "I don't know if we're trying to attract *that* young of people."

"Of course you are," Vi insisted. "You don't want another guest dying, do you?"

Zo bit her lip to keep from smiling. She decided now was the perfect time to change the subject. She held up the blue baby booties. "Look what we found in the attic. The problem Enid wrote about had to have been an unexpected pregnancy. Lilly must have thought she would adopt Griffin. It would explain your dreams and the color blue."

"I don't go in for all that spirit mumbo jumbo, but I'll admit Lilly was a complicated person," said Vi. "If she wanted to communicate—which would be a first—she'd send smoke signals like these."

Zo didn't dispute it. Lilly had been a complex person. She had also been a careful person, especially when it came to her loved ones. "What I really want to know is how this information helps us with Enid's death. Is Lilly saying Griffin is the murderer?"

The words hung in the air unchallenged. All clues pointed toward Griffin. He'd argued with Enid, he'd found her the morning after, and he had the most to gain from her death. He must be the killer.

A door opened upstairs, and Zo glanced at Beth and Vi. "We've solved one mystery. I'm going to try to make it two. Do you have the continental breakfast laid out?"

Beth nodded.

"Let's wait in there," said Zo.

As Beth and Zo walked to the dining area, Vi hollered she had twenty-two likes already. Zo laughed. Vi would have business booming again in no time.

Zo picked up a chocolate chip muffin, poured herself a mug of coffee from the caffeinated carafe and sat down at a table near the window. She glanced out at the canyon. *If there were ever a time she needed a spirit, it was now.*

"Here they come," whispered Beth as she joined her with a croissant.

Kaya, Sarah, Jennifer, and Allison walked into the dining area still smelling like shampoo. They formed a single-file line near the coffee carafes, looking slightly glum. Zo wondered if it would be hard for the longtime friends to exchange good-byes. They looked closer than ever. Their strong bond had been renewed during their weeklong stay.

"Good morning," said Beth. "I hope you slept well."

"Like the dead," said Jennifer, sitting down in a chair next to their table. Allison gave her a look as she joined her. "Sorry. Was that inappropriate?"

Kaya and Sarah joined them. "Just a bit," said Kaya. Her leather jacket squeaked as she sat down. "But that's why we love you."

"What time are your flights?" asked Beth.

"Not until late this afternoon," said Kaya. "Allison's giving us a tour of Homestake Mine before we leave. I've always wanted to see that place."

"Before you go, I think you should know the police are fingerprinting the money," said Zo. Sarah's eyes grew as wide as her plate. "They're zeroing in on the thief."

Allison cleared her throat. "I'm sure you must be worried, then." She directed her statement at Beth.

Zo kept her cool. They might be protecting each other, but she was protecting someone too: Beth. "They'll be able to match up means with motive, and everyone knows at least one of you needed the money."

"I think it's time to take our breakfasts to-go," said Kaya. Her voice was as dark as her leather jacket.

"They're also fingerprinting the stationery that was found in the original envelope," said Zo. "Someone's missing an awful lot of paper from their hotel room notepad."

The room was silent for a moment. Jennifer dropped her head and moaned into her folded arms.

"We know it was your stationery," Zo said to Kaya. "And the police do, too."

Sarah sat up straighter in her chair. "I'll take the blame. I've got a clean record. The police will be more understanding of me."

This was a surprise. Zo thought the admission would be the other way around.

"No!" said Kaya. "It was my stationery, and the cops will know it when the test results come back."

"Sarah's right," said Allison. "The prosecutor will treat her more sympathetically. She's a mom with a sick child who needs her at home."

Jennifer lifted her head. "Just shut up. We all did it. We all stole the money."

Again the room went quiet. Zo decided it was the sound of the truth coming to the surface. "But why?"

Jennifer crisscrossed her legs, her sweatpants stretching tightly over her knees. "Our sorority mom is being evicted from her apartment. She owes thousands of dollars in back rent because her Parkinson's disease takes all her money."

"Jen..." said Allison.

"What?" said Jennifer. "They're going to find out anyway. They might as well know it was for a good cause."

Zo remembered the picture of them with Sandy. Now living alone as a senior, she couldn't make ends meet. Her prescriptions must have cost as much or more than her rent. Their hearts were in the right place. "How did you do it?" asked Zo. It made more sense now that she knew it was a coordinated effort.

"I saw the money when Enid checked in," said Allison. "I helped her with her door—it was jammed. I told the group."

"I stole the money when Enid went downstairs," said Jennifer. "Snoopy old bird."

"I filled the envelope with paper," Kaya put in.

"And I put it back when we found out Enid's death was being considered a murder," said Sarah. "I didn't know Beth would be arrested. I swear I didn't. That's why we put it in the closet, a neutral location."

"Sorry, Beth." Jennifer offered a contrite look. "I guess you hate us."

"I don't," said Beth. "I would do the same thing for my mom."

"You did the right thing by telling us," said Zo. "Thank you."

"So, what now?" said Sarah.

"I'll call my friend Max." Zo paused for a moment, realizing she'd called him her friend. That was a surprise. "He's a forest ranger and a lot nicer than Brady Merrigan. He could help you get this sorted out."

Sarah looked at Kaya. "And all of us will admit to the crime."

"Agreed," said Allison. "Jennifer?"

"I've heard jail time can do wonders for your waistline," said Jennifer.

"None of us is going to jail," said Kaya. "We returned the money, and I know a good defense lawyer. He'll get us off."

Zo glanced at the cuckoo clock on the wall. She still needed to drop off her column at *Canyon Views*. Though she'd sent it via email last night, her editor also asked for a hard copy because of ongoing network problems at the office. If she didn't get her article in by noon, the column wouldn't print, and any publicity Beth might receive would be put off another week. Plus, her editor didn't tolerate missed deadlines. She'd fire her on the spot.

"I have somewhere to be in town," Zo said. "I can call Max on the way."

"Let us spend our last morning together, okay?" said Allison. "Beth can call him before we check out."

Beth nodded. "Okay."

Zo stood to leave. The group had done the right thing. They'd admitted to the theft. It'd be nice if doing the right thing were enough.

Chapter Thirty

Canyon News was housed in a squat building a few blocks from Main Street. Built in the 1970s, the newsroom had a false ceiling, half a dozen cubicles, and a large wooden desk that belonged to her editor, Harriet B. Hobbs. Hobbs did it all. She wrote; she edited. In essence, she *was* the newspaper. A stout woman with smooth brown skin, Harriet was smart, and it showed. Her eyes were sharp, like a hawk's, and she had no patience for slackers. Everyone under the age of fifty was a slacker, according to her. She, herself, was exactly fifty. Her short hair was brown but thinning early at the temples, and she wore dark eyeliner that accentuated her eyes. Today her gaze was fierce as Zo rushed up to her desk with the column.

"Hey, Harriet. It's my column," said Zo.

Harriet looked at her watch, a men's Timex with three time zones on its face.

"Of course, you know that," added Zo.

Harriet scanned the typed paper in a matter of seconds. She took out a red pen from behind her ear and scratched two lines under a word. "Hemingway. One M. Don't assume you know how to spell things; look them up."

"Sorry." Zo winced. The error physically hurt. She'd written that Hemingway would have appreciated the creek behind Spirit Canyon Lodge. It was filled with rainbow trout.

"The attachment?"

"Sent last night," Zo confirmed.

Harriet pushed back her chair. The formal inquisition was over. "I saw you on the news last night—and heard your quote: 'She didn't steal the stupid money.'"

"Really? I didn't see it."

"Yep. Ten o'clock." She took out a fresh pack of cinnamon gum and popped a piece in her mouth. She'd quit smoking a few years ago and chewed Big Red gum like it was the last pack in town. "If Beth didn't kill Enid, who did?"

Zo leaned in. "I think it was Griffin."

Harriet tossed her wrapper in the trash. "Griffin is a big mama's boy."

Zo took a breath. "You sound like Brady Merrigan."

"Tell me why you think Griffin did it then."

Zo relayed the information in the letter and her idea of a shotgun wedding. Griffin had to have been unplanned. It explained the clues Aunt Lilly was leaving Vi. Plus, Griffin had strong motives: money and freedom.

"So, a ghost told you?" Harriet said with a smile. "Hardly a reliable source."

Zo crossed her arms.

"It's easy enough to find out. We can get Griffin's birth record." Harriet stood from her desk and walked over to a young man who was shutting down his computer for lunch. He stopped when he saw her approaching. He clicked and typed for a few minutes before Harriet called Zo over. She pointed to the computer. "I told you. Griffin isn't your man."

Zo squinted at the screen. According to the record, Griffin had been born in Spirit Canyon thirty-nine years ago. *That's right.* He'd told his mother he was *almost* forty years old and could make his own decisions. He was nowhere near Denver, Colorado, forty-five years ago.

"Sorry, Zo," said Harriet. "It looks like you have some work left to do."

"Don't I know it," mumbled Zo as she left the office. Outside, it was beginning to rain. Large round drops plopped from the sky. *Perfect.* She didn't have her umbrella, so she kept her head down, practically running into A.J. on the side street. Dressed in a hoodie to protect his face, he was taking long strides to get out of the rain.

"Sorry!"

"I'm so glad you remembered," said A.J. "Come in before you get soaked."

The truth was she'd forgotten all about the jump drive but luckily had her backpack with her. She didn't really feel like going into KRSO, where she could run into Justin Castle, who might want another quote or try to get her on camera. But she might as well get it over with. At least it would get A.J. out of a jam.

A.J. sidestepped a group of tourists. "How's Beth? I saw the station in Rapid City ran a story on Enid's funeral. It mentioned the lodge. Tough break."

"I know," she said. "She's had a few cancelations."

He stopped in front of the door to KRSO. The building was a classic on historical Main Street, complete with arched windows and tin ceilings.

But inside, it was a collection of separated rooms. "I've got a few pictures of my own from the chuck wagon. Would they help?"

"Thanks. Anything might help at this point." Zo stepped inside the small front office, where the receptionist was gathering her purse for lunch. Zo wished she were going for lunch. A big piece of lasagna from Lotsa Pasta sounded perfect right now. She imagined taking a bite of warm garlic bread. Heaven.

A.J. pointed out the studio and the control room, with its thick glass walls, as they passed. One controller pushed buttons, another turned a script, and someone else typed in the text on the bottom of the screen. Zo didn't realize it took so many people to produce the noonday program.

"Pretty cool, huh?" said A.J.

"It is. Do you ever work in there?"

A.J. shook his head and kept walking. "I work on feature pieces mostly. I'm back here."

They walked to a room with no windows and lots of cords and equipment. Zo thought it looked more like a supply room than an office. But there was a desk with a computer and a file cabinet. A.J. sat down and unlocked the computer with his password. He opened up a folder and pulled up a photo of the lodge from the rear. He clicked the right arrow so she could see them all.

"Look at that one of the creek," said Zo. "Gorgeous."

"Thanks," he said. "You want me to email them to you?"

"Could you send them to Beth?"

"Sure. What's her email address?"

Zo gave him the information, and he started compiling the pictures as attachments. He didn't want Beth's email server to reject them because of the size, so he sent them in batches.

It took a few minutes, and Zo glanced around the room as she waited. Anything to distract her growling stomach. On the corner of a bookshelf she noticed a nameplate: Aeron James Miller. An interesting spelling for sure. Something tugged at the back of her mind, another name. Then she remembered it was *Griffin*. It was Welsh, like Enid's name.

A.J. saw her looking at the nameplate. "All finished."

"Thank you so much." Zo turned to leave.

"Wait, what about the drive? I need that back."

Zo opened her backpack and glanced through it. She knew she needed to get out of the room, but she didn't know why. Not at first. She was simply stalling for time—and words. She couldn't think of a thing to say to get her out of the office. "It's not in my backpack. I must have left it in my car. I'll go get it."

"I'll come with you," he said. "I was on my way to lunch."

As he followed, she could hear him breathing. He was that close. She searched for a way to create some distance between them, but her mind was busy grappling with the new information. Spirit Canyon was a small town. If A.J. was Welsh, as the spelling of his first name suggested, he had to be connected to Enid and Griffin. But how? And why was he so desperate to retrieve the jump drive? Something important must be on the video, something he didn't want her to see. She thought back to the footage of the lodge: the great room, the staircase, the guest rooms.

Suddenly it clicked, and she quickened her pace. When she got to her car she would gun it, leaving him standing at the curb. Then she would go straight to the police with the drive. Beth needed Max at Spirit Canyon Lodge. Brady would have to do.

The rain was falling in sheets now, and she was soaked by the time she got to her car.

A.J. surprised her by getting in the passenger's door. "You don't mind, do you? It's really coming down out there."

She shook her head but no words came to her lips. Instead she glanced through the cup holders and middle console, but of course the jump drive wasn't there. It was in her backpack; it had been there all along. The video was the evidence she needed to clear Beth, and she wasn't about to give it back now. A.J. had access to the rooms the night of the murder. In fact, he was the *only* one in the house while everyone else walked to the chuck wagon. That must have been when he tainted Enid's water.

"Drop the act, Zo," A.J. said as he pulled a handgun from the front pocket of his hoodie. "I knew this was a pretense to get out of my office. You know why I want the drive back, don't you?"

"I have no idea what you're talking about," said Zo. She couldn't take her eyes off the shiny black pistol. It was pointed right at her stomach. "I don't know why you have a gun pointed at me."

"You're a smart woman. You don't do very well playing dumb." He wiggled the gun. "Drive."

She started the engine. "Where?"

"Head to the Homestake Mine."

She turned down Main Street, thankful that the mine was several miles away. It would give her time to come up with an idea. If he were going to shoot her, he would have done it already. He must have a reason for taking her to the mine. "Why the mine?"

"It's a big crater in the middle of the earth," said A.J. "It's an easy place to kill someone. And if Allison killed once, she might kill again, right?"

"You must think so," said Zo. "That's why you planted the digoxin in her dresser drawer. You wanted to make it look like she murdered Enid."

"See, you *are* smart. Allison's not quite as smart as she thinks—or maybe she's just lonely. She fell hook, line, and sinker for my act. I had to get into her bedroom somehow. All I had to do was quote Jules Verne, and I was in." He shrugged. "It's really not my fault. If it hadn't been for the storm, I would have left after the chuck wagon and been miles away from the murder. But since Justin made us stay overnight, I needed a fall guy." He huffed. "Damn Justin."

"And what about Robyn?" Zo asked. The rain was pummeling her windshield, and she turned her wipers on high. "Is that how you seduced her? With quotes from writers?"

"There was no need to seduce Robyn," said A.J. "She was more than willing to go to bed with me. She didn't ask any questions."

Zo turned onto the highway. "That's because she never dreamed you were Griffin's half brother. You slept with her to get revenge on him, just like you got revenge on your mother."

A.J. remained silent.

"Enid *was* your mother, wasn't she?" asked Zo. "Your name is Welsh, just like hers and Griffin's."

"Speed it up, or I'll shoot you right here."

She didn't recognize the new aggressiveness in his voice, and she feared for her life. Automatically, she pressed down the gas pedal. A minute later, she slowly let it up. "You killed her to get back at her for leaving you and your dad forty-five years ago and starting a new family."

A.J. released a shaky breath, and Zo wondered if he was questioning himself. She decided to try empathizing with him. Maybe he would be more hesitant to kill someone he saw as an ally. "Believe me, I get it. Some days, I'd like to kill the person who left me at the police station. Being alone, fighting for every little thing I got." She shrugged, trying to appear casual. "It's a miserable way to grow up. But I overcame it. You can, too."

"Don't you get it?" said A.J. "I wasn't abandoned just once. I was abandoned again and again. For forty-five years she wanted nothing to do with me. It never ended, so I ended it."

"But your *dad* wanted you," said Zo, her voice pleading. "He must have begged Enid to let him take care of you. She agreed, but she couldn't stay away from your dad completely. She allowed him to manage Serenity Hills so that she could stay close to him—maybe even you."

"No! She didn't care about us," said A.J. The car was quiet, only the patter of rain hitting the roof. "All she was interested in was her new family, her *legitimate* son."

"Things were different then," said Zo. "Unexpected pregnancies are handled with more sympathy now."

"And what about my dad?" A.J. demanded. "He deserved *something* in return for taking care of me all those years, and I knew the old hag promised him the lodge. He deserved his own life. Now he's free, and so am I."

Zo took the exit for the mine. The road was desolate because of the bad weather. She curved around the mountain without seeing a single car. "If you're free, why am I here?"

"Because you know too much." He shook his head. "My dad can never find out. It would kill him."

"You're a good son, A.J. Don't do this."

"It's too late," he said. "Pull over right here."

The mine was a huge hole, eight thousand feet deep, looming before her like a rocky chasm of death. She hated heights. She always had. She couldn't imagine a worse way to die. *If there were a fence*, she thought to herself, *I might have a chance*. But they were a ways from the visitor center; yelling wouldn't help. She racked her brain for a plan. All she could think about was falling into the gigantic crater before her in the cold rain. There had to be something she could do.

She gazed at the Black Hills, which had been home all her life. Dark and beautiful, they'd made her who she was today: independent, resilient, and strong. Strong. Like the trees, like the earth, like the wind. She'd survived a dozen foster homes. She'd survive this. She had to.

"Get out," he said.

A thought came to her. "What about the jump drive? You don't want to leave evidence behind. You broke into my house to get it. It was you, wasn't it? You realized you'd given me footage of your whereabouts the night of Enid's murder."

"You're right." Blinking, he seemed happy she reminded him. "Give me your backpack."

Slowly, she reached into the backseat, grabbing the sack. A.J. didn't realize how much stuff she carried around in the bag, but she did. It was the reason she didn't carry a regular purse.

Instead of handing it to him, she threw it at his face, temporarily disarming him. She heard him swear as she burst out the door. Then he was running after her, his long legs closing the distance.

Zo ran up the hill toward the visitor center because she didn't know where else to go. The grass was slick with rain, and her legs burned from the steep incline. If she got to the main road, she might find a forest ranger or a scientist who could help her. The rain made it difficult to see, and she wasn't familiar with the area. She noted a fence; she was getting closer to civilization. She wouldn't be going off the edge of the mine any time soon. He'd have to shoot her if he wanted to kill her.

As if reading her mind, A.J. fired his gun, and a bullet hit her arm. Her skin exploded in a million pieces, but her legs were still working, sort of. She was running sideways now, as if the bullet in her arm had put her entire body off kilter. When she heard a voice, she thought it was her imagination. She was ready to pass out, and an angel was calling her name. Then she realized the angel was a large woman with a gun. It was Kaya, and she was telling Zo to duck out of the way. That's right! Allison was giving them a tour of the mine today.

Zo lunged toward Allison's Durango, and her knees met with the asphalt parking lot. She turned her head in time to see Kaya shoot A.J. in the leg. He doubled over like a wilting flower and fell to the ground.

Kaya walked up to him and kicked his gun out of his hand, stepping on his fingers. She stuck his gun, and hers, in her waistband and walked back to Zo. "I guess they'll give anyone a gun these days."

Zo couldn't agree more.

Epilogue

A knock at the hospital door startled Zo. The nurse was gone, and Zo must have dozed off. The bullet had left a flesh wound, which had been stitched and bandaged. It was her leg that really hurt, the asphalt from the parking lot deeply skinning her shin. But she was lucky to have escaped at all. She never imagined A.J. would try to kill her. It was like Robyn warned her: it was the quiet types that surprised you, and he'd certainly done that when he pulled a gun on her.

"Come in," she called.

Beth popped her head in and rushed to her side. "Are you okay?" She didn't wait for Zo's answer before hugging her.

"I'm fine," said Zo, underneath Beth's pile of chestnut hair. "My arm hurts a little."

Beth quit hugging her and took a step back to look at the arm.

"It's fine," said Zo. "It's just a flesh wound."

Beth frowned. "It looks big."

"It's the bandaging."

Beth perched on the end of the bed. "Kaya said A.J. shot you. What happened?"

Zo told her the story. When she was finished, she asked Beth to look inside the small room closet for her backpack. She'd made the EMTs get it before taking her in the ambulance.

Beth handed her the bag. "So, someone did break into your house that night."

"Yep," said Zo, unzipping her backpack. "He was looking for this." She held up the jump drive. As she did, a man ran past her door, stopped, and turned back. It was Max Harrington, winded and red-faced, but still Max.

"Zo! I..." He coughed. "I was looking for you."

She smiled. It was kind of fun seeing him rattled. "You found me."

"I came as quickly as I could," said Max.

Zo sat up taller in bed, remembering the stolen money. "What happened to the group? Were they arrested?"

He took the chair next to her bed. "They're fine, better than fine. Kaya's being hailed a hero." He nodded toward the door. "They're in the lobby right now talking to the press. Hopefully in light of the new development, the DA won't press charges about the money, but we'll see." Max motioned to her arm. "Did A.J. really shoot you?"

She nodded. "Kind of crazy, huh? He was the one who broke into my house that night." She gave Max the jump drive. "The video footage puts him at the scene of the crime."

"But why kill Enid?" he asked.

Zo reiterated the story, explaining that Enid was his mother.

"No wonder she left Serenity Hills to Henry," said Max. "It makes sense, but I never would have figured it out."

"I guess all those years at the *Star* weren't in vain." Zo smiled. "When did you know I was in trouble?"

"When Beth saw the pictures A.J. sent her," said Max. "In his email, he said you were at the station, dropping off the jump drive. Beth didn't think you'd return something she'd paid for without talking to her first. She sensed you were in trouble, so she called, but you didn't answer. That's when she called me."

"Ah," said Zo. "No service at the mine."

"I was on my way to the television station when I heard the distress call." Max smiled. "And you know the rest."

"I guess this means Allison and A.J. are officially broken up," said Beth.

"Yep," said Zo. "Looks like you're going to have to wait a little longer for a wedding."

"Actually," said Max, "It might not be as long as you think."

Zo and Beth looked at him for an explanation.

"I heard Griffin and Robyn are planning a summer wedding," said Max.

Beth tapped her fingers. "I wonder if they've found a venue..."

"Jack will make you admit he was right," said Zo. "You know that, don't you?"

Beth sighed. "I know. But the lodge would be a beautiful place for a wedding. Don't you agree?"

"I do," said Zo and Max at the same time. They looked at each other and laughed. It was like Beth had said: her love bug was almost contagious.

Almost.

Zo Jones's S'more Bar Recipe

Ingredients:
1 c. butter
1 c. baking cocoa
2 c. sugar
1 tsp. salt
3 eggs
1 1/3 c. flour
1/4 tsp. baking soda
1 tbsp. vanilla
1 1/2 c. Golden Grahams
1 3/4 c. mini marshmallows
1 c. milk chocolate chips

Directions:
1. Preheat oven to 350. Spray 9-x-13 pan with nonstick cooking spray. (I recommend a glass or light-colored pan.)
2. Melt butter in a large saucepan. Remove from heat.
3. Whisk in sugar, cocoa, and salt.
4. Add in eggs one at a time, mixing well after each addition.
5. Stir in flour and baking soda.
6. Add vanilla.
7. Pour into prepared pan.
8. Bake 25–30 minutes. Brownies are done when a toothpick comes out almost clean. Do not over bake.
9. Remove brownies, and turn oven to broil.
10. Sprinkle brownies with Golden Grahams and marshmallows.
11. Put back into the oven, and broil on high until marshmallows are brown, about 30 seconds. Watch carefully so that the marshmallows don't burn.
12. Remove brownies, and sprinkle with chocolate chips.
13. Cover with foil 5–7 minutes, or until chips start to melt.
14. Remove foil. Cool before cutting.

Acknowledgments

Starting a new series takes work, and lots of people put time and effort into this book, including first readers Amy Cecil Holm, Sharon Engberg, Elena Hartwell Taylor, and Samantha Schroeder. Thank you for your feedback, advice, and encouragement. It also takes a support system, and mine is my family, Quintin, Madeline, and Maisie. Your love makes anything possible. As I wrote, I had many questions about the Forest Service, and Black Hills National Forest rangers patiently answered every one of them. Their time is much appreciated. Also appreciated is the dedication of my agent, Amanda Jain. Thank you for believing in this story. Likewise, thank you to Norma Perez-Hernandez and Kensington for taking a chance on this series. You've been a joy to work with. Finally, thanks to readers, who also take a chance when they try a new series. I hope you love it as much as I do.

Meet the Author

Photo credit: Julie Prairie Photography

MARY ANGELA is the author of the Professor Prather and Happy Camper cozy mystery series. When Mary isn't penning heartwarming whodunits, she's teaching, reading, traveling, or spending time with her family. She lives in South Dakota with her husband, daughters, and spoiled pets. You can find out more about her loves, including her writing, at MaryAngelaBooks.com.

Printed in the United States
by Baker & Taylor Publisher Services